A Shadowed Spirit

Works by Sara C. Snider

Tree and Tower Novels

The Thirteenth Tower
A Shadowed Spirit

Other Publications

The Forgotten Web
Hazel and Holly
a web serial at saracsnider.com/hazel-and-holly/

A SHADOWED SPIRIT

SARA C. SNIDER

Double Beast Publishing
Stockholm, Sweden

ISBN 978-91-87657-06-1

Book design by Ray Rhamey

Cover art by Ferdinand D. Ladera

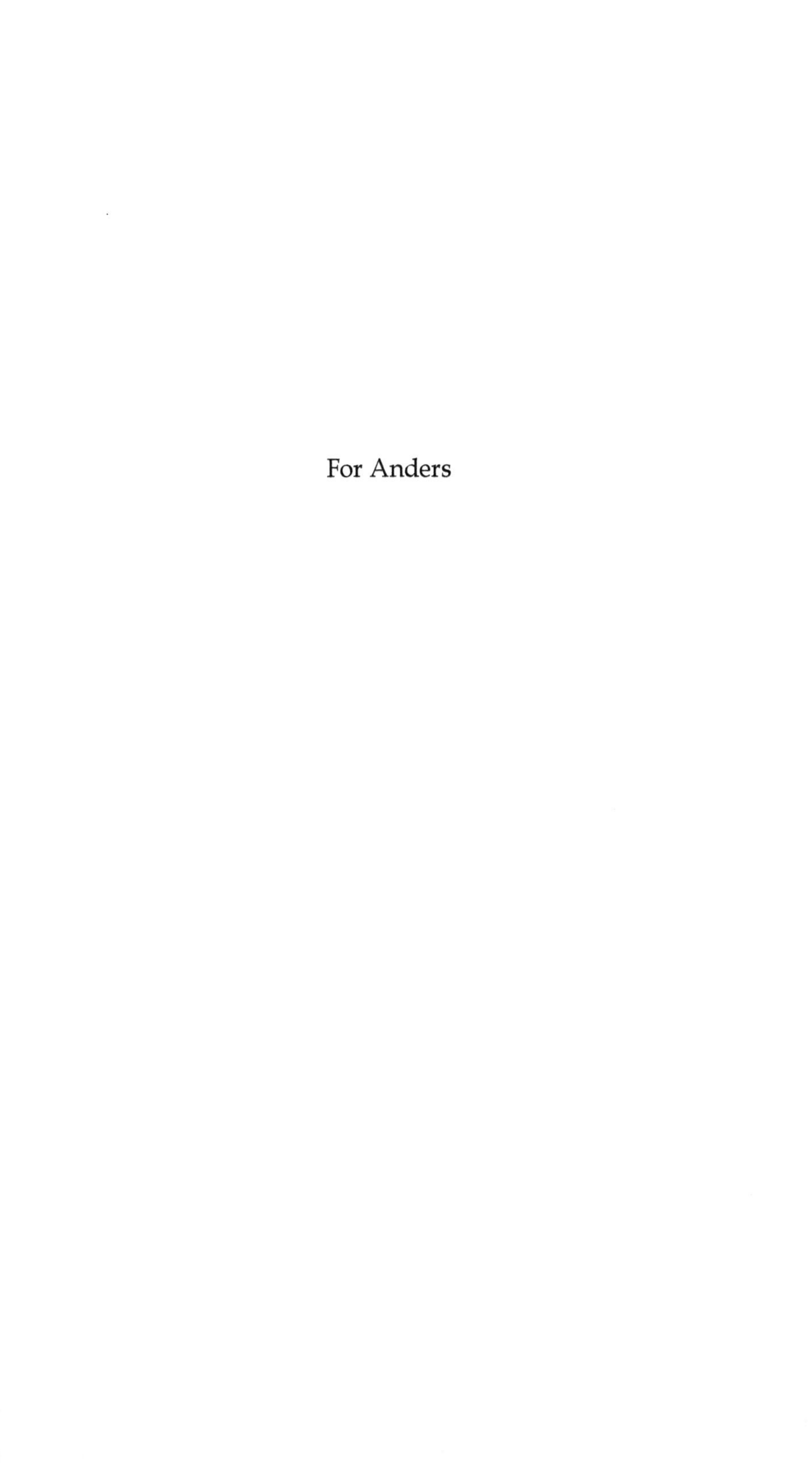

For Anders

It's as though a blanket has been pulled over my mind. Where the Art should be is only a stifled mass of woolen thoughts.

—From the journal of Addigan Moore

Chapter I

Siyan called the wind. Above her, the branches of a towering oak began to sway, rustling in the breeze like a hoarse whisper. She smiled, enjoying the cool spring air against her cheeks. Then her smile faded and pleasure turned to determination. She focused her attention and willed the wind to be something more—to cause the branches to lash with storm-like fury. But even as the thought entered her mind, the focus faded and slipped from her grasp, and the breeze stilled and died. Siyan clenched her jaw.

It was the same every time.

She studied the branches, now still against the clear morning sky. Control of her ability continued to elude her. Her power came easily enough with simple things—calling a gentle wind, turning a faded leaf green—but she was capable of so much more.

Siyan could control the weather and change the earth beneath her feet. Heal wounded flesh. She had done all of these things, but they had been during frantic moments of fighting for her life that had, at the time, seemed as simple as anything. Now, when she tried to repeat such feats, she couldn't do it. She didn't understand why, and that troubled her.

She toed a narrow edge by remaining near a city where so many Magisters lived. Magisters had taken her mother and tortured her until they broke her mind. They might have done the same to Siyan had she not escaped their grasp. Even though it lay several leagues away, the tall spiraling stone Magister Tower seemed to cast a heavy shadow.

The morning had grown late, so Siyan turned her back on the tree and walked through the grassy field as she returned to the Falconry Guild. It was a drab place with russet-colored stone buildings and hard-packed earthen grounds. Plant life seemed to shun it, keeping to the surrounding fields and giving the Guild a wide berth. It looked out of place in such green surroundings, like someone had dropped it there and then forgotten it.

Siyan crossed the expansive courtyard, surrounded by tall towers echoing with the calls of falcons and hawks. A couple of men traversed the grounds, each carrying a falcon on a gloved fist. She stayed clear of them, weaving between wooden posts and poles as she made her way to the other end of the compound, taking care to nudge the occasional stuffed leather decoy out of her path with her foot.

When she saw Master Sorrel speaking with a visitor, Siyan turned and hurried away. He was undoubtedly boasting of the prowess of his trained birds. Men from Roelith would often visit the Guild, touring the grounds as Master Sorrel regaled his birds' capabilities, which he promised would make any man into a superior hunter. But only if they joined the Guild, whose yearly fees were, of course, a modest investment that any serious huntsman would be pleased to pay. She edged along the courtyard, hoping to remain unnoticed.

"Siyan!" Master Sorrel cried and waved her over.

Siyan closed her eyes and let out a breath. Why couldn't he call over one of the men? She wasn't in the mood for this particular little performance.

As she approached, Master Sorrel said, "I was just telling Mr. Jash—"

"Please," the man said. "It's just Jash." He had copper-colored hair that had been pulled back in a short tail. A rapier hung from his belt at one hip, and a flintlock pistol at the other.

"Ah, yes," Master Sorrel said. "I was just telling *Jash* here that falconry is extraordinarily simple. Be a dear and demonstrate just how simple it is."

Siyan tightened her jaw, wondering what Master Sorrel would do if she told him no. Yet he was still her employer and, despite these embarrassing demonstrations he insisted upon, a good man. He had given her a job when she had needed one, and he paid her well—better than some of the men in his employ. Glancing at Jash, Siyan then looked to the sky and whistled.

From the roof of the tallest tower, a falcon took flight. Siyan put out a leather-clad arm, and the falcon circled ever downwards, perching at last upon her limb.

Master Sorrel laughed and brought his hands together in a thunderous clap. "You see?" he said, turning to Jash. "Falconry is so easy that even a woman can do it!"

Siyan bit the inside of her cheek. She wished for the day Master Sorrel would stop parading her around like a prized pony.

Jash looped a thumb in his belt and smiled, his gaze lingering on Siyan. "Clearly. And where did you find such a woman?"

Siyan shifted her feet, uncomfortable under his gaze.

Master Sorrel waved a hand. "Before me, she was nothing. A pathetic vagabond. Now she is a mighty huntress! All because I taught her everything she needs to know of falconry."

That was all false, of course. Master Sorrel hadn't taught her a thing of falconry, other than how to put on the leather sleeve that protected her skin from sharp talons. The falcon resting on her arm was wild and had never—much to Master Sorrel's distress—seen the inside of his aerie. Siyan had saved the bird from a trap two years ago, and he had been following her ever since. Fal—that was what she had taken to calling him—seemed tame around her, but he was still a wild animal that largely came and went as he pleased. The fact that Siyan was able to use her power to interact with him didn't really diminish that. She certainly didn't compel him to return to her—nor did she truly understand why the bird obeyed her commands. That he did any of these things only made Siyan all the more grateful for his presence. She only wished Master Sorrel wasn't so eager to exploit her and the bird.

"Impressive," Jash said.

Master Sorrel drew himself up and pointed at the flintlock pistol hanging at Jash's hip. "Far more impressive than hunting with one of those things. Abominable creations. More likely to kill you from misfire than hit your mark. You'd be better off using it as a paperweight and leave the hunting to my birds."

"And such fine birds you have," Jash said. His gaze lingered on Siyan, pushing her discomfort to the edge of alarm. Why was he looking at her like that, with that half-smile as if he were privy to some secret? She wanted to leave.

"The finest!" Master Sorrel said. "You'd be hard-pressed to find better."

"I agree completely," Jash said, "and see no need to continue the search."

"Wonderful!" Master Sorrel said. "I can draw up the papers today, officially marking your enrollment in the guild, which will give you access to our birds and to training. I . . . uh . . . assume you'll prefer to pay the enrollment fees at once, correct?"

Jash pulled his gaze from Siyan to look at him. "Of course," he said, causing Master Sorrel's face to light up. "Once I speak to my patron, that is." He glanced at the Magister Tower and then winked at Siyan.

She froze as her stomach clenched into a knot of ice. Had he something to do with the Magi?

"Oh, I see," Master Sorrel said. His voice sounded distant, difficult to hear over the thundering of Siyan's heart. He mentioned something about drawing up the papers and having them ready for Jash's return, and Siyan felt sick at the thought of seeing him again, his patron in tow.

Siyan stared at the man. Had he been searching for her? She wracked her mind, trying to remember an encounter, a strange look that suggested she had been recognized, but nothing stood out. Jash smiled at her. He bowed low, keeping his gaze locked with hers.

"Have you gone daft, girl?" Master Sorrel's sharp voice pulled her out of her thoughts. He waved his arms at her. "I said off with you now. Shoo!"

Siyan cast another glance at Jash and then lifted her arm and Fal took flight. Keeping her back rigid, she turned and hurried away. Siyan resisted the urge to look back, feeling as though Jash's gaze was on her until she opened the door to the servants' quarters and stepped inside.

She leaned against the door as she took a deep breath in an effort to calm her racing heart. Jash had recognized her. She didn't know how or where—all she knew was that his glances were more than passing admiration. And the fact he seemed to know Magisters just made everything so much worse. Why was he here? What would he do when he left?

Siyan peeked out the door, but Jash had gone. She stepped outside, looking around, but saw only Master Sorrel.

"Didn't I tell you to get to work?" he said. "Why are you standing there gawping like that?"

"That man, Jash. Is he still here?"

Master Sorrel pulled the waist of his pants up over his protruding gut. "No. Said he needed to go find his patron. I told him I'd take that pistol of his as collateral for the dues, but he wouldn't have it. And I was being generous, too. Those things are all but worthless. Everyone knows that."

Siyan's gaze moved over the field and to the road that led towards Roelith, but Jash was nowhere in sight.

"I have an errand I need to run," Siyan said as she headed towards the road.

"Errand? I don't pay you for errands, girl!" Master Sorrel called after her.

"I won't be long!" Siyan called back. She rustled through the grassy field until she reached the main road and there, further down the way, walked a copper-haired man. Siyan swallowed as Jash rounded a bend and fell out of sight. Part of her wanted to let him go; she shouldn't be following a man potentially in league with the Magi. But she couldn't leave. She needed to know. So she followed him.

A sinking dread settled in Siyan's gut as she drew closer to Roelith. Why had she stayed here so long? She hadn't really intended to. It was only supposed to be temporary—she'd intended to stay long enough to earn some money to buy some supplies before she headed back into the forest to find her mother's people. But then nearly two years had passed and she still hadn't left.

She told herself it was the comfort of routine, the security of steady work and decent wages. The others at the Guild even seemed to hold a measure of respect for her and—having once felt invisible when she had worked as a housemaid—that meant something to Siyan.

But there was more to it than that. She was afraid of what she might find should she go searching in the forests. She knew what she wanted it to be. She wanted to find her mother's family—a clan of forest folk that lived somewhere out in the wilds. She wanted to find love and acceptance, a place to call home. She wanted to understand herself and this power that eluded her. But she knew from past experience that what she hoped to find was not always what came to pass, and she was afraid of going out there and having her heart broken all over again.

Siyan quickened her step, trying to ignore another deeper, uncomfortable truth that continually nagged at her mind.

She felt drawn to the Magister Tower.

There was an energy about it—a tingling on her skin and a humming in her ears. She had felt the same energy when she had approached her mother's Tower, and she felt it now. It was faint, given the distance to Roelith's Tower, but it was there. It pulled at her in a way she couldn't explain. Almost like an intense curiosity, though she knew better than to go anywhere near it.

She lost sight of Jash once he reached Roelith and passed through the gates. Siyan hurried after him and, once in the town proper, she stopped and looked around.

Massive stone houses with tall arched windows and wrought iron balconies loomed overhead. People bustled up and down the streets, while fountains bubbled from one of the many gardens that followed the city wall. Jash was nowhere in sight. She scanned the roads, hoping to find his distinctive coppery hair, but saw nothing.

Her heart sinking, Siyan turned off the road and followed narrow alleys and side-streets until she got to the well-maintained, though primarily empty, road that led to the Magister Tower on the outskirts of town. She had hoped she'd been wrong—that she was just imagining Jash having recognized her. Yet when she passed through Roelith's eastern gates and saw a coppery-haired man on the road ahead of her, Siyan's stomach clenched into a hot little ball. Her palms began to sweat and she wiped them on her breeches. She shouldn't be so close to the Tower. She needed to turn around and head back to the Guild.

And yet she kept on walking. Why was Jash going the Magister Tower? Who was he going to meet? What would they discuss? The pull from the Tower seemed to intensify along with the prickling on her skin. Siyan had never come this close before. She'd thought about it and all the things she'd like to say or do when she got there, but she'd never dared.

What would she find if she did? In Fallow, Magisters had taken the forest people into their Tower where they were never seen again. Would she find forest people here, locked up and forgotten by the outside world? Maybe that's why it had been so difficult for her to leave. Maybe, deep down, she thought she should be locked up with them.

Siyan bumped into someone and staggered back.

"I'm sorry," she said and then noticed the man was wearing a Magister's robe.

"Quite all right," he said.

Siyan froze, unable to breathe. When had the air suddenly become so stifling?

"Are you well?" he said and reached towards her.

Siyan's entire body tensed as she staggered back another step. Overhead, the clear sky clouded over.

"Do you need help?" he said as he took her arm.

Siyan yanked her arm away and lightning flashed in the darkened sky.

The Magister looked up just as rain started to fall. Her heart racing, Siyan turned and ran.

Chapter 2

Addigan sat in the Tower library as she wrote in her journal. The vast room was largely empty save for a pair of Magisters leafing through tomes and a group of young apprentices who were fetching books in accordance to whatever was written on their slips of paper. She pretended not to notice the glances they cast her way, or the seemingly innocuous rasp of their whispered voices. She knew they were talking about her. The others in the Tower always were.

"Silent," they sometimes called her. "Mute." The notion was absurd. She wasn't silent or mute. Had anyone dared say it to her face, she'd tell him as much and half-again over. But she knew it wasn't her ability to speak that they meant. No, they meant her ability with the Art. Or rather, the ability she had lost.

Addigan looked at her hand, her skin mottled with a bruise that refused to heal. It engulfed half of her body, stretching from the right side of her face down to her right foot. It was an ugly bruise—more so than usual—with purple veins that branched and snaked just below her skin. They reminded her of broken spider legs, scrambling across her body in a twining, tangled mass. It wasn't painful, though, just slightly numb, as if her skin had grown a little too thick.

She continued writing in her journal, focusing on the scratching of her pen rather than the whispers. Her strokes were too forceful, and she tore the paper on which she wrote. Taking a breath, she ripped the ruined page from the binding and started again on a new leaf.

It is more than coincidence, the similarities between the different sites of the Towers. Trees of a certain power and their so-called And'estar keepers—they seem to have always been present where Towers have been built. What that may mean, however, I do not yet know. There is knowledge to be obtained and I mean to find it. The Grand Magister will be made to see, and he will be made to know that I am one with whom he must reckon.

Addigan lifted her pen and stared at the page, remembering her confrontation with the Grand Magister and his dismissal of her research. She wondered if his indifference towards her was because she was a woman or because she wasn't a Magister. Maybe it was both.

She put down the pen and flexed her hand. Again and again, she made a fist and then relaxed it, enjoying feeling her muscles work, remembering the time when they hadn't. She had come a long way, overcome more than anyone else in the Tower. She deserved to be there. She'd make them see that.

"Addi," a hushed voice said from behind.

Addigan turned to find Malvin walking towards her. She turned back around and returned her pen to the paper.

"Addi, I've been looking for you."

"Well, you found me. What do you want?"

He was quiet a moment. "Why must you always be like this?"

Addigan forced herself to face him, taking care not to look at the vibrant red Magister robe he wore. "I must be 'like this' because it is who I am. If you don't like it, you are free to leave." She turned back to her journal, not wanting to see the hurt expression in his eyes.

Addigan attempted to resume writing when Malvin said, "You have a visitor. He's waiting in the garden."

She thought about asking who it was, but decided against it. Addigan suspected she knew, and she'd rather not discuss such matters with Malvin. "Thank you."

When he remained, Addigan raised her eyebrows at him.

"What are you doing, Addi?"

"I don't know what you mean. I am writing in my journal. Surely that is not a grievous offense."

"You know what I'm talking about."

Addigan gazed at him, clenching her hand in an effort to keep her face calm. "My affairs are my own."

"I know you feel like you have something to prove—that your failure in the Threshing doesn't mean you're worthless."

She narrowed her eyes and said in a low voice, "You wouldn't know anything about that."

Malvin glowered at her. "You think everything that's happened has happened to you alone? You almost died, Addi! You think that hasn't affected me? You think that I don't have a say in the matter, after everything we've been through?"

Malvin's rising voice had carried, and the others in the library threw them questioning glances.

"Keep your voice down," Addigan whispered.

He grabbed hold of her wrist and leaned in close. "I know you better than anyone here. I know you're up to something and, knowing you, you're likely to overlook the consequences of your actions in order to prove a point. I'll not have anything happen to you, Addi. Not again."

Addigan wrenched her wrist out of his grasp. "Don't call me that. And what I do or don't do is not for you to decide. You think you know me, but you don't know anything about the world in which I live. That you keep pretending you do insults us both." Taking her journal, Addigan rose and walked out.

Malvin. He meant well, but his good intentions often came across as overbearing. Especially now. He no longer had any right to comment on her affairs.

Addigan walked down the broad hallway, past tapestried walls and candelabra sconces. She came to a stairway and followed it down before traversing another hallway and descending another set of stairs. She passed sturdy wooden doors that led to quarters and to research rooms, and the occasional narrow, latticed window that looked out over the rolling hills surrounding Roelith. The way was winding, but she knew it well and eventually left the spiraling stone Tower and made her way to the garden.

The day was clear, though the air still held a sharpness reminiscent of winter. Malvin hadn't said where in the garden the visitor would be waiting, but Addigan suspected she knew.

She turned off the pebbled path and headed towards a hedge maze. She wound through the labyrinthine twists and turns of the tall bushes, now pale green with the first leaves of spring. The maze was one of four massive runes that circled the Tower, all of which served to amplify the power of the Art. But at a glance, the hedges were deceptively mundane, and Addigan liked that.

When she heard a trickling of running water, Addigan rounded another corner and came to a marble fountain sculpted in the form of a naked woman. In one arm she held a baby who suckled at her breast. In the other she held an urn from which the water of the fountain poured into the basin below. Just as she expected, Jash stood there, gazing up at the sculpture.

As Addigan approached, he turned towards her and smiled. "I've always liked this statue. How does the water pour out of the urn like that?"

Addigan thinned her lips. She'd never liked the man. The less she had to speak to him, the better. "Why are you here? Have you learned something?"

Jash's smile widened. "Perhaps. I suppose you'd like to know, just as I'd like to know how that fountain works."

She frowned. "I pay you with money, not trivial information."

Jash waved a hand as he turned back to the statue. "Money isn't everything."

Addigan snorted. "Said the banker to the beggar."

"*I'm* not a beggar. Are you?"

Addigan thinned her lips again. Talking with Jash tended to be a frustratingly circular affair. It was usually best to just give him what he wanted, lest he babble on to the brink of driving one mad. Except . . .

Jash grinned. "You don't know, do you?"

Addigan glowered at him. "Of course I know."

He folded his arms. "Well then?"

Addigan tightened her jaw and flailed a hand towards the fountain. "Something about the water source some distance off being higher than the fountain here. It's all very complicated and highly irrelevant."

"But . . . is it magical?"

"What?"

"The fountain. Have you Magi waggled your fingers the way that you do to get the water to spring forth?"

Addigan stared at him. "Of course not."

Jash slumped a little. "Well, that's disappointing."

"Why are you here?"

Jash looked off in the distance and pointed. "The other mazes, do they have fountains as well?"

Addigan tightened her grip on her journal and took a

breath. "No. The northern maze has a pair of statues, but they are not fountains."

"Are they like this one? With a lady?"

"No. They are two shrouded men."

"And the other mazes? What do they have?"

"Nothing, just hedges."

"Huh." He turned to her and grinned. "Guess we're in the best one, then."

Addigan glared at him, wondering if he was done with his incessant questions.

"Anyway, I found someone you were interested in," Jash said. "A tree-keeper, or whatever you called them."

"And'estar?"

"Yeah, that. I found her."

"Her?"

Jash glanced to the side and shrugged. "Yes, her. Why? You expecting someone else?"

"No, I . . . I suppose I didn't know what to expect."

"She was at the Falconry Guild outside Roelith. Pretty little thing with bright blue eyes the color of the sky, just like you said."

"That's it? Just her eyes? She didn't do anything?"

Jash shrugged again. "She demonstrated her falconry skills. Why? What should she have done?"

Addigan rubbed her temple. "I don't know. Just . . . something. How can we be sure she is an And'estar? Maybe she just has very blue eyes."

"Not my problem. You told me to find someone with eyes that reflect the color of the sky, and I did."

Addigan doubted the man could find his way through an unstarched shirt, let alone find someone she had been unsure even existed. Still, this was what she had been waiting for, and what her research depended upon. She couldn't let the opportunity pass, however unlikely its validity. "Take me to her, then."

The following day, Jash and Addigan made the journey to Roelith's Falconry Guild. She peered around the courtyard and at the unwashed men working there. What a disgusting place. How anyone could choose to live so closely with a throng of filthy animals, Addigan would never know.

The man in charge—Master Sorrel—scratched at his head, sending his disheveled hair into further disarray. He probably had lice. Addigan took a step back.

"I told you, she's gone," Master Sorrel said.

Addigan narrowed her eyes. "People don't just disappear. If she left then that means she had to walk out of here to do it, and that means someone should have seen her."

Master Sorrel chuckled and shook his head. "We're not watch dogs. We don't raise an alarm whenever someone comes or goes. The girl's gone. Said she had an errand to run and never came back. She never even received the last of her wages. She'd not have given up her pay without good reason. Either she wanted to leave without being noticed, or something happened to her." He eyed Addigan and Jash. "Maybe she knew you folks would come calling and didn't care for the visit."

Addigan unclenched her jaw and opened her mouth, intending to illuminate for the man just how unpleasant this visit would be, when Jash stepped forward.

"Thank you, Master Sorrel," he said while giving Addigan a pointed look. "I'm sure we'll find her, regardless."

Master Sorrel glanced between Addigan and Jash and then grunted. Turning to Jash, he said, "If this is your patron, you let me know when you find a different one." He turned and left.

Jash grinned.

Addigan frowned. "Well, he was useless."

"You say that about everyone," Jash said as he walked past her.

"Because it's true."

Jash kept on walking, making his way across the guild grounds to the surrounding field.

Addigan hurried after him. "Where are you going?"

He glanced back at her. "You want to find your tree lady, don't you?"

"Yes, but we don't know where she went."

"These things can often be found out."

"Found out? How?"

Jash kept on walking and said nothing.

She grabbed him by the arm. "You will answer me."

Jash shrugged his arm out of her grasp. He looked down and kicked dirt onto her boots and the hem of her skirt. "Tracks, my overbearing lady. If you'd bring your nose out of the sky, you'd see that the ground is covered in them."

She frowned, backing away from the dust he was kicking up. "Are you saying you'll be able to follow her?"

"I might if you quit yapping and let me get on with it."

Addigan swallowed her annoyance along with a sharp retort. She swatted at her skirt with a gloved hand, trying to get the dust out of the fabric, though it seemed to be a futile endeavor. She stood there, rigid and awkward and wishing she was back at the Tower.

Except that wasn't true. Not really. She wanted to be at the Tower, but only when the Magisters learned to respect her. They never had and they never would, not unless she did something about it. She had to see this through, no matter how dirty or demeaning the task. Proving to them this connection between the Towers and the mysterious And'estar would be worth it, in the end.

Growing increasingly uncomfortable from the glances she was receiving from the men around the courtyard, Addigan followed Jash, though she stayed a good distance away, not wanting to intrude upon whatever he was doing. His gaze remained fixed upon the ground, and he stopped from time to time to touch a piece of grass or to put his hand to the dirt. Addigan didn't know how he could possibly find the girl after she had already gone, but she remained quiet and let him get on with it.

The day waned as Jash plodded and poked around the grounds and into the surrounding field. Addigan began to fear they'd spend the night at that frightful place when Jash finally straightened and turned towards her.

"She went that way," he said, jerking a thumb over his shoulder towards a hill in the field.

"What? Are you sure?"

He looped his thumbs in his belt and straightened his back. "Of course. Single set of tracks lead through the field there. Small ones. A woman. Don't know who else it'd be."

Addigan licked her lips, growing excited. It was happening. She was tempted to head off right then, to see where the trail led. But that would be foolish. "We'll need supplies," she said, pacing back and forth as she thought. "Though not too much. We need to travel light. Haste is imperative if we are to catch up with her."

"You're over-thinking it," Jash said. "All we need is some food, something to carry water, and a flint and steel. I know a guy. We can leave tomorrow."

Addigan blinked at him. "Tomorrow?" It seemed both too soon and too far away.

From behind, a man said, "What is happening tomorrow?"

Addigan spun around, her mouth falling open as Malvin approached them. "What are you doing here?"

"What is happening tomorrow?" he repeated.

"You'll answer my question."

Malvin settled his sharp gaze on her. "You'll answer mine."

Addigan knew that look. Malvin was often an easygoing man, but when he had that look in his eyes she knew he would never budge, not even if the earth shifted below his feet. "I've found a lead on something that should prove interesting to the Grand Magister. I'm going to investigate it."

"What lead? What are you doing?"

"I'd rather not say."

Malvin glowered at her and set his jaw. "No. You're coming back with me. I don't know what you're up to, but it's likely foolish if not dangerous. I can't let you do it."

Addigan clenched her hands as she fought down her rising anger. How dare he come here, telling her what she could and couldn't do, threatening to take her back like an unruly child? "You have no say on the matter."

"I have more say than you'd like to admit."

Addigan's anger withered as if he had just punched her in the stomach. Suddenly the gap between them seemed very wide, the red robe he wore almost painful to look at.

It must have shown on her face, for Malvin's grim look of determination faded, replaced by remorse. He took a step towards her. "I'm sorry. It's just . . . I worry about you."

Unable to look at him, Addigan kept her gaze fixed past his shoulder. Then the anger again smoldered within her gut, hot and sickening. She'd not give him the satisfaction of seeing her defeated, and so she stifled her anger and fear and hurt, stifled it deep within her so that the sickness turned to numbness.

She looked him in the eyes. When she did, she no longer saw the man she had once cared about, the man that had once set her heart racing. She saw only a figure in a red robe with dark eyes and hair. He could have been anyone, and so she stared at him, as vacant and distant as if he were a stranger on the street.

Malvin put his palms to his face and rubbed his eyes and forehead. He looked tired, but Addigan didn't care about that any more than she would have cared about a farmer exhausted from his daily toils.

At length, he said, "Fine. Just . . . let me speak with your man first, all right?"

Saying nothing, Addigan turned and walked away. She heard their murmured voices as Jash and Malvin spoke. She didn't know what they were talking about. She didn't care. She just needed to keep walking—away from Malvin, away from the Tower. She needed to get away from all of them before this empty, dead feeling that was inside her became the only feeling she would ever know.

Chapter 3

Siyan sat on a fallen tree, nibbling on an under-ripe wild onion bulb that served as her breakfast. After her encounter at the Magister Tower, Siyan hadn't dared return to the Falconry Guild. She got close, but there had been too many men walking around and she hadn't wanted to risk running into one of them—especially Master Sorrell. There would have been uncomfortable questions about where she had gone, why she wanted to leave. She wouldn't be able to answer truthfully, and she hadn't wanted to lie to Master Sorrel. She doubted she'd have been convincing anyway. So she had left.

Siyan swallowed a mouthful of fibrous onion, ignoring the way it scratched her throat, or the bitter aftertaste that lingered on her tongue. This wasn't how it was supposed to be—she had planned for the day she'd leave to find her mother's people. She had stashed a bundle of supplies under her bed—dried fruit and meat, cracker bread and crumbly cheese. She had thought herself prepared, that everything was under control. Instead, she had been terribly foolish.

What had she been thinking, following Jash so close to the Tower? She should have left long ago. If she had more courage—if she'd been stronger—then she would have never been in this position.

She looked to the sky, searching for Fal, but he was nowhere in sight. It had been two days since she sent him away to scout, yet he still had not returned. Until he did, she was on her own. She finished her onion and then rose and strode into the forest.

Days passed. Then a week. Without any supplies, Siyan had to forage for her food, but the season was early and her knowledge limited. She ate what she could find—roots that tasted of earth and left grit in her teeth or bitter leaves that left her mouth feeling waxy and numb. She hadn't succeeded in finding any more wild onions. She almost missed the woody, bitter taste.

Her hunger grew and her strength waned. When Fal at last returned and dropped a squirrel at her feet, Siyan thought she might weep from relief. She made a fire and cooked it, her tension easing as she ate.

She continued on, now following the falcon as it flitted from tree to tree. The forest grew darker and denser, the foliage seemingly soaking up more of the sun. Yet for all of that, the air seemed warmer, the wind less harsh. Spring appeared further along, and Siyan even found a few small, unripened berries that tasted bitter and tart.

She walked on, her footsteps muffled by thick, spongy moss beneath her boots. Twigs snapped as she moved, but it sounded suffocated, distant. In fact, the entire forest sounded eerily quiet. She stopped and listened.

The wind gusted, sending a cascade of pine needles fluttering down from the trees. They stuck to Siyan's hair, but she made no move to brush them away. Ahead, a collection of crimson fireflies swirled around a bush. She'd never seen anything like it—either fireflies being out during the day or having such a deep red glow.

Siyan started towards them, but then a twig snapped and she turned and found a man with a bow drawn, aiming an arrow at her.

She swallowed as her heart raced. She lifted a hand as if that would stop him from releasing the arrow straight into her chest. "Hello," she managed to say.

The man said nothing, watching her with intense, dark eyes. He had long black hair, part of which had been woven into two thin braids that framed his face. His clothing was of rough leather, deerskin maybe. It was a style Siyan had seen once before.

"I'm looking for the forest people," she said, feeling stupid. But she didn't know what else to say. "My name is Siyan. My mother was one of you. I'm . . . one of you. I'm hoping you can help me."

The man watched her a while longer before lowering his bow. He walked towards her. His hands were stained with blood, and he had a sheathed knife strapped to his thigh.

Siyan took a step back as he approached, but then she clenched her jaw and forced herself to stand her ground. He stood close to her, the metallic smell of blood clinging to him. He was short for a man—not much taller than she. Though his features looked young, they had a careworn look about them, suggesting he was older than her in years—perhaps nearing thirty. Braided into his hair were strands of little white shells. They reminded Siyan of a little girl from long ago, and the beads that had hung on her dress. She swallowed, the memory of it sharp in her heart.

He looked her up and down, slowly, as if examining every detail about her. Siyan gritted her teeth, hating being scrutinized, but refusing to back down. At last his gaze locked with hers, and they stood there watching each other for what felt like ages.

Then, for the first time since their encounter, something like emotion passed over his features. Was it . . . disappointment? Anger?

Then he spoke. "Come." He turned and headed deeper into the forest.

Siyan hesitated. She didn't want to follow him. Not him. He unsettled her, and she tried to think of a different way, but nothing came to mind. She had wanted to find the forest people, and now it seemed that she had. Was she to run away simply because a man made her feel uncomfortable?

Letting out a breath, Siyan hurried after him before he disappeared from sight.

He walked up to a dead rabbit lying on the ground, its belly cut open. He placed it in a satchel that lay next to it and slung the strap over his shoulders. He then wound through the trees, coming to a stream that he used to wash his hands. He never spoke to Siyan as they walked. Never even looked at her. She kept a fair distance from him—close enough to keep him in sight, but far enough away for her to escape should she need to run.

They passed more clouds of crimson fireflies, circling monstrous ferns as tall as Siyan's waist with fronds as long as her arm. Vines of ivy twined around trees and trailed from low branches that swayed in the breeze like ribbons. Siyan stared, wondering how the forest could look so different so quickly. She glanced back, but the man pressed on and Siyan was forced to follow or be left behind.

They came upon a camp with a score or so of huts framed with wooden poles and draped with overlapping lengths of oiled hide. Men looking much like the man who led her gathered around, watching as she passed by. The women all had long dark hair and wore dresses of rough leather. They reminded Siyan of her mother, and her heart was again stabbed with a pang of sorrow. She fixed her gaze ahead, no longer able to meet their eyes.

The air rustled with their whispers. Then the man stopped at a hut with a thin trail of smoke twining out of a hole in the roof. He pushed aside a leather flap and ducked inside. There was a murmured exchange, then the flap was pulled back and the man stepped out, followed by a woman.

She was shorter than Siyan, her hair mostly grey save for a few wisps of black marbled throughout. The lines around her eyes and mouth showed a life long-lived. Yet for all of that, she exuded a certain vitality that belied her aged exterior—a strength that suggested that if she and Siyan were to come to blows, this woman would undoubtedly emerge the victor. Siyan's heart raced as she looked at her, for this woman looked at her with eyes a grey color that matched the clouded sky above. She was an And'estar.

Siyan's mind went blank. All the questions she had wanted to ask had now flown from her mind, and it was all she could do to stand there and breathe.

The woman regarded her. Then her gaze then flicked past Siyan's shoulder as though looking for others.

"I'm alone," Siyan said, finally regaining some of her wits.

Her gaze moved to Siyan's arm. "This thing," she said, patting her left arm as she gazed at Siyan's right. "What is it?"

Siyan looked down at the thick leather sleeve she wore. Then she looked to the trees and whistled, smiling as Fal flew down and alighted on her outstretched arm.

The woman watched her a moment longer. Then she turned to the man that had guided Siyan and gave a slight nod. When he left, she lifted the flap to the hut and motioned for Siyan to step inside.

Siyan let the falcon fly back to the trees and ducked inside. It smelled of smoke and dirt, of spices and oil. On the ground lay heaps of furs and skins around a fire that burned within a circle of stones.

The woman let the flap drop and the hut darkened, illuminated only by the fire and the feeble light that filtered through the leather. She pointed to a heap of furs and Siyan sat down. The woman sat opposite her.

The woman's features looked obscure in the gloom. She could have been anyone then. She could have been Siyan's mother, and the more Siyan thought about it, the more she thought she saw Iyen sitting across from her. She closed her eyes.

The woman asked, "What is your name?"

"Siyan."

"Siyan," the woman said, as though trying out the words. "I am Emora."

Siyan nodded. "Emora."

"Tell me, why have you come?"

Siyan hesitated. She had so many reasons for coming, but she didn't know what to say without sounding crazy or desperate. "I . . . my mother was one of you . . . one of us. I'm looking for her kin. My kin."

Emora regarded her with a raised chin. "To which clan did your mother belong?"

"I don't know."

"Did she not tell you?"

"No. I was raised by someone else. I only just found her a couple years ago. She had . . ."

"She had changed?"

Siyan blinked, swallowing as her heart leapt into her throat. Emora couldn't know about Iyen's transformation, could she? "What do you mean?"

"She became a tree, did she not?"

Siyan stared at her. "How could you possibly know that?"

"It is the way of things."

Siyan frowned. What was that supposed to mean? "There is so much I don't understand."

Emora smiled. "That is also the way of things." She got up and placed a blackened kettle over the fire. As it warmed, it filled the hut with the smell of spices. She poured the hot liquid into two cups and handed one to Siyan.

Siyan lifted it to her nose. It smelled a little like cinnamon but different, more pungent. When she sipped the liquid it was bitter on her tongue.

Emora sipped her tea. "Your mother, did she leave her clan? Live with outsiders?"

Siyan nodded. "Yes. She married my father, who's not one of us. She lived with him in the woods until . . ." Until the Magi took her and drove her mad. But Siyan couldn't bring herself to say those last words.

Emora frowned, looking a little sad. "Then she also didn't understand."

"Understand what?"

"Her duty. Her purpose."

"What purpose is that?"

"To protect. To guide. To remember."

"Remember what?"

"Everything."

Siyan frowned again. Maybe Emora thought she was being clear, but Siyan only grew more confused the more they talked. "What does that mean?"

"We are And'estar. It means 'spirit walker' or 'one who is spirit.' In time, we change; we become something more."

Siyan could only sit and stare. "What do you mean, we become something more?"

"You saw it with your mother."

Siyan remembered the great white tree that her mother had become—twisted and grotesque, yet beautiful all the same. She'd never spoken of it to anyone. She tried not to even think about it, though she had been less successful in that endeavor. It was a memory that haunted her—

her mother's lost humanity and the nightmares she had unleashed upon the world. Siyan had blamed the Magisters for her mother's transformation, but Emora seemed to suggest otherwise. "She . . . became a tree. You're saying that happens to all And'estar?"

Emora nodded.

Siyan's stomach sank into her boots. She put down her tea and rested her forehead against her clammy hands.

Emora was quiet a moment then said, "It is not so sad. Such an occasion warrants more celebration than mourning."

Siyan peered at her through the haze of smoke and her own welling tears. Was the woman serious? "I don't know how you can say that. If you saw what she became, what she did, you wouldn't be celebrating. And now you're telling me I should be glad I'll become the same thing?"

Emora regarded Siyan a moment before saying, "The day grows late and you have undoubtedly traveled far. You will rest for tonight. We can speak more of this tomorrow." She rose and stepped out of the hut, holding the flap open for Siyan.

Siyan remained sitting as she stared at the woman. How could Emora so calmly tell her she was going to become an abomination? And then dismiss her as if she hadn't just shattered her life? Siyan bit the inside of her cheek, refusing to cry. She got up and left the hut.

Siyan spent the evening with a woman named Nidia and her young son. They spoke very little, but they fed her, for which she was immensely grateful. Siyan tried to control her hunger, but she still ate eagerly and in greater quantities than was likely appropriate.

She slept fitfully that night, her mind returning to her mother and the horrific form of the tree she had become. When Emora fetched her the following morning, Siyan felt like she hadn't slept at all.

The man who had been Siyan's guide the previous day stood nearby, a satchel slung across his shoulders and a bow in his hand. Siyan glanced at him, but he kept his gaze fixed ahead. When she and Emora headed off into the forest, the man trailed after them.

They walked in silence for hours, stopping once to take a meal of greasy cakes made of dried meat, fruit, and fat. It was barely palatable, but it was filling. Once they finished, they continued on. There was still plenty of daylight left in the sky when the man stopped, hunkering down on his haunches as he rummaged through his pack.

"Come," Emora said and continued walking.

"Isn't he coming with us?" Siyan said as she followed Emora, realizing that she still didn't know the man's name.

"He will wait for our return."

They walked a short while longer before coming to a great tree. Emora stopped and rested her hand upon the trunk.

The tree looked similar to her mother's in the Tower—the pale golden bark, the vibrant green leaves. But this one was different. This one was healthy and robust, not the twisted, misshapen tree that her mother had become. Siyan looked closer, looking for any sign that this had once been a person, looking for the outline of a human form that had been all too apparent in that tree in the Magister Tower. But she saw nothing. There was maybe a shape of a face in the swirls of the bark, but she wasn't sure. It was like seeing figures in the clouds. If she looked hard enough, she'd probably see a dog and a rabbit, too.

"This is Minan," Emora said. "My mother."

Siyan flinched, feeling as if she had just been slapped. "No," she said, much more coldly than she intended. Why did she feel so angry?

Emora frowned, looking concerned. "Was your mother not also the same?"

Siyan wanted to laugh, to find a way to keep her throat from constricting and to keep the tears from rolling down her cheeks. She wanted to pretend that this discussion didn't cut at her heart, especially since Emora didn't seem troubled by it. Instead, all she could manage was another feeble, "No."

"Yet you say she had changed."

Siyan shook her head. "She didn't look like this. The coloring was the same, once the sunlight came in, but the tree was . . . twisted. I could see her . . . her body, twisted in the wood. Her face . . ." She wiped at her eyes, angry at her weakness.

Emora was quiet a moment. "Was she not ready to die?"

Siyan blinked. "She's not dead. I . . . I've seen her. Spoken with her. She . . . creates things, makes things happen."

"Yes, which is why it is not so sad and is cause for celebrating. We are fortunate in that our loved ones are not lost to us. They remain, making the world richer for their presence."

Siyan scoffed. "Richer? By unleashing nightmares on the world? By attacking innocent people, leading them to some unknown fate? How can you say they make the world richer?"

Emora hummed a song, a shrilling of notes that pierced the air and echoed around them. The wind stirred, and light sparkled around the pale tree. Emora put out a hand and a sparkling, luminescent form flitted to it. She stepped towards Siyan, showing her a butterfly with wings that glimmered like sunlight.

"To be an And'estar is to remember and to dream," Emora said. "And this is what And'estar dream when their dreams are pleasant. This and other beautiful things. This is why we must tend to them—to keep them from sleeping too deeply and forgetting the world, but also to keep them from growing lonely. For an And'estar that is unhappy, her dreams can become like nightmares, as you said."

Siyan eyed the glowing butterfly and then Emora. "How do I know you didn't create this yourself?"

Emora smiled—a broad grin that seemed to suggest she was quite pleased with the notion of such trickery. "How many nightmares have you seen since you have been here?"

"I haven't been here very long," Siyan said, stubbornly holding to an argument she was already losing in her heart.

Emora smiled again and wiggled her fingers, sending the butterfly back to its companions fluttering around the tree. "I do not know why your mother's passing was so difficult, or why she took the form she did. Perhaps she did not understand what was happening, and that she, in her fear, fought against the inevitable."

Siyan thought of her mother, dying alone in the dark. How frightening it must have been. She shook her head, not wanting to think of it.

"Is there anyone looking after your mother now?"

Siyan nodded. "My father."

Emora smiled. "Good."

Siyan cast a sideways glance at the tree, at the sparkling butterflies that surrounded it. Was that how her mother should have looked, instead of the misshapen form she had taken? Was Siyan supposed to find comfort in that? Because comfort still eluded her.

Emora followed her gaze. "I think I understand now, your confusion and fear. To have been raised as you have been by outsiders, to know nothing of the way of things. It must have been upsetting to learn of it in this way. It is unfortunate that your mother did not also understand, for it would have been much easier for her if she had."

If Emora was trying to console her, then she was doing a poor job of it. "How do you know she didn't understand?

She grew up among her people; she only left when she married my father."

"If she understood, she would not have left."

"How do you know?"

"Times have changed for us from how they used to be. Before, we all understood our purpose. We told our stories, tended our loved ones, and they returned our love by bringing our stories to life. Before, our world was wondrous, filled with the beauty of these butterflies here, hundreds of times over. Now, there are few of us who remember and will do what is required. Most others have forgotten and do as they please."

"Why have so many forgotten?"

Emora looked at Siyan with eyes that had grown golden with the setting sun. "Men from the south, they come here building tall towers, cutting groves and trees and sending our people to scatter across the land. Their cities grow larger and more numerous, and places we once called home are ours no longer. We wander, then, searching for new homes and for And'estar to tend. But the years become long and we forget the home we are searching for, and the loved ones we were meant to look after. Now, most of us live for no other reason than to exist. We have no purpose, and the beauty of the world has dimmed because of it."

Siyan considered a moment. "Men from the south? You mean Magisters?"

Emora nodded.

A Magister had told her the forest people were nomadic, but Emora made it sound like they only started wandering because of the Magi's arrival. She wondered if the Magister knew this and had withheld it, or if he had misunderstood.

"Did they know about the And'estar trees?" Siyan asked. "What they really are?"

Emora lifted a shoulder in what might have been a shrug. "I would think not. If they did, they would not have cut them down. But then, these men are foreign to me, so I cannot say for certain."

Then Siyan remembered something else a Magister had told her. "I was told once that all forest people have magical capabilities. Is that true?"

"You mean the Ilvar."

Siyan blinked. "What?"

"You called us forest people, but we call ourselves the Ilvar. As to whether or not we can all call spirit, I cannot say for certain. Only And'estar can do so in a way we can perceive. But I will say it feels . . . right . . . that others might also do so in less perceptible ways."

Emora left the tree, and they returned to the man who had followed them. While they had been gone, he had built a fire and flattened the surrounding brush into a camp for them to spend the night.

Siyan walked up to him. "I'm afraid I never got your name." She held out her hand. "My name is Siyan."

The man cast her a cursory glance before feeding more wood to the campfire.

"That is Enon," Emora said. "My son."

Siyan put down her hand, wondering if she had said or done something to cause offense.

They ate another meal of those greasy, meaty cakes, then sat in silence around the campfire. Siyan glanced at Emora. The woman was an And'estar just like her. She might not get another chance like this.

"I have many questions," Siyan said.

"You may ask," said Emora.

Siyan licked her lips and glanced at Enon, but the man just sat and watched the flames. She wasn't even sure if he was listening.

"I don't understand this power we have," she said. "When I got my ability I was able to do amazing things, but then it faded. It almost feels like I've forgotten it, but I haven't. I know it's still there. Yet when I try to look at it, to make something grand happen, it slides away. I don't understand why."

"You never 'got' your power. You have always had it. And it has not faded. You simply have not needed it."

"Why does that matter?"

"To use our power to our greatest extent requires us to surrender. We must forget ourselves—this idea we have about ourselves—and become something more. The mind does not like this, and so it resists. This is why you have difficulty in recalling how to use your power; it is because your mind does not want you to use it. It wants you to carry on just as you always have, without rocking the boat and splashing the water. When your need is great, however, the surrendering becomes easier. Splashing the water is no longer a concern when the boat is sinking."

Siyan stared at the woman. "How do you know this?"

Emora smiled, though her eyes looked sad. "It is knowledge that has been passed through generations. From mother to daughter, father to son. It is the knowledge all Ilvar should be sharing with each other, only most have forgotten the stories to tell. So I am sharing it with you, and you will share it with others."

Siyan blinked. "I . . . what?"

"I was unsure at first of your purpose here. At first I thought you came here as a daughter, one to replace those I lost. One who could protect our people after I had gone and would continue the And'estar tradition with daughters of your own."

Siyan's throat tightened and she coughed. She stared at Emora. Had the woman completely lost her wits?

"But I am not certain that is your purpose," Emora continued. "You come here with a falcon on your arm and questions in your heart. Your purpose is that of seeking and finding, and that is what you must continue."

"By teaching others? I . . . I can't do that."

Emora frowned. "It is your purpose."

"I only just arrived. I'm just learning of all this myself. I can't go out there and teach others. It's not my place. I wouldn't know what to say."

"You have adopted the outsider perspective of wishing to do as you please rather than as you are expected. What you are meant to do."

Siyan stifled her annoyance. She had grown up a servant, always doing what others expected of her; what she wanted had never been considered. Now this woman was accusing her of selfishness and it angered her. She didn't know what Siyan had been through. She didn't know what she had endured for nearly two decades.

"*I* decide what I'm meant to do," Siyan said, her voice tight.

"Yes," Emora said. "I wonder if you will remove the blindfold and see it."

Chapter 4

The following morning, Siyan, Enon, and Emora ate a quick breakfast before heading back to the Ilvar camp.

Siyan trailed behind them as they walked, wondering what to do. Part of her wanted to oblige Emora and help these people who were, in a way, her people. But how could she? Emora wanted her to teach to others what she herself barely understood. The very idea of it seemed absurd, and she didn't understand how Emora could possibly think the idea a good one.

They walked in silence a long while, then Siyan said, "There has to be a better choice than me. You, for example. You know all of this; you should be the one to teach others about it, not me."

Emora glanced back at Siyan but kept on walking. "My purpose is to stay and protect my people, and to tend the few And'estar trees that still remain. I will teach those who come to me, but I will not abandon my duty. You, however, have chosen to wander. You have a falcon as a companion whom you have taught to find others for you. That you are the one to do this is clear. It is the purpose you have chosen for yourself."

"But I haven't chosen it." Siyan rubbed her forehead. It was true that Fal helped find things for her, but not this. "I only wanted to find my mother's people, to get answers about myself. I've barely gotten any answers at all and now you want me to try and teach others? How can you possibly think that's a good idea?"

"You already know more than most, and there is not much more I could teach you. It is enough to let others know that there is more in life than they are aware; that there is a purpose they have forgotten. It will be more than they have now, and that is enough."

"Surely you haven't taught me everything you know. I still have so many questions."

"Being an And'estar is not something that can be taught. Your command over your power is something you must find for yourself, over time. You already know all you need."

Siyan wanted to refuse, but she kept silent. Then she remembered something Emora had said the previous night. "What did you mean when you said you thought I might be a daughter to replace the ones you lost?"

Emora stopped. Enon, glancing at his mother, kept on walking before stopping a short distance away.

Fixing her gaze on the surrounding trees, Emora said, "The And'estar tradition is usually only passed from mother to daughter, from father to son. My three daughters all died before they could walk. My son is all that remains to me, yet he is not gifted with the trait. When I am gone, there will be no one to continue the tradition, to protect our people or to guide them. I . . . worry for our future." She glanced at Siyan. "When I first saw you, I thought you could be the one to continue it. But I see now it is not the purpose you have chosen."

Siyan's heart sank. It saddened her to hear of Emora's lost daughters. It saddened her even more to hear Emora had considered calling her a daughter, but then decided against it. The pain she had felt for so many years from being abandoned by her parents now resurfaced; that deep-down fear that she was, at her core, unlovable. It was a pain Siyan thought had healed, but she now realized it hadn't. Maybe it never would.

She looked at Emora. The woman seemed convinced that Siyan's purpose was to wander, that it was a choice she had made for herself. But it wasn't. Not really. She just wanted to learn about this ability of hers that confounded her.

She wanted to find her mother's family—her own relatives—if there were even any to be found. Most of all, though, she wanted to belong. She wanted to stop feeling awkward and out of place, afraid of being herself for fear of others finding out who she really was and what she could do. She wanted peace—a calm in her mind and heart that she had never known. A calm that would let her simply be, and in that peace she would find happiness. Siyan wandered only because she wanted these things, and she didn't know where to go to find them.

What would Emora say to her if she asked to stay? If Siyan told her she wished to make a life for herself here among these people? Would they welcome her? Or would they cast her out like the outsider she was? Siyan was afraid to ask—afraid to bare her heart only to have it wrenched and cast aside, to be told she didn't belong, that she wasn't one of them.

So what could she do? She could leave. But where would she go? To her parents? To her mad, metamorphosed mother who, on a bad day, might try to kill her? To all the sorrow that the thought of her parents always brought? No, she couldn't go back there. And if she left, she'd be alone again, without any purpose to give her life any meaning or direction. She didn't agree that her purpose was what Emora said it was, but maybe it was better than nothing.

With a sinking stomach, Siyan nodded. "All right. I'll do it."

They returned to the camp, and Siyan readied to leave the following day.

The next morning she stopped by Emora's hut to say goodbye and found Enon standing there, his satchel packed, a bow in his hand and a quiver on his back.

"I am going with you," he said.

It was the first time he had spoken to her since that first day. Siyan's mouth worked soundlessly for what seemed an excruciatingly long moment before she managed to stutter, "No . . . I . . . that's not necessary."

Emora ducked out of her hut. "It is. Your journey is of great importance, and the dangers are many. It would be best if you did not travel alone."

"I can take care of myself."

Emora smiled. "Yes, but even an And'estar cannot foresee all dangers, and an extra pair of eyes and hands are always to be valued. Take him, if not for yourself, then for me, and help ease this old woman's worry."

Despite the woman's advanced age, "old" somehow seemed an inappropriate description. Still, as much as Siyan would have preferred to travel alone, she found it difficult to refuse. Even if she did, she wasn't sure that Enon would heed her. He had a look of grim determination about him—one that suggested he had a task, and he meant to carry it out. Not knowing what else to do, Siyan nodded.

She said goodbye to Emora and thanked her for her hospitality. Then she left, thinking sing Emora would like some time to say goodbye to her son in private. Instead, Enon gave a slight nod to his mother, which Emora returned, and that was it.

Siyan wound her way through the forest while Enon trailed after her. He made no move to speak with her, or to walk beside her. They traveled a while in awkward silence before Siyan realized she had no idea where they were headed.

She turned to Enon. "Do you know where we ought to go?"

Enon looked at her a moment, his expression unreadable. "You are the one who finds things."

Siyan tightened her jaw. That she "found things" wasn't exactly how she would have described herself. And yet that seemed to be the whole premise of this journey they were on. She couldn't help but wonder if the whole endeavor was a big mistake.

She held out her arm and whistled. After a moment, Fal flew down from the sky and perched on her outstretched limb. Siyan stroked his breast while eyeing Enon. The man watched her and the bird, but said nothing.

It felt strange trying to use her ability while others watched. She never used her powers in front of anyone, not if she could help it, and Enon was no different. She had always thought her reluctance stemmed from being so different from everyone else, and that it would be unwise to draw unwanted attention. Enon, however, knew all about her power; his own mother was an And'estar, just like her. She ought to be able to trust him. Yet having him standing there watching her with those dark, impassive eyes just made her feel . . . exposed.

"I don't like being watched," she said.

Enon looked at her a moment longer. Then he turned and walked away a short distance.

Siyan continued to watch him, wondering why he unsettled her so much. Then she lifted her arm and brought the falcon level with her face. Looking into his black eyes, she whispered, "I need you to find someone for me. People like me, like Enon here. Ilvar that have forgotten their ways. They need our help, and I need your help to find them."

Fal turned his head, looking at Siyan with a single eye. Then he flew off and disappeared over the trees.

Siyan remained still a moment, enjoying the quiet solitude. She closed her eyes, breathing in the cool spring air. Exhaling, she opened them and turned towards Enon. He stood a stone's throw away, his back turned.

"Let's go," she called to him.

Enon turned and looked at her, and then looked to the sky. His gaze fell back on her, his eyebrows knitted in a quizzical manner. Siyan thought he might speak to her, but he remained silent. By the time he reached her, his face was impassive yet again. He stopped, waiting for her to lead the way.

Suppressing a sigh of exasperation, Siyan turned and continued walking. Without Fal, she had no idea in which direction they ought to travel. It would take some time before he returned—days, maybe even weeks—and until then they would only be wandering aimlessly. It would, perhaps, be wiser to set up camp and wait, but Siyan couldn't bear to sit for days on end in the company of a man who barely acknowledged her existence. Nor did she want to return to Emora's village and further impose on her hospitality. She didn't belong there. Not yet, anyway.

The days wore on, long and filled with silence. Each evening after setting up camp, Enon would venture out on short hunting excursions. Many nights he returned empty-handed and shared with Siyan some of those greasy meat and berry cakes he kept in his satchel. Though such fare wasn't particularly pleasant, it was better than nothing, and so she was grateful.

Without Fal, Siyan's ability to hunt was minimal, and she depended upon her own meager ability to forage to find any food. If not for Enon, she imagined she'd have spent many of the passing nights hungry. And so, despite the uncomfortable silence that hung between them, Siyan began to appreciate his presence.

He was away hunting one evening while Siyan remained in the camp, preparing some thistle buds she had found earlier in the day. The buds were still young, having not yet blossomed and thus relatively free of thorns. When roasted over a fire, the thistles were actually very tasty, and were one of Siyan's favorite things to eat out in the forest.

She had just finished paring away the spiky tops of the buds with her knife when Enon returned with a rabbit in hand, and Siyan smiled at the sight of it. She roasted her thistles while he gutted and skinned the rabbit, and they ate the thistles while the rabbit, in turn, roasted over the fire. After the rabbit was done and they had eaten, Siyan sat staring into the fire, feeling full and content. It was the happiest she had felt in a while, and her happiness made her bold.

She turned to Enon. "You're not much for talking, are you?"

Enon glanced at her out of the corner of his eye but remained silent.

Siyan pursed her lips—now he was just being rude. "Where I'm from it's considered impolite to ignore people who talk to you."

"We are not from the same place."

Siyan frowned. "I was just trying to make conversation."

Silence.

"Have I done something to offend you? Or are you this hostile to everybody?"

Enon looked at her. "If you think me hostile, then you are a greater fool than I thought."

Siyan blinked. "If I'm such a fool, then why did you agree to come along?"

"It is my duty. That I understand this and you do not is the difference between us."

"So, you don't like being told what to do. Is that what this is about?"

"No one has 'told' me anything. What I don't like is you."

Siyan set her jaw and raised her chin, pretending his words didn't feel like a slap in the face. "You don't even know me."

"I know enough."

"And what is it you think you know?"

Enon turned towards her, resting his arm on the fallen tree he had been leaning against. In the firelight his eyes looked black, and Siyan suddenly wished she had never spoken to him.

"I know you are an outsider," he said. "You might have the eyes of And'estar, but you are not one of us. You dress as an outsider, you prattle on with meaningless words as all outsiders do. You are not content to just sit and listen and find peace from within. Instead you burden those around you with your need, and want, and fear. You are not worthy of the And'estar name, of the responsibilities that lay at your feet. You don't even know what those responsibilities are. I doubt you care."

Siyan swallowed. "I care."

"You care for yourself. That is the only reason you have accepted your duty. You do not care for us, or what becomes of us. You only seek to find the other clans because it benefits you, and you alone. The other clans will see you as I do, and they will not accept you, and it angers me that such responsibility has fallen to you.

"As a boy, I watched my mother weep as she buried each of her daughters—each time losing hope for our future. I wished I could be what she needed me to be. I wished I had died rather than my sisters, so that our hope may live on in them. None of these things came to pass, and I came to accept it. But what I cannot accept is an ignorant outsider making a mockery of our ways for her own selfish benefit. I will do what is expected of me and see you safely to your destination. I do it for my mother and for my people. Not for you." He turned back towards the fire.

Siyan swallowed again. The whole time Enon had spoken, his voice had been even, calm. He hadn't shouted or become angry, and somehow that made what he said all the more hurtful. She wished he had yelled at her. Then she could have hidden her feelings in indignation or dismissed his words as rash and ill-spoken. Instead, his calm words ate their way to her heart, echoing in her mind even though she wished she could brush them aside and forget they had ever been spoken.

He had called her selfish. Siyan thought herself many things—weak, abnormal, inadequate—but never selfish. Her entire life had been spent in the service of others. Even now she was on a quest that she would rather have not undertaken, yet had anyway. How could he say she was selfish? The idea of it hurt her and made her angry. She wanted to yell at him, tell him he didn't know anything about her. But she couldn't bear to have those dark eyes of his looking upon her again while he calmly tore her apart. She was weak—always so weak—and that angered her most of all.

CHAPTER 5

ADDIGAN SAT ON A blanket spread out on the forest floor, her legs stretched out with the skirts of her dress carefully arranged so as not to leave any parts of her anatomy exposed. The forest was such a foreign place with the rustling of the wind, the creaking of branches, and the squawking of birds. She missed the quiet of the Tower library, the smell of dust and leather and paper. She missed the scratching sound her pen made whenever she wrote. The pencil she now used to write in the journal resting on her lap was vulgar and crude. It was an instrument for school children not yet entrusted with valuable ink.

She shifted her weight, trying to find a reasonably comfortable position on the cold, uneven ground, and continued to write.

To be traipsing through such inhospitable surroundings while in the company of an insufferable fool is almost beyond bearing. How odd that, in my strong desire to flee the Tower, I now wish to return there. No, that is not entirely true. I wish to return victorious. I wish to see the look on all of their faces when they realize I am worthy of respect. However demeaning the task, I must remember that this journey is a means to an end, and not the end itself.

Leaves rustled behind Addigan. She turned and found

Jash standing behind her, peering over her shoulder and at her journal. She frowned and closed the book.

Jash smiled. "Writing about me, are you?"

"It's none of your concern."

"If it's about me, I'd say it is."

"It's nothing to do with you."

He chuckled. "You're a terrible liar."

Addigan frowned as her cheeks burned. "I do not pay you to be looking over my shoulder, reading my private correspondence."

"Then you've nothing to worry about. I can't read."

Addigan blinked. "Then what were you doing looking over my shoulder?"

"A man's got a right to be curious."

Addigan put the journal away in her satchel. The man was impossible, as always. They had been traveling through these wilds for nearly two weeks, and each day was as the last—with Jash putting his nose into her affairs, as pleased as could be with himself all the while. She got up and stretched her legs.

"I've business to attend to," she said.

"You mean you need to piss," Jash said. "Go on, you can say it. I won't tell anyone you were *unseemly*."

Tightening her jaw, Addigan turned away as Jash's laughter rang around her. Insufferable, indeed. Addigan didn't know what was worse—having to put up with that man or having to live in the wilds like savages. It was almost more than she could bear, and again she wondered if she was doing the right thing. Maybe Malvin was right, maybe she was being rash and foolish.

What if none of this mattered? What if these supposed "tree keepers" she had read about turned out to be simple gardeners, if they even existed at all? Then all of this incessant wandering would have been for nothing.

But what else could she do? She couldn't return to the

Tower. The very idea of seeing those smug, judgmental smirks of the Magisters would be enough to keep her wandering until her legs gave out. No, she couldn't return.

Having relieved her bladder, Addigan returned to the camp and found Jash squatting on the ground as he rummaged through her satchel.

"A-D-D-I," he said, squinting at a piece of paper.

Addigan stormed up to him and snatched the paper from his hand, tearing it in the process. "How dare you!"

"Addi," he said, sounding thoughtful. "Is that you?"

Addigan glared at him. "I thought you couldn't read."

Jash shrugged a shoulder. "I know how to string a few letters together. Wouldn't exactly call it reading." He smiled. "That's your name, though, isn't it? Addi."

"To you, it's Miss Moore."

Jash screwed his mouth to the side and tilted his head. "No, Addi sounds better. Much more fitting for a lovely woman than 'Miss Moore,' don't you think?"

Lovely. It had been a very long time since anyone used that word to describe Addigan. She wondered if Jash was having yet more fun at her expense. She picked up her satchel and said in a low voice, "Stay out of my business and out of my things, or our arrangement will be at an end."

She started to walk away when Jash said, "Well, if your business is anything like the business you do out in the woods, I'll be sure to stay clear of it."

With a straight back and stiff jaw, Addigan walked to the other end of the camp. She looked at the paper in her hand. It was an old letter from Malvin, back before the Threshing, when he had been away in Sunbridge. Her heart ached to see it crumpled and torn, and for a moment she hated Jash for touching it.

But that was foolish. It was just an old letter—a crushed memory of what used to be. It had no more bearing on her life than the ink with which it was written. Addigan had never been one for sentiment; she was not about to start now. She stuffed the letter back into the satchel.

They continued their journey through the forest. Most of their supplies were stowed in a pack that Jash carried on his back, though Addigan had a satchel in which she kept her journals and letters. Jash had mocked her for taking along what he thought to be useless things, but they weren't useless to her. Her journals were a part of her, the core of her being. They helped her make sense of a sometimes dark and confusing world. They were her comfort in times of fear and loneliness. Above all, they were her salvation.

In her paralysis after the Threshing, Addigan's desire to keep writing was what had driven her to heal, to recover and take back that which she had lost. And it had been a long and arduous road. She had to relearn everything—how to walk, how to hold a pen, how to chew her food. She had been an invalid, and it had been as horrific as it was humiliating. She still had the journal from that time, packed away in the satchel she now carried. The penmanship in it was appalling, and its contents a near-incoherent tirade of her fears and anguish. She had thought about burning it on several occasions, but she could never bring herself to do it. As much as it pained her to look at that journal, it was a marker of all she had accomplished. She had fought, and she had won. And it was that lesson Addigan never wanted to forget.

She watched Jash as he wound through the forest. He'd stop from time to time, examining the ground and bushes and trees. He said he was following a trail, though Addigan could never see what he claimed was there. On occasion she would see a stray print set in some mud or moss, but that was all. Certainly nothing she would call a trail, nor was it a clear indication of where this girl they were seeking had gone. But Jash was known in Roelith as a man who could track people down, particularly those who did not wish to be found. She had to remind herself repeatedly to trust him on this matter. Yet trust did not come easily to Addigan, especially when the man in question had the wit of an adolescent.

Two long and monotonous days later they came to a wide clearing where the ferns and underbrush had been flattened and broken. Addigan and Jash separated as they walked around. Addigan came upon some blackened rocks, coal, and ash.

"It's a camp," she said.

"That it is."

"We're getting close, then."

Jash scratched his neck. "Maybe."

"What do you mean, 'maybe'?"

He smiled and spread out his arms. "Do you see any-one here?"

Addigan frowned.

"It's a pretty big camp," Jash said. "So far we've been following a single set of prints, but this place looks big enough for . . . I don't know, two score of folks or so. Maybe more. This camp was not made by the girl we've been fol-lowing."

"But she came here, right?"

Jash nodded, his gaze still fixed on the ground. "Oh yes, she definitely came here. The question that remains is where did she go?" He wandered off, staring at the ground as he went.

Addigan also looked around, though as usual she couldn't find anything. After a while, she gave up and sat on a rock while she waited for Jash to finish his survey.

Eventually he returned and stood before her.

"Well?" she said.

Jash looked down at her, shifting his weight to rest upon a single leg. "So, what happened to your face?"

Addigan flinched. "What?"

He rubbed one of his cheeks. "Your face, it's all purple. Why?"

"It's none of your business."

"Probably not, but I'm curious. And you're curious to know where that girl has gone. So, you tell me and I'll tell you." He flashed her a bright smile. "A trade."

"I'm paying you to tell me where she's gone. There's nothing to trade."

Jash squatted down as he looked out towards the forest. "There's always something to trade, and money's not everything. What would you do if I left? What will your money buy you then?"

Addigan narrowed her eyes. "You wouldn't dare."

Jash smiled again—a carefree grin that might have been charming if it hadn't been so infuriating. "You sure about that?"

Addigan felt nauseated. "Why do you care?"

He shrugged. "Just curious. I like to know the people I travel with."

Addigan stared past him. She didn't know where to start. She had never talked about her injury to anyone, not even Malvin. How could she tell Jash of the Threshing—a gauntlet of horrors that challenged would-be Magisters in both mind and body? It was a test designed to force one to think quickly on one's feet and to wield the Art at a certain level of power. And it did—exceedingly well. One either passed the Threshing or one died. The fact that Addigan had done neither made her an anomaly—a fact she had spent the subsequent years trying to forget along with the horrors she had endured. She didn't know if she could talk about it, even if she wanted to. "Then leave if you must."

She kept her gaze glued to the trees, refusing to look

at him. He probably thought it a harmless question, but it ate away at her heart, leaving her feeling exposed and violated. Her bruising was a constant reminder of her failure, of all that she had lost. She hated that she had to bear her weakness so openly for all the world to see.

Addigan suddenly wished that Jash would leave. She no longer wanted to be near him, to look at him, to hear him prattle on. A slow death alone in the forest seemed preferable by comparison.

After a while, Jash said, "Well, it looks like your girl and whoever was in this camp have gone separate ways. Except for one. Judging by the prints, it looks like she's now got a man with her."

His words seemed distant, inconsequential. Addigan found it difficult to care, even though she knew that she should.

"It could mean trouble for us," Jash said. "Might make things messy."

Addigan closed her eyes, burying the hurt that Jash had so casually unearthed. Then she forced herself to look at him. "We'll not have any trouble."

Meaningless words. She had no idea if they'd have trouble or not. At that moment, she didn't care. She just wanted to continue on their journey. Anything other than sitting there in the presence of a man she was growing to despise.

Jash stood and readjusted the pack on his shoulders. "Right," he said and continued walking.

Addigan put a hand over her eyes. She needed to get a hold of herself. Taking a deep breath, she followed after him.

CHAPTER 6

AFTER THAT NIGHT BY THE FIRE, Siyan did not try speaking to Enon again. They continued their journey in silence, ate their meals together in silence. It was unbearable, and Siyan regretted all the more having accepted this fool's errand. She had wanted to find her mother's people, but Emora and her clan weren't them. She should have moved on. She might have relatives, aunts and uncles and grandparents. Finding them was what mattered, not trying to teach these other clans what they had forgotten.

Siyan agreed with Enon on one thing—the other clans would not accept her. Nor did she want them to, not really. Teaching them of ways she herself barely understood was not her responsibility, nor did she want it to be. So why had she agreed to do it?

Enon had said she was doing it out of selfishness, but that wasn't true. She just hadn't had the courage to tell Emora no. The woman seemed to have pinned her hopes on Siyan, and she didn't have the heart to dash them. It wasn't selfish, it was weak. Was it better being selfless and weak, or selfish and strong? Siyan was unsure, but at that moment the latter seemed preferable.

The days wore on, fading into each other in indistinguishable monotony. When Fal at last appeared in the sky, Siyan felt as if her heart would soar up to meet him. They altered their course, following the falcon as it flew above, coasting on the wind. Another week passed as they followed the bird, and traveling became less onerous. Siyan was glad to have a purpose, a goal she could focus her attention upon rather than stumbling through the wilderness in leaden silence.

When they at last came upon a camp, Fal came down to perch on Siyan's outstretched arm. She caught a brief quizzical look from Enon, but the man said nothing, as usual.

Siyan hesitated, unsure of what to do. Was she to just walk into their camp, unannounced and uninvited and start telling them all of what they had forgotten? Siyan didn't know much about these people, but she suspected that such an entrance would more than likely be unwelcome.

She turned to Enon. "What do we do?"

Enon said nothing for a while, keeping his gaze on the camp ahead. Then he looked at her. "We go and talk to them."

"Just like that?"

"That is usually the way of talking."

"I mean, we don't just walk in there, do we? Don't we need to . . . I don't know . . . introduce ourselves first?"

Enon looked away again. "Do what you think is best."

The man was no help. Siyan wondered why Emora thought it so important that he follow her.

She hoisted her arm and the falcon again took flight. Casting a final glance at Enon, Siyan then started towards the camp.

The camp was bigger than Emora's had been, though it looked much the same. Huts of leather hide draped over wooden poles served as homes, with thin trails of smoke twining upward as fires burned within. People wandered about the area, working and talking with each other. Some were tanning hide into leather, others were curing meat and fish on wooden racks. As Siyan drew closer, several noticed her approach and stopped their tasks as they watched her.

She slowed, wondering if her arrival was an unwelcome intrusion, if someone would step forward to stop her, but no one did.

As Siyan approached the center of the camp, a man walked up to her. He was in his elder years, his white hair braided much like Enon's, his eyes brown.

He regarded her in silence, and so Siyan also remained silent. She didn't know if she should speak, or if her words would be an unwelcome intrusion, as Enon seemed to think they were. The Elder looked at her, then at Enon who stood behind her, and back to Siyan again. Then he said, "An outsider comes with a distant brother. This is either a boon or a burden. Which are you?"

Siyan glanced back at Enon. "A boon, I think."

"Yet you are unsure."

They stared at each other a moment when the Elder asked, "Why have you come?"

Why, indeed? "I've . . . come to teach you. Of things your people have forgotten." Siyan stared at the ground, unable to bring herself to look at the man.

"And what would an outsider know of such things?"

"I'm not an outsider. Not really. I'm one of you, I only grew up among outsiders. I'm an And'estar—a spirit walker, or . . . one who is spirit."

"You speak these words as if you know their meaning, but your actions tell me you do not."

Siyan had already felt like an impostor; now she felt even more like one. She made herself look at him, ignoring the twisting feeling in her stomach. "I'm learning."

"One who is learning cannot hope to teach others."

"I don't see why not. If I've learned something your people have forgotten, what's the harm in my telling you about it?"

"And what, exactly, would you tell us?"

Siyan faltered. She had thought she'd know what to say, but her mind had gone blank.

He nodded and started to turn away.

"Your ancestors," Siyan said, blurting out the first thing that came to mind. "You've forgotten them."

The Elder looked at her, frowning. "We have forgotten nothing."

His gaze was unsettling, but Siyan clenched her hands and stood her ground. "You have. You've left them behind, forgotten them, and so they've forgotten the world."

The Elder's eyes sharpened, his voice angry. "I will not have an outsider tell me of our ancestors. You know nothing, understand nothing."

"I understand more than you," Siyan said and then regretted it.

He straightened his back, his face reddening. "You are not welcome here."

Siyan remained still, trying to think of something to say that could convince him, something that could salvage the conversation, but again her mind went blank. She turned to Enon, but the man did nothing other than watch her and the others from the camp that now gathered more closely around them. Some held long spears, others bows. Children hid behind their mothers' legs. Everyone watched her with eyes that had turned distant and cold.

"You will leave," the Elder said. "Now."

Not wanting to find out how they might handle an unwelcome visitor, Siyan left.

She crashed through the ferns and brush, hurriedly trying to get away from the Ilvar and her failure. From the sound of his footsteps, Enon followed close behind. She couldn't bear to look at him. He had told her she would fail, and she had. Was he taking pleasure in her defeat? She wished he would leave her alone.

But he didn't leave her alone. He just kept on following her in silence. Always in silence.

She rounded on him. "I suppose you're glad that I failed. You said I would, and I did, and I bet that just makes you pleased as pie."

Enon frowned. "Pleased as pie?"

With an exasperated sigh, Siyan turned and kept on walking. Enon followed.

She walked until her legs grew tired and her hunger increased. It had been many hours since they had last eaten. She should be putting her efforts into finding food, and not fretting over something she couldn't change. So she hadn't convinced the Elder to let her teach him. So what? She hadn't wanted the responsibility anyway. But then why did her failure feel like a stab in the gut? Why did she care so much?

Siyan stopped and leaned against a tree. Enon stood behind her.

After a long moment of silence, Siyan said, "What do we do now?"

"You teach them of what they have forgotten, as you said you would."

"I tried, he didn't want to hear it. He got angry at me. I don't think I'd be welcomed back."

"Then you find a way."

"How?"

Enon said nothing.

Siyan looked at him, but the man just stood there. She turned back around, watching as the fading sun illuminated the forest in a mottled, golden light. She wanted to be alone. She couldn't think with Enon standing there, watching her.

"When I was a boy," Enon said, "I left our camp and headed into the forest to undergo the Cerias, or Bleeding. I was, by all reason, too young. Not older than six. Usually it is a boy's father that decides when he is ready for the ritual.

But since my father had died, I decided that the decision fell to me alone. I thought I was ready, and so with a knife, a bow, and a quiver with only four arrows, I set out to make a kill that would mark my entrance into manhood.

"It was spring after a particularly harsh winter, and game was scarce. I wandered for three days, drinking from streams and eating what leaves and berries I could find. I was very hungry and thought myself a more skilled hunter than I was. My attempts with the bow were rash and unconsidered, and I soon depleted the four arrows I had brought with me.

"I was unsure what to do. I couldn't turn back, not without being shamed for my failure. Yet if I stayed, I would surely perish from hunger. Considering these two outcomes, I decided that perishing would be the preferable course, and so I stayed." He shifted his weight, glancing at Siyan before returning his gaze towards the surrounding trees. "I don't think I believed it, though, that I would perish. I don't think I truly understood what that meant. I thought it some brave deed, something men did that was later spoken about in stories with awe and admiration. To die bravely sounded much like undergoing the Bleeding. My father had died bravely, and so it was what I would do, and everyone would be proud and speak well of me.

"And so I wandered. I still had my knife that I used to try and catch squirrels or spear fish. But I failed in that as well, and so my hunger grew. The more I wandered, the hungrier I became, and soon I could not wander at all and had to rest beneath a tree until my strength returned to me. I remember thinking then that dying there alone in the forest, with pain in my belly and fear in my heart, didn't seem all that desirable anymore. I wanted to be home with my mother. I wanted to be warm underneath the furs in my hut. I started to cry, and I knew that when I died, I would not have died bravely, and all of it would have been for nothing.

"I do not know how long it was after that when they came, but she was there, my mother, together with a group of men from our clan. She picked me up and carried me until we returned home. As happy as I was to have been found, I also felt ashamed and foolish at my weakness. I waited for the others to taunt me, to mock my failure, but if they did, it was outside my knowing.

"When I was stronger, my mother came to me and asked me why I would wander off alone into the forest with only a knife, a bow and four arrows, and none of the knowledge men need to survive in the wild. When I told her, she just looked at me for a long time, and I wondered if I was in trouble—if I should have remained silent or told her something else.

"Then she said to me something I have never forgotten: 'To die brave is a lie spread around by foolish men who are too frightened to look into their hearts and know that they have fallen short and wasted their lives. So they cling to the notion that they are somehow courageous to accept their own death, rather than fighting to stay alive. If you want to be viewed as a man, then it is not the Bleeding that will make you one, but rather your resolve to survive and to never lie down and accept your defeat.'"

Siyan and Enon watched each other. She didn't know what to say to him. It was the most he had ever spoken to her, and she was touched that he had shared such a personal story. It was kind. It was . . . confusing. Siyan no longer knew what to make of this man that followed her through the forest.

"You will not lie down and accept your defeat," Enon said. "You will fight, and you will succeed." Taking his bow in hand, he then wandered off into the forest.

Later that evening, Siyan and Enon sat around the campfire as the smell of roasted meat hung in the air. Enon had returned with a bird that looked like a pheasant, but with black feathers that gleamed blue and green in the firelight, save for the long tail feathers that were white as snow.

She wondered what to do. Enon was right—she couldn't give up. But she didn't know what to do to get the Elder to listen, and Enon wasn't providing any suggestions. So she continued to sit by the fire, hoping an idea would come to her.

They sat in silence, ate in silence, and, once the meal was finished, lay down to sleep without a word being exchanged. The silence didn't bother Siyan as it once had— she was too preoccupied with her own thoughts. Such thoughts, however, made sleep difficult, and she had only managed a fitful slumber when sunlight once again broke through the trees.

They breakfasted on what was left of the bird. Once finished, Enon started picking through the feathers, trimming the finest of them into fletches for arrows. Siyan left him to his task and walked further into the forest. After she had gone a ways, she put out her arm and whistled and waited as the falcon soared down and perched upon her limb. She liked feeling the weight of the bird, always a little nervous that the sharp talons would pierce the leather sleeve that protected her skin, but they never did. She reached out and stroked the back of the falcon's head with a finger, enjoying the softness of the tiny feathers. Standing there in silence, she could almost forget Enon and Emora and the Elder of that clan who had never given her his name.

Twigs snapped behind her and Fal took flight. Siyan turned and faced a woman and a man. The man had short coppery hair and a pistol at one hip, a rapier at the other. Siyan's stomach tightened.

"We mean you no harm," the woman said as she took a step forward. She had russet brown hair that had been wrapped into a bun behind her head. She wore a long dress—the hem at her feet caked with mud—with long sleeves and a high neck. Her features were plain and prim, utterly unremarkable save for the deep purple bruise that marred one side of her face. At least she wasn't a Magister.

Siyan looked at Jash. "Why have you followed me?"

The woman said, "*I* am the one who has sought you out. This man is in my employ."

Siyan frowned, her hands tensing. "Why?"

The woman raised her eyebrows, looking at Siyan as if the answer was quite apparent. "I have questions."

"And how is that a concern of mine?"

"You are an And'estar, are you not?"

Siyan tensed further, her heart beating faster. "What would you know about that?"

"Admittedly very little, which is why I have sought you out. I have questions, and you will supply me with answers."

Enon appeared nearby with his bow drawn and an arrow nocked, aiming it at Jash.

Jash, seeing Enon, drew his pistol and pointed it at Siyan. "You shoot me, I shoot her. Simple as that."

Enon said nothing and kept his bow drawn.

Siyan narrowed her eyes. Who were these people? "You have an unusual way of requesting help from strangers."

The woman caught Siyan in a level gaze. "I am requesting nothing."

Siyan crouched, ever so slightly, closer to the ground. "I don't take orders from anyone."

The woman tilted her head back as her lips twitched. She looked amused. "Everyone takes orders from someone."

Siyan crouched closer to the ground. "I think you ought to leave now."

"We needn't make this difficult. Surely you're not so threatened at the prospect of answering a few questions?"

"I'm threatened by having a pistol aimed at my head and you making demands as if you're the Queen of Sunbridge."

The woman pursed her lips. Then, to Jash, she said, "Lower your weapon."

Jash glanced at her but kept his pistol raised. "I'll lower mine when he lowers his."

The woman lowered her voice. "Put down your weapon and he'll do the same."

Jash remained still.

Growing angry, the woman turned to him. "Put down your weapon, I command you!"

With her attention diverted and Jash watching Enon, Siyan crouched to the ground and put her hands to the earth. She burrowed her fingers through the fallen needles and leaves and into the soil.

A rustling came from the surrounding trees, and Jash adjusted his grip on the pistol as his gaze darted from side to side. The woman turned and emitted a startled gasp when a great stag emerged from the forest. It was massive, with legs that were almost as long as she was tall, its snout towering high above them. The stag was crowned with antlers that branched upwards and outwards as if trying to encompass the entire world within their bony limbs. The stag looked at them and huffed, and white mist plumed from his snout.

Both Enon and Jash seemed to have forgotten each other and lowered their weapons as they stared at the animal. The woman stumbled backwards as the stag moved towards her, looking at her with big black eyes. It huffed again, and again a white mist plumed from its nostrils, hanging in the air like a foggy haze.

"Do something!" the woman said.

Jash seemed to remember his pistol and raised it at the animal. "I've only got one shot with this thing, and I don't know how well my sword will fare against those antlers."

The stag lowered his head, baring the broad rack of antlers while he stamped at the ground. His breath quickened, and the mist from his nostrils billowed around him.

"Jash . . .!" the woman said, sounding panicked.

The mist from the stag grew and coalesced, spreading from the animal to Jash and the woman and eclipsed their forms. When it passed over Siyan, the air grew cold and heavy. The world quieted. The others sounded distant and muffled, as if they stood beyond a thick pane of glass.

Siyan removed her hands from the earth and rose. The fog obscured the trees, reducing them to little more than vague shadows. Enon and the others remained shrouded in the haze, though Siyan could still see them. Their forms glowed from within the mist, figures of gentle light that moved and wandered. Except for one. Siyan walked towards Enon, who had remained still during the entire event. He did not see her approach, and the fog dampened her footsteps. When she put a hand on his arm, he started and reached for his knife. Then he relaxed.

Saying nothing, Siyan pulled him by the sleeve as she led him away. Beyond in the mist, the muffled sound of Jash and the woman grew quieter until all was silent.

CHAPTER 7

ADDIGAN WANDERED THROUGH the damp, cool mist. The air felt heavy and thick, making the simplest of movements labored and strained. Despite the chill air, sweat broke across her brow. Memories of her previous paralysis flashed through her mind, and her stomach constricted in that horribly familiar twinge of panic and fear. It was happening again. She was losing herself again.

She squeezed her eyes shut, flexing her hands open and closed. Open and closed. She could still move. She was still herself. Whatever was happening, it wasn't happening to her alone. Addigan forced herself to breathe deep, despite the wet air that threatened to gag her.

She listened for Jash, for any sounds of movement, but everything sounded so distant and muffled—as if the world had been reduced to a muted memory. The only clear sound was her blood rushing in her ears.

"Jash?" she called. Her voice sounded stifled and foreign.

What had the girl done? That stag had been an abomination, as was the mist. She tried not to think about what it meant for her to be breathing it, or what might be lurking out in the haze. Was the man with the bow still out there? How long until she felt the stabbing pain of an arrow piercing her flesh?

Despite her efforts to keep calm, Addigan's heart quickened.

"Jash!" she called again, putting a harshness in her voice that she hoped masked her fear. How could he not hear her? He had been standing right next to her. Had he left? Or had he been dragged away by that animal?

" . . . Addi . . .?"

Addigan froze, listening. There was a faint popping sound, a snapping of twigs, maybe. Then all was quiet again.

"There you are," Jash said.

Addigan spun around and found Jash standing there as if he had coalesced out of the mist itself. "Where were you? Why didn't you answer when I called out?"

"I did, didn't you hear me? And I didn't go anywhere, you're the one that wandered off." He grinned. "What would you do without me?"

"Live an easier life, no doubt."

"Easy lives are fine for wives, but strife and toil makes men."

Addigan scowled at him. "I always hated that saying."

"Because you are not a wife?"

"Because everyone wants an easier life, only men pretend they don't."

"Not me. I'd love an easy life. I'd even become a wife, but I've not yet found a man who'll have me."

"You're a buffoon."

"I do try."

Addigan turned around. "This mist is wrong. Where did it all come from?"

Jash chuckled. "From the cavernous nostrils of that stag, if I remember correctly."

She frowned at him. "That's exactly my point. Since when do monstrous wild animals breathe such an otherworldly mist? And at such a fortuitous time for the And'estar to escape?"

Jash raised an eyebrow, hooking a thumb in his belt. "You're joking, right? You Magi are always making the impossible happen. Now when someone else does it you're baffled?"

"I'm not a Magister. And that's not how the Art works. Magisters don't . . . summon animals."

Jash shrugged. "A Magi came into a tavern once. Had a little too much to drink and ended up lighting a chair on fire with no more than a few spoken words. I really don't see the difference between this and that."

Addigan narrowed her eyes. "Well, there is. A big difference."

"If you say so."

She paced around in the mist. She had caught up with the And'estar; she had spoken with her. Now she was stuck waiting for the mist to clear while her quarry got further away. Worse still was that the And'estar now knew they were looking for her. She might go into hiding, and Addigan would once again have failed to prove herself. It galled her.

"Stop pacing," Jash said. "It's annoying."

Addigan rounded on him. "Annoying? What's annoying is putting up with you day in and day out. It's annoying having caught up to our quarry only to have her disappear right under our noses. And perhaps most annoying of all is having you standing there telling *me* what to do! Why don't you make yourself useful for a change and start finding out where they've gone instead of standing there like the useless heap of flesh that you are!"

Jash's jaw tightened, but he said nothing.

Addigan clamped her own jaw shut, both out of frustration as well as to keep herself from speaking further. Part of her regretted what she said; part of her knew she had gone too far. But her temper, like always, had gotten the better of her, and her pride refused to let her back down. She stiffened her back, glaring at Jash while wondering what he'd say.

Jash was silent a long while, looking at Addigan before gazing out towards the misty trees. He closed his eyes and rolled his shoulders. He arced his head from side to side, popping the joints in his neck. He returned his gaze to her. "I'll find the trail as soon as the mist clears and then we'll be on our way." He started to walk away before adding, "Miss Moore."

It was the most civil response she had ever heard from him, yet somehow it felt like the worst of insults. She let him go, telling herself that she did not feel bad for what she had said. She did not feel bad about it at all. If she told herself enough times, she might even come to believe it.

CHAPTER 8

SIYAN CONTINUED TO LEAD Enon by the sleeve until they emerged from the mist. She let go of him, glancing back to see if they were followed, but no one was there. Siyan hurried on—she wanted to get a good distance away from Jash and that woman he was with.

Who was she? She knew about the And'estar. She knew that Siyan was one and had tracked her though the forest to find her. That was the most disturbing part of it all. Siyan had thought she was hidden away in the forest, but apparently she could still be found. Quite easily, it seemed. She was beginning to understand the Ilvar's inclination to wander, and that maybe it really was the only way to live in relative peace and safety.

They kept on walking. Only when the sun began to set did Siyan finally stop to rest upon a fallen tree. Enon crouched down in front of her, watching her with those unsettling dark eyes of his. He was quiet a long while, but in time he spoke.

"The stag, it was you that called it?"

If Siyan hadn't known better, she would have thought he looked unnerved. "Yes."

He nodded, looking down at the ground.

"Why do you ask?"

"I have never witnessed it before. The spirit-calling. Not like that. It is . . . not what I expected."

Siyan frowned. "Surely you've seen your mother's magic? Her . . . spirit-calling?"

Enon shook his head. "Not like that. She usually only calls upon her power while alone. She says it is a private matter between her and the trees, the earth and sky, that no one else need concern himself with. The few times she has used it in my presence it was much more . . . subdued. More of a denseness of the forest, or a darkness of night. Never a stag so great it defied imagining, or breathed mist so thick it nearly eclipsed all sight and sound." He smiled, and it occurred to Siyan that he smiled too rarely. That was a shame, for his entire being seemed to light up when he did.

"I needed to do something," she said, shrugging. "I don't know what they wanted, or why they've followed us, but I didn't see it ending well. So . . . I made a diversion."

Enon nodded. "It was well done."

Siyan smiled, feeling silly that her heart felt so lightened for such a few simple words. Then her smile faded. "They know about the And'estar."

Enon looked at her but remained silent.

"How could they know about that?"

Enon shook his head. "I do not know."

Magisters had known about her mother's power and knew about Siyan as well. But they had never mentioned the And'estar. Had they withheld that knowledge from her? Even if they had, Jash and that woman were not Magi. So where had they learned of it?

More than that, how much did they know? They came to Siyan looking for answers, but she was unsure she had any to give. Her own knowledge of the And'estar was tenuous, and this encounter only served to strengthen her doubts that she really understood anything at all.

Siyan didn't want to be teaching others, she wanted to be learning. She wanted to understand what it truly meant to be an And'estar, but there was no one to teach her. Emora had already told her all that she knew, but it wasn't enough. Siyan wanted more.

Enon rose and said, "We should camp here." He took his bow and headed off among the trees.

Siyan watched him leave before getting to her own feet. She put out her arm and whistled, but Fal did not appear. She was on her own.

Siyan wandered through the forest as the light of the setting sun faded into twilight. She didn't know if there would be a moon that night. It didn't matter—she no longer needed it to light her way.

As the sky grew darker, the trees around her grew brighter. It was a muted light, gentle and cool, that seemed to come from the trees themselves. It was as if they had a light all their own, deep beneath the bark that could only be seen once the brilliant light of the sun had faded. It was beautiful and, even though her sight had been like this for nearly two years, Siyan still hadn't grown used to it. Each time night came, her breath still caught as she looked at the world around her.

Siyan glanced at some of the bushes as she walked, but she felt distracted. Despite her hunger, food somehow seemed unimportant. Something else was tugging at her mind—a nagging curiosity, an intense desire to see what lay just a little farther ahead. The more she walked, the stronger this feeling grew until she gave up on the pretense of foraging altogether.

She hurried through the brush, pushing aside branches as she passed. All around her the trees glowed in faded brilliance, like a memory of color that had waned in the telling of it. It made Siyan feel like she was also fading, drifting away to some distant place. She thought she should feel frightened, but she only felt sad, her heart aching with a curious longing. It caused her to quicken her step as she pressed forward, ducking underneath a canopy of low branches and into a small clearing.

A great white tree towered above her—thick at the base and pale as bone, with gnarled, twisted branches that reached towards the sky. Siyan's stomach sank as she remembered her mother's tree, hidden away in a dark, decrepit Tower. But unlike her mother, this tree was wide and robust like a great white oak.

The tree shone in the darkness, brighter than the other trees around it, yet duller than her mother's had been. That tree had exuded a light all its own, pale and bright like the moon. This tree seemed shadowed.

Siyan walked up to it and placed her hand upon the trunk. The wood was hard and smooth, just as her mother's had been. She looked for a face in the wood, a trace of who this And'estar used to be, but there was nothing. A swirling of grain that maybe looked like a mouth or an eye, but she was unsure. Maybe it was only what she wanted to see.

Siyan's hand lingered on the wood and she frowned. Her mother's tree had felt . . . different . . . under her fingers. Alive, somehow. She remembered how it had shivered when she had touched it. But this tree felt . . . heavy. Just like any other tree. It felt wrong, even though she didn't know why.

She walked around it, running her hand over the smooth wood. Her gaze roamed up the trunk to the knobby branches and to the green leaves that shivered in the breeze. They looked dark and murky in the shadows, but green all the same. She circled around until she again stood before the swirl of grain that might have been a mouth or an eye.

Then it occurred to her: the tree was sleeping. It was an And'estar that must not have been tended to for some time and had slipped into slumber. That had to be why it seemed darker than her mother's, or why it seemed like there was no life in the wood beneath her fingers. The tree was sleeping, and Siyan knew then that she needed to wake it.

She hesitated. How does one wake a tree?

Siyan reached out and rapped on the wood. "Hello?" she whispered. Then she felt ridiculous. What did she expect? For a door to open where the And'estar herself would come strolling out? Stupid girl.

But what else could she do? She had no idea how to wake a slumbering And'estar. Enon might know, but the idea of asking him made her uneasy. And she didn't want to return to Emora without completing her task.

Siyan knelt down in front of the tree. She put her hand to the bark, sending her thoughts into it like she would when changing the color of a leaf, or calling the wind. Simple tasks—ones that didn't require Siyan to forget herself, if Emora was to be believed. Only instead of changing its color, Siyan willed the tree to waken—even though she was unsure what that meant.

She removed her hand and leaned back. The tree still looked darkened and shadowed. She sighed. Minan's tree had seemed so much brighter, made all the more so when Emora had hummed her tune. She could almost hear it, the shrilling melody that had made the air alive with light. And then another melody surfaced in her mind—the hollowed notes of a flute as her father played for her mother, and how her mother had calmed when she heard it.

Could it really be so simple?

Siyan rubbed her hands on her legs. She hadn't ever been one for singing. She had been raised to keep silent until bidden, and that songs were for fools and heartsick lovers. She didn't know how to sing, nor did she know of any songs save for a few childhood rhymes and a couple of tavern chanties, neither of which seemed particularly appropriate.

She closed her eyes and listened to the crickets chirping and to the wind rustling in the branches. She thought of her mother and the twisted form of her body in the wood—of all the pain and fear she must have felt dying alone in the dark. She thought of her own childhood and of her quest for answers, and her desire to find a family that loved her. It was a desire she carried with her still. Even though she had found her parents, the love she felt for them also carried pain. Siyan wanted to feel love that didn't hurt, that didn't want to make her cry whenever she thought about it.

She hummed a tune. Feeling awkward and unsure of hearing her own voice, Siyan's song was halting at first. But the more she hummed the more comfortable she felt, and the more she opened her heart to it.

She wove into her song her own feelings of love—pure and unblemished by pain or regret—and the hope she held to one day feel that pureness of love come back to her. She wanted to forget her sorrow and all the expectations that had been placed upon her. She wanted to feel happy and safe. She wanted to just . . . be.

Siyan stopped singing, realizing only then that her cheeks were wet. She wiped her eyes, feeling silly and grateful that no one was watching her make such a fool of herself. She looked at the tree. Though it was still dark and shadowy, it looked a little brighter than it had before. But maybe that was only what she wanted to see, just like she wanted to see a face in the swirls of the grain.

She got to her feet and made her way back to where Enon had left her. He was there, attempting to start a fire with a flint and steel. He glanced at her before returning to his work. Siyan looked at the ground near his feet but saw only brush and fallen pine needles and leaves. He had been unsuccessful in hunting, then. She dreaded another meal of greasy meat cakes, especially since she was unsure of how many they had left.

Siyan walked up to Enon and sat down on a nearby rock as he struggled to light the wood. "I can get the fire going, if you want."

Enon looked at her and then looked beyond her. He remained still, his gaze fixed on a point in the darkness. Then he reached for his bow.

Alarmed, Siyan turned. A small white rabbit hopped through the brush. It stopped and stood on its hind legs, looking at them with colorless eyes.

Enon nocked an arrow and took aim.

"Wait," Siyan said.

Enon glanced at her. "Why?"

"It's not a rabbit. I mean, not like you think."

Enon's pull on the bowstring slackened as he frowned at her. "What do you mean?"

Siyan said nothing, reluctant to say too much and make an even greater fool out of herself than she already was. She had only a suspicion about the rabbit, nothing tangible other than a feeling in her gut.

She walked over and crouched down in front of it. The rabbit remained sitting on its haunches as its nose twitched in the air. Siyan put out her hand and the rabbit sniffed at it, its whiskers tickling her palm. She giggled.

Enon crouched next to her, his eyes inquisitive. The rabbit hopped away as he drew near, though it stayed within sight.

Siyan, watching the rabbit as it nibbled on a leaf, whispered, "I think it's an And'estar."

Enon's perplexed look turned to one of incredulity. "What?"

Siyan couldn't help but feel a flash of satisfaction at seeing the stoic man so unsettled. "I'm not certain. But there was a tree not too far off, an And'estar tree. I think it was asleep. It seemed darker than the others. I . . . tried to wake it."

Enon stared at her in what seemed to be a mixture of horror and awe. "You woke an And'estar?"

Siyan shifted her weight under his gaze. "I think so. I wanted to wake it, but I didn't know how. I thought I failed. But now this rabbit . . . It has colorless eyes. I saw that once before, with my mother." Siyan didn't want to talk about that experience, and so she was grateful when Enon said nothing, his gaze shifting back to the rabbit sniffing along the ground.

Yet the lengthening silence concerned her. "Was it wrong of me?" she asked. "To wake it?"

Enon smiled and exhaled a short breath—almost a laugh. "No."

Siyan relaxed. She wished she didn't care so much what he thought of her, but she did.

They sat in silence for a time as they watched the rabbit hop to the unlit firewood and nudge the branches with its nose. As amazing as it was having seemingly awoken an And'estar, the creature before them was still just a rabbit. It wasn't a great stag that breathed mist; it wasn't a tall pale woman wielding an ivory spear. It was just a little rabbit, and if Siyan hadn't felt so certain in her heart that this was an And'estar, she might have doubted it.

"Is this how it happens when your mother awakens the trees?" she asked.

Enon shook his head. "My mother has not woken any trees for a very long time, if she ever did. We travel from place to place so that she can tend to the few trees that are already awake. We had thought the trees that slumbered to be lost to us, and that it was all we could do to not lose any more. As far as I know, the awakening of an And'estar has not happened for a very long time; I had feared it was no longer possible."

Enon made it sound like she had accomplished an impossible feat. But as Siyan sat there watching the rabbit, it didn't feel so grand. Had she done something wrong? Was she missing something?

"I want to return to the tree." She got to her feet and started walking.

Enon followed her, stumbling over brambles and roots, and Siyan remembered that he couldn't see as well at night as she. She took his hand and led him through the darkened forest until they returned to the pallid tree. Was it brighter than it had been before? Siyan couldn't be sure. It still wasn't as bright as it should have been.

Behind them the brush rustled, and out came the rabbit as it hopped into the clearing.

Enon walked up to the tree and put his hand on the wood. The rabbit followed him and circled the trunk, sniffing at the ground as it went.

Siyan watched Enon a moment before asking, "What do you see?"

Enon looked at the branches above him. "I see an And'estar tree, just like the others I have seen."

"Does it look different to you somehow? Darker, maybe?"

Enon frowned. "No, it looks as the others looked." He turned towards her. "What do you see?"

Siyan said nothing. She also walked up to the tree and put her hand to the trunk. It had felt so heavy before, though she still didn't know how she could tell such a thing by touch alone. Now it just felt like a tree; nothing remarkable about it other than the smoothness of the wood. Had she imagined it before? Or was it really different?

"It's different somehow," she said. "Darker, even though it's so pale. It doesn't seem right. I don't know why. It just doesn't."

"What did you do to awaken it?"

"I . . . sang."

"And what happens if you sing for it again?"

"I don't know."

"Could you try?"

Siyan rubbed her forehead. The idea of using her power in front of Enon was an uncomfortable one. Adding singing to an already awkward moment just made matters worse. But she wanted to try; she wanted to see what would happen.

Siyan moved around the tree so that it blocked her view of Enon. She closed her eyes, trying to imagine she was alone, and hummed a melody. She didn't know the song, not really. It was just something she made up at that moment, a happy little tune that made her think of sunny days and flowered fields. The wind stirred in the branches above her and Siyan opened her eyes and found the rabbit had come to sit at her feet, looking up at her with its glass-like eyes.

Enon came around the tree and looked at her, his expression curious.

Siyan looked between him and the rabbit and shrugged. "I don't think it worked. I don't think anything happened."

Enon tilted his head back as he regarded her. Then he glanced at the tree before heading back in the direction they had come.

Despite Enon stumbling through the darkness, Siyan remained behind him. It gave her time to think. Somewhere out in the forest, a man and woman were following them, looking for answers that Siyan was unsure she'd be able to provide. Now she had found an And'estar tree that she thought she had woken, but even with that she remained unsure. It only served to deepen her doubts about her ability and who she really was.

And'estar. What did that mean, anyway? Enon called her ability spirit-calling. She called it magic. Emora said that when her need was great enough, she could do remarkable things. And when she died, she'd turn into a great white tree which could either be tall and magnificent, or twisted and grotesque. Beyond this, Siyan knew very little, and that frustrated her.

What would it be like being an And'estar tree? Emora said they dreamed, but Siyan felt there was more to it than that. In her mother's more lucid moments, Siyan had been able to speak with her. Was that all supposedly a dream? A vague and fluid occurrence that was forgotten as soon as it ended? Or had her mother known what was happening? Did she remember the conversations they had shared, even though several seasons had since passed?

Siyan didn't know. She hadn't thought to ask her mother these things when she had the chance. Now Siyan was leagues away and burdened with a mission to teach others of the And'estar—a word she barely understood—while being hunted by a pair of strangers.

What a mess.

If she could awaken this tree—completely waken it—maybe she could get some answers about herself. If she could truly come to understand this power of hers and what it meant to have it . . . well . . . maybe then she'd feel worthy of being able to teach others what they had forgotten.

Maybe then she'd stop feeling so lost.

CHAPTER 9

ADDIGAN TRAILED AFTER Jash through the forest. They had been walking for three days and still had not caught up to the And'estar or her companion. Addigan didn't understand it. It had taken a few hours until that otherworldly mist cleared, but once it had, Jash had quickly found their trail and they resumed the pursuit. Addigan figured they would catch up to the girl later in the day, or maybe the next day at the latest. But now three days had passed and still they had found nothing.

"Explain to me again how we have not yet found them," Addigan said. "You've led me to believe you've found their trail, yet there is still no sign of them. How can that be possible? Unless you're a greater fool than I thought and can't tell a footprint from a hole in the ground."

Jash turned around and grinned. He spread out his arms. "If you think you can do better, then be my guest. I've forgotten what peace and quiet sounds like. I think I might rather like getting reacquainted with it."

"If you'd do your job, then you'd have all the quiet in the world."

Jash grunted in what almost passed for a laugh, but not quite. He continued walking.

Addigan followed him, thinking about what had happened when they had encountered the And'estar. She had spent a lot of time thinking of it, trying to understand what she had seen. She'd like to dismiss it all as some odd coincidence. That the beast was a rare and strange creature, but real all the same, and that it had only happened upon them by a random turn of events.

But Addigan knew that wasn't true. Fool though he might be, Jash had been close to the truth. It was the Art that had brought that animal into being, but not by a Magister's hand. That And'estar apparently had capability with the Art, yet in a way Addigan had never thought possible. She wanted to return to the Tower—to the books and scrolls that had mentioned the And'estar and comb them anew for some kind of explanation. How could she have missed such a thing in all her research? Had she overlooked it? Or was the information itself lacking in the tomes, overlooked by everyone that had encountered these people through the years. The thought that such a thing could happen was . . . unthinkable.

Voices carrying through the trees pulled Addigan out of her thoughts. Jash kept on walking, right towards the sound. He didn't hesitate or look back at her. She was about to tell him to stop and show caution when they came upon camp of men, and that's when she saw Malvin.

He was sitting on a folding chair, leafing through a book as a serving boy poured steaming wine into his cup. There were other men in the camp as well, either tending the horses, cooking over fires, or doing other camp-related activities that Addigan didn't really care about. No, her gaze was fixed on Malvin—his handsome profile as he read, dressed in his fiery Magister robe.

Jash walked up to him, took the cup of wine out of his hand and drank it. He handed the cup back. "I've brought you your lady back. Safe and sound, just like I said. Though, I think I ought to get paid extra for putting up with that mouth of hers."

Malvin frowned at Jash. Then he looked at Addigan. "Addi . . ."

Addigan looked at Malvin, at Jash, at Malvin again. She took a step back. "What's going on? Why are you here?"

Malvin rose from his chair and took a step towards her. "Addi, I can explain."

"Let *me* explain it to you," Jash said. "Love-struck robe-boy here wanted me to keep an eye on you. Told me to look after you while you have your fun in the woods, and then bring you back here, safe and sound." He turned to Malvin. "Which I did, so I'll be taking my payment and wishing you a very happy life with your crazed wench."

Of course. She should have known. Addigan straightened her back. "I was not 'having fun.'"

"That makes two of us," Jash said.

Malvin clenched his jaw and closed his eyes. He turned to Jash and grabbed him by the shirt. "Leave us. You'll . . . get your payment. Just leave." He let go of Jash with a bit of a shove.

Jash straightened his shirt, took one last look at Addigan and, shaking his head, wandered over to the supply sacks and started rummaging through them.

Addigan stared at Malvin. He had made a fool out of her. She should have known, yet somehow it still came as a surprise. "How dare you?" she whispered.

Malvin at least had the decency to look abashed. "I'm sorry, Addi. It's just . . . I spoke with the Grand Magister. He told me what you were researching—some nonsense about Tower sites and trees and savages in the woods. He told you he'd look into it, but that wasn't good enough for you."

"The Grand Magister is a pompous idiot!"

"See? That's what I'm talking about. You think everyone is wrong, that everyone is a fool and that you have to do everything yourself, without stopping to think about what it is you're actually doing. These woods are dangerous, Addi. I didn't want you wandering off to the middle of nowhere without some kind of assurance that you would be safe."

"So Jash is my keeper now?"

Malvin said nothing.

Addigan closed her eyes and shook her head. When she spoke again, her voice was quiet. "Out of everyone in the Tower, I thought that you still believed in me. That you still thought I had something worth saying when everyone else thought I should be cast aside."

"I do think that." He took a step towards her. "Addi—"

"Don't lie to me! You couldn't possibly think that or you wouldn't have done . . . *this!*" She waved her arms towards the camp. "You're just like everyone else. You think I lost my wits along with the Art in the Threshing. That I'm some wounded bird you need to coddle. Well, I'm not! I'm not wounded, and I'm not yours to protect!"

Malvin reached towards her but she moved away. She walked over to Jash, who hunkered down on his haunches, eating dried olives. He looked up at her just as she kicked him in the chest and knocked him down. As he went sprawling backwards, she pinned him down with a booted foot.

Jash grinned. "If you wanted me on my back, you could've just asked."

Addigan made a disgusted sound and, reaching down, took the pistol from his belt. She moved away, leveling the gun at him and Malvin as she picked up a sack of supplies and hoisted it over her shoulder. She started to back out of the camp. "If you won't help me, then I'll find this And'estar on my own."

"Addigan, don't be stupid," Malvin said.

"Don't try to follow me," she said, still backing away. "If you do, then I'll shoot you."

Jash got to his feet, grinning like a fool.

Malvin shook his head and rubbed his eyes. "What do you think you'll accomplish, Addi?"

"I don't know," Addigan said. "But I intend to find out." She continued backing away until, satisfied they were not following her, she turned and ran.

CHAPTER 10

SIYAN AND ENON REMAINED near the And'estar tree for several days as they waited. It felt like they were trapped in a nebulous existence, unable to move for indecision. Jash and that woman were following them, after all. It wouldn't do to return to the Elder and his clan and lead the two strangers to the unsuspecting Ilvar. Part of her felt like she was waiting for them to return so she could again confront the scarred woman as she demanded answers. Mostly, though, Siyan simply didn't know what to do. Even if she and Enon weren't being followed, the fact still remained that she had no idea how to convince the Elder into letting her teach him of the And'estar and their forgotten ways.

How was she supposed to change that?

The little white rabbit hopped around her in the underbrush. She supposed she could return to the Elder and show him the creature. It was a manifestation of an And'estar, after all. But it was unlikely they'd see that. They'd probably just see a harmless little animal and send Siyan on her way.

No, the rabbit by itself wasn't enough. She needed something more. Perhaps she could perform a feat of some kind—a display of her power that would show them she was worth listening to. Then again, what if she couldn't?

Control of her power still eluded her, and she doubted they'd be impressed with the wind stirring in the trees.

Siyan rubbed her eyes. She was tired and hungry, and her wandering thoughts only added to her weariness. She gazed out towards the trees, looking for movement. Enon had gone hunting—all was still save for the rabbit hopping around in the underbrush as it nibbled and explored.

And'estar. They were the same, she and the rabbit. Somehow, there was a person behind this creature that crept through the brush, and she wondered what stories this And'estar had to tell. What dreams could he or she share with the world? What would Siyan dream, when her time came? Would she create wondrous and beautiful things as Minan had? Would she create nightmares like those from her mother? Or would she fall somewhere in between and innocuously travel the world as a harmless woodland animal, unseen and unimportant?

It all sounded too familiar. She had spent her whole life unseen, dismissed as unimportant. She wasn't that girl anymore, though. Her life was now open to her, waiting for her to shape it as she pleased. She could make others see her, do something meaningful, but only if she had the courage to try.

She waited for Enon to return. The hours stretched and the rabbit disappeared into the bushes, and she was left only with her winding thoughts for company. Day faded into twilight, and only when the trees had succumbed to shadows did Enon return.

His face was grim, his hands empty. He knelt down to the ashes of the campfire, throwing some kindling onto the coals as he attempted to coax the flames back to life.

"We need to leave," Siyan said.

Enon looked up at her and nodded. "We will leave at dawn."

"We need to leave now."

He blinked at her before gazing out to the trees beyond. He was probably concerned over Siyan's sudden desire to leave, wondering if they were in danger.

"I don't want to wait any longer," she said. "I've been putting off what I need to do, waiting until it becomes easier. But it's not going to get easier, and sitting here isn't helping us. We need to leave, and it's better to leave now."

"It is too dark."

"I can see fine."

"I cannot."

"I'll help you."

Enon watched her a moment before shifting his gaze back to the coals of the campfire. Then, putting his hands to his knees, he pushed himself up. "Very well."

Siyan grinned, glad to be on their way—glad to be doing *something* other than sitting and waiting.

Twilight had since turned to night, and though Siyan could still see, she had always relied on the sun to tell her where east and west lay. "I'm not sure where to go. Where the other clan was."

"They were to the south and east of us," Enon said. "That way." He pointed away from the And'estar tree, back towards where they had come.

Siyan nodded and took his hand in her own. She was mindful that he couldn't see as well as she, and so she kept a slow pace. She watched out for rocks and exposed roots, and took care to tell him whenever she saw such hazards. It worked well for the most part, but as the night wore on, Enon stumbled and slowed regardless.

She stopped, wondering if they should set up camp for the night, even though she was reluctant to do so. They just needed a little bit of light, but the moon was waning and too dim to filter through the trees. If she could, she'd carry the moon in her hands and light the way for Enon.

She looked at him. Despite the darkness, Siyan could still see him clearly—the lines of his face, the shells in his braided hair. Though he was looking at her, the distant, unfocused look in his eyes told her he did not see her well.

She wanted to keep moving. She wanted to give him light.

Siyan put her hand to a tree, and beneath her fingers the bark glowed. The light spread from her hand and up into the branches, like flame crawling up a sheet of paper.

Enon gasped. Siyan was also taken aback, looking up at the tree that now shimmered with silver light. It reminded her of her mother, and she closed her eyes, afraid of the tears that always came with such thoughts.

When she felt calmer, she looked at Enon, finding he had been watching her. She put on a smile. "I thought you could use some light."

"It is beautiful," he said, his voice quiet. He still held her hand, and Siyan wondered if she should pull away now that he could see. But she didn't want to. She liked the way his hand felt around her own. She almost felt guilty about it, like it was a pleasure she wasn't allowed to have.

And so, hand in hand, they continued on. Siyan touched the trees and bushes along the way, making them glow as if infused with moonlight. They dimmed shortly after she and Enon passed. It was like walking into a new world, leaving the old one behind to be consumed by shadows.

They traveled through the night and arrived near the Ilvar camp late the following day. Siyan hesitated long enough to wonder if she should wait until morning. Perhaps the Ilvar would consider it rude to come calling so close to evening, but she dismissed the thought. If she waited, she might lose her nerve. And, given her past encounter, she suspected her presence would always be an unwelcome intrusion regardless of the time of day.

So, taking a deep breath, Siyan walked into the camp. Once again, her approach was unhindered. Once again, she met the clan Elder. They regarded each other for a time in silence. Growing fearful that he would tell her to leave, and growing more aware that she had no idea *what* she should say, Siyan instead bowed before him.

"Forgive me, Elder," she said, staring at the ground near his feet, "for my previous rudeness."

When there was no reply, Siyan straightened and looked at him.

Then the Elder said, "It is forgotten." He was quiet a while, then added, "You and your companion look weary."

"We've traveled far with little food. We are tired and hungry."

The Elder nodded. "Then you will eat and rest." He pointed to a woman standing nearby. She nodded and walked inside one of the huts. A few minutes later she emerged with a bowl in her hands. She handed it to Siyan.

Siyan looked down at the food—a stew of some kind— steaming and smelling of onions. "Thank you."

The woman nodded and walked away.

The Elder said, "If you wish, you may sleep here." He pointed towards the edge of the camp. "There, under the stars. You have not yet proven yourselves as friends, and so you may not share the same fire as us, or sleep under the same furs. Time will tell if you ever will." He turned and disappeared inside a hut.

Despite his dismissal, Siyan felt encouraged. He had given them food and told them they could stay—even if it was out in the cold. It was certainly an improvement over their previous encounter.

With the bowl in hand, Siyan walked to the edge of the camp and sat on the ground. There was no spoon and no bread to scoop up the stew, so she and Enon took turns slurping from the bowl. It tasted bland, and the meat was tough and gristly, but warm and filling nonetheless.

Once finished, she and Enon then set about gathering wood for a fire. Feeling cold and tired, Siyan didn't wait for Enon to light it with his flint and steel and used her power instead. Then it occurred to her she that could have used the fire as a means of demonstrating her power as an And'estar. But the deed was done, and she didn't feel like dragging someone over there to watch her do it all again. No, it would be better to be quiet this evening. She had tried to tell them too much too quickly last time. It hadn't worked then, so she'd need to be more careful about it this time around.

When morning came, the same woman that had given them food returned with a bowl of porridge. Again there was no spoon, so she and Enon used their fingers to eat. The meal was thick and sticky and made of a grain that Siyan didn't recognize.

She was at a loss what to do next. The camp was coming alive with women cooking over fires, sewing clothes or tanning leather. Men strung their bows and fetched their spears before heading off into the forest—some of them, at least. Others remained behind, watching Siyan and Enon with shrewd, unapologetic eyes. Their gazes made her uneasy, and made her even more reluctant to approach the Elder. So she was relieved when the Elder came to her.

"Why have you come here?" he said.

Siyan licked her lips, nervous about saying the wrong thing. She glanced at Enon, but the man just looked back at her, silent as ever.

"I'm looking for guidance," she said.

The Elder's brow twitched into a frown. "Guidance?"

"For myself." It wasn't a lie. She was wandering, wondering what to do with her life, trying to find where she fit. But it wasn't the whole truth, either. She hoped to be able to tell him the entire truth later.

"Why do you think I can help you?"

"We are the same. My path through life has taken me far from the forest. I want to come back. I want to find where I belong. I . . . want to stop feeling so lost." It hurt her to speak of it so plainly—a wound she wanted to hide, not bear openly for all to see. She kept her gaze fixed on the Elder, not daring to look at Enon. She was afraid of what she might see in his eyes.

The Elder watched her a while. He opened his mouth, as if to speak, when a woman stumbled out of the forest and came crashing into the camp. Her bruised face held a crazed expression, and her hair that had once been pulled back in a bun was now a disheveled mess. She had a wild look in her eyes that unnerved Siyan as the woman turned her gaze upon her.

"You . . ." she said and took a step towards Siyan.

Ilvar men stepped towards her, raising their weapons.

The Elder turned to Siyan, his expression dour. "Do you know this woman?"

Siyan wasn't sure how to respond. She didn't know her, not really, but that answer didn't seem entirely truthful.

The woman spoke first. "I've come for her," she said, pointing at Siyan.

"Then you do know her," the Elder said.

Siyan said, "No, but she's been following me."

The woman looked at the Elder. "I have no quarrel with you. It's her I want. Give her to me and we shall both go away from here."

"I am not his to give away," Siyan said, her voice tight.

The woman pulled a pistol from a pocket in her skirt. She leveled it at Siyan. "You'll come with me."

The Ilvar, bearing their weapons, closed in on Siyan and the crazed woman.

Enon stepped forward, nocking and drawing an arrow in his bow and aiming it the woman.

She glanced at him. "Don't do anything foolish. If you care for the girl then—"

Enon released the arrow and the shaft plunged into the woman's shoulder.

She cried out and reeled back, firing the pistol into the air as she lost her footing and fell.

Women screamed. Those with children grabbed them and ran. Some of the men that had been brandishing their weapons at the woman and Siyan now turned them on Enon.

The Elder paled. The way he looked at Siyan made her want to crawl into a hole. She had brought this upon them.

The woman writhed on the ground, staring with wide eyes at the arrow protruding from her skin.

"You . . ." she huffed, spittle flying from her paled lips. "You . . ."

Enon, drawing another arrow, took a step towards her, but stopped when a man leveled a spear at him.

Siyan, glancing at the Elder, walked over to the injured woman. Her wild eyes had taken on a vacant look, as if she no longer understood what she saw.

"Leave her alone," Siyan said to the men that had crowded around her. "Let her breathe." She crouched down and put a hand to the woman's shoulder.

"You . . ." the woman repeated. "I . . . why . . ."

"You've been wounded," Siyan said. "You need to lie still so I can pull out the arrow. It's going to hurt, I reckon, but I'll be able to heal you afterwards."

The woman put a clammy hand on Siyan's. "No . . ."

"It's the only way." Siyan wrapped her hand around the shaft of the arrow, all wet and sticky with blood.

"No . . ." the woman said.

"Don't you dare touch her!"

Siyan turned to find Jash in the company of a Magister, his scarlet robe embroidered with golden runes. Siyan rose. Slowly.

"Get away from her," the Magister said.

Siyan backed away.

The Magister walked up to the woman, his hands clenched as he looked at the arrow in her shoulder. "What have you done?" His voice was quiet, and Siyan was unsure of to whom he spoke.

"She pointed a pistol at me," she said. "We were only protecting ourselves, though I didn't want this to happen."

The Magi glowered at her.

The woman groped at the Magister's robes. "Malvin . . . It's her . . ."

He bent down and pried her hand from the hem of his robe, holding it afterward. "Hush, Addi. Lie still."

That seemed to agitate her. Grimacing, she propped herself up on her unwounded side. "It's her . . ." she said again, her face ashen and grey. "The And'estar. It's her."

Malvin frowned and looked up at Siyan. "What is she talking about?"

"I don't know," Siyan said, hoping her face kept still through the lie.

The Elder stepped forward. To Siyan, he said, "You have brought danger and trouble to us. You say you are lost, and I see the truth in your words. But your path is not here. You must leave. Now."

"Please," Siyan said, taking a step towards him. "This is all a misunderstanding. I didn't mean for this to happen."

"Yet it has."

Malvin said, "We will leave at once." He leaned over the woman—Addi he had called her—and put his arms beneath her legs and neck. The arrow in her shoulder pressed against him when he lifted her, and she cried out.

Addi put her hands to his chest, as if trying to push herself out of his arms. "No! Not without her."

Malvin sighed, his face looking worn and tired. He turned to Siyan. "Come with us."

"No."

"You will leave," the Elder said. "You will not stay here."

"No, but I'm not going with him, either."

Addi thrashed around in Malvin's arms as she tried to push away, and he very nearly dropped her.

"Jash!" Malvin cried, his voice strained.

Drawing his rapier, Jash walked up to Siyan. "Don't make this any harder than it needs to be."

Enon started towards her but stopped when one of the men from the clan touched the tip of his spear to Enon's abdomen.

"You will not hinder their leaving," the Elder said to Enon. Turning to Jash he said, "Take her and leave us."

Smiling, Jash grabbed her by the arm.

Siyan tried pulling her arm free, but his grip was firm.

Enon raised his bow, but before he could draw an arrow, the spear-wielding Ilvar plunged his weapon into Enon's stomach.

Siyan cried out. The wind around her kicked up and the sky clouded over. She pulled free from Jash and started towards Enon when pain struck her head, and all went dark.

CHAPTER 11

Siyan awoke on the ground, her faced pressed against dirt and dried pine needles. Ferns towered over her, bright and green in a patch of gleaming sunlight. She pushed herself up and winced as her head pounded. She put a hand to it as if that would help stop the pain. It didn't.

She found the Magister sitting nearby, watching her. Then she remembered what had happened.

Her heart quickening, Siyan looked around. "Where's Enon?"

Malvin regarded her a moment longer before extending a hand behind him and pointing to a figure lying on the ground underneath a blanket.

Ignoring her pounding head, Siyan got to her feet and walked over to him. Enon looked pale, his brow beaded with sweat though he lay shivering.

"I didn't want to bring him," Malvin said. "But the old man in that camp insisted we take the both of you. Addigan was interested in you, but him I have no use for. I expect he'll die soon, at any rate."

Siyan put a hand to Enon's brow—it was hot with fever. Trembling, she lifted the blanket that covered him and gasped. Strips of cloth had been tied around his waist to staunch the bleeding, yet blood had still soaked through the rags. The smell was metallic and sweet and rank.

"Enon . . ." she whispered.

Enon stirred at her voice, though he did not seem to fully wake. He touched her arm with a hot hand.

Siyan was vaguely aware of the Magister that stood nearby, watching her. She knew that what she was about to do would pique his curiosity in a dangerous way. But it didn't matter. She had to help Enon. She couldn't let him die.

She pushed the blanket aside. Enon groaned and grasped for it, but it was out of his reach. She fumbled with untying the rags that had been wrapped around his waist. It seemed to take ages. The cloth was sticky and squelched with blood as she pulled at the knots, and her trembling hands only made matters worse. Yet somehow Siyan managed to get them off of him. She lifted his shirt and gasped, once again, when she saw the gaping wound beneath. It looked like a hole filled with dark blood. Not wanting to look too long or too closely, Siyan put her hands over his injury.

She closed her eyes and imagined him healed, all the skin and muscle whole and unbroken. She imagined the bleeding to stop and for his fever to subside. She imagined him hale and vigorous, just as he had been for their entire time together. She wanted him back on his feet, watching her in silence as was his way, speaking only when there was something worth saying. He was meant to be in the world, and she realized then how much the world would pale without him in it.

Siyan lowered her head and then remembered herself. She remembered where she was and who was watching her. But she couldn't bear to look up. She didn't care what the Magister saw, just as long as Enon would live.

She lifted her hands from Enon's stomach and smiled when she found his wound closed, lacerated with a fresh scar.

"What have you done?" Malvin said, his voice quiet.

Siyan ignored him. She couldn't look at him yet. Not yet. She touched Enon's brow with bloody, shaking fingers. His skin was cool, his shivering had stopped. Enon opened his eyes, blinking as he peered at her in a groggy, unfixed gaze.

"Siyan," he murmured.

Siyan bit her trembling lips and forced a smile. It was the first time he had ever said her name. Overcome with fear and relief and happiness, she leaned down and hugged him, burying her face in his neck as she cried.

Enon brought a hand to her head. He stroked her hair, once, then let his hand rest on her back. They remained there for a time until, from the evenness of his breathing, Siyan knew that he slept. She rose, wiped her cheeks, and turned towards Malvin.

He was watching her, of course. He had been watching the entire time; he had seen everything. Yet for all of that, Siyan was grateful that he had not interfered. That he had left them alone until Siyan was ready to face him.

She faced him now, but the Magister simply looked at her and remained silent. His gaze traveled from Siyan, to Enon on the ground, to Siyan again. He looked puzzled, surprised, and a little curious. But still he remained silent.

Siyan got tired of waiting. Clasping her hands in front of her, she said, "I healed him."

Malvin narrowed his eyes. "So it would seem."

"What do you want?" she said, hoping to change the subject. "Why have you been following us?"

"I want nothing. I was simply following my friend, making sure she didn't do anything foolish. It was she who was following you. I didn't know why she was so interested in you before, but now I understand."

Wind rustled in the trees around them as they stood staring at each other. In the distance, a bird chirped.

"Are there others like you?" Malvin said. "Others who share your . . . capabilities?"

Siyan said nothing.

Malvin smiled. "You need not be afraid. I, too, have capabilities." He reached up and plucked a leaf from a tree, spoke a word, and the leaf glowed as if imbued with sunlight.

Siyan was unimpressed. "I know your kind. You needn't try to dazzle me with your tricks."

Malvin raised his eyebrows. "Oh? And what 'kind' would I be?"

"Dangerously curious. You think you have a right dominate everything, especially those things you don't understand. You don't care who you hurt as long as you get what you're looking for."

Malvin's arched eyebrows collapsed into a frown. "You seem to think you know much about Magisters."

"I know more than I care to."

"And how did you come to know such things?"

Siyan remained silent. Then, against her better judgment, she said, "I knew a couple of Magisters, once. They hurt my mother and father in their maddened pursuit of knowledge. They would have hurt me, too, if I had let them."

Malvin rubbed his chin. "I've never heard of this. Who are your mother and father? More to the point, who are *you?*"

"None of your concern."

Malvin smiled again and chuckled. "You're cautious, I'll give you that. No matter. I'll let Addigan do the questioning. It was she who was after you, she's the one who should hear whatever it is you have to say."

"I've nothing to say," Siyan said. "And we're not staying."

"I think you are." He nodded towards Enon. "Your man doesn't look to be in any condition to travel, even though you healed him, as you say. I don't think you'll be able to carry a grown man with determination alone. Do you mean to leave him behind?"

Siyan tightened her jaw. "I told you, I've nothing to say."

Malvin waved a hand and turned away. "We shall see."

He walked over to Addigan, who sat on the ground, her eyes closed, resting against the trunk of a tree. The arrow had been removed and her shoulder bandaged. When Malvin crouched down next to her, she opened her eyes and frowned. Siyan wondered if they were truly friends, or if Malvin had his own reasons for trailing after this woman through the forest.

Siyan looked around. The camp they were in boasted a half-score of tents and around a score of men, including a young boy. Everyone tended the camp in some way—feeding the pack ponies and horses, poking the campfires, or tightening the ropes to the white canvas tents. None of them wore red robes, at least.

"You look a fright," a man said.

Siyan turned and found Jash standing next to her.

He held out a wet rag. "Here."

Siyan frowned at him.

"Your face," he said, waving a hand near his own. "It's all bloody. Just thought you'd like to clean up, is all." He held out the rag to her again.

Still frowning, Siyan carefully took the rag. She put it to her face and wiped at her cheeks and forehead.

Jash nodded towards Enon. "He going to be all right?"

Siyan paused her cleaning as she studied Jash. She had difficulty believing he could possibly care. "I think so."

Jash smiled and nodded. "Good. Hate to see a man die for no good reason."

Siyan frowned harder still. "I wouldn't think you'd care. Especially considering he threatened to shoot you not that long ago."

Jash shrugged. "He was doing what he thought he needed to do. I can respect that."

"Is that why you've been tracking us? Because you think you need to?"

"Need to? No. But it's a job. A man's got to make a living."

"A man ought to find different work."

Jash tilted his head as if he were actually considering it. "No. I'm good at this, and I like it reasonably well. Not much else for me to do, otherwise. I'm not skilled in a trade or got any land to farm upon. Haven't got the smarts, either, for any scholarly pursuits. No, tracking people and finding folks who don't want to be found is really the only thing a man like me can do. That and thieving. Tried my hand at that for a while. Liked it well enough, I suppose, but I like this better."

"And why is that?"

Jash grabbed hold of his jacket and stood straight and tall. "I'm respectable now." He grinned—a kind of cat-who-ate-the-custard type of grin that looked anything but respectable.

"And how does a thief manage to find such 'respectable' employment?"

"Just sort of happened, really. See, I turned to thieving as a boy to help put food on the table for my ma and sister. Da was a drunkard and only ever spent his wages on more drink. He was also a bit of a thief, though nothing noteworthy—cut some purses in the market square. Me? I was good. Managed to break into some of the grander manor houses in Roelith. Found some nice things that managed to put a fair bit of food on the table. Even had some left over for myself. It was good times. But Da was getting older and drunker and meaner. He made life for Ma and my sister . . . well . . . unpleasant. He was a useless, dangerous burden. He needed to go; I just didn't know how to make him leave.

"Then, on one of my . . . uh . . . escapades, I found this fancy egg. I never seen anything like it. Looked just like a regular old egg, but one that had been decorated with gemstones and gold. Who would want such a fancy, useless thing? Figured it'd fetch a fair price, though, so I pocketed it. Turned out it was some kind of family heirloom, and the folks I took it from were quite upset over it gone missing. Made up all kinds of a fuss in trying to get it found, even offered reward money to anyone who turned in the thief.

"So, one night, I waited until Da passed out from his usual bout of drinking. I put the egg in his pocket, then fetched the authorities and turned him in." He chuckled. "Quite genius, really. Truly my finest hour. Got rid of the useless lout and got paid for it besides. After that, it seemed I developed some kind of reputation. Folks seemed real impressed that a boy would turn in his own father for 'justice and the greater good.'" He laughed. "People started contacting me a short while after. Folks looking for someone that had wronged them, or the occasional estranged daughter that had run off with a poet and taken the family silver. Most of these people I was sent to find were thieves, though, and I knew how to find them. And I did, and got paid for it. Got paid nicely. Folks came to think of me as an upstanding citizen of sorts. Respectable, even, as I said. I like that, and so here I am."

Siyan scrunched up her nose. "You turned against your own friends?"

Jash chuckled and shook his head. "Weren't any friends of mine. Just folks I knew that I was able to earn some money off of by telling other folks where they were. Isn't anything wrong with that. Had they been in my place, they'd have done the same."

Siyan closed her eyes and shook her head. "Why are you telling me this? How do you know I won't turn you in for what you've just told me?"

He smiled and shrugged. "I don't get to talk about it much, and I like talking about it. And it'd be my word against yours if you told anyone. But you won't. You're like me. You don't want to bring too much attention to yourself. You like to keep to the shadows, and the fewer people that notice you, the better."

Siyan scowled at him. "You don't know anything about me."

Jash tilted his head back and smiled. "I do. I might not have the smarts of a scholar, but I know people. I know you have no place in a city like Roelith—that you belong out here in the wilds with the likes of him." He nodded towards Enon. "I think I know this better than you do, otherwise you wouldn't have been in Roelith in the first place. I would have never encountered you, and we wouldn't be standing here having this conversation. You wouldn't be in this whole mess if you had more conviction in who you are. It's kind of funny, if you think about it."

Siyan didn't think it was funny at all. "Who I am or who I think I am has nothing to do with why I was in Roelith."

Jash smiled and shrugged again. "If you say so." He turned and left.

Siyan was tired of being dismissed by these men that acted like they knew more than she did. The sooner she and Enon left this camp, the better it would be for both of them.

Chapter 12

Siyan remained by Enon's side. He slept for the remainder of the day and through the night, for which she was grateful. Siyan's own sleep had eluded her, and so she sat and watched as day once again broke behind the trees, and the camp came to life as men lit the fires and cooked breakfast.

Smoke filtered through the dim morning light, shrouding the trees in a shifting haze that smelled of roasting meat and spices. It made Siyan's stomach growl, though she refused to ask them for food. So she was surprised when the boy from the camp came over and handed her a bowl of porridge and a mug of tea.

"Thank you," she murmured. She didn't want to accept it, but she was hungry. The porridge smelled of apples and nutmeg, the tea sharp and pungent. She woke Enon and helped him sit up. He winced as he moved and, once upright, lifted his shirt and looked down at his stomach. He touched his skin, moving his fingers over the dried blood and fresh scar.

"What happened?" he said.

"You don't remember?"

He thought a moment. "I was wounded."

Siyan nodded. "I healed you."

Enon looked at her, but his expression was unreadable.

"Does it still hurt?" she asked. "I've never healed any-one before. Not like that."

He tried to move and winced again. "It feels like my insides have been turned out."

Siyan handed him the porridge and tea. "Here, eat this. Hopefully it will help you recover, and then we can leave."

Enon looked around as he took the food. His gaze fell on Addigan and Jash and Malvin. "Why are we here with them?" he said, his voice low.

"You were hurt, and when I tried to help you, I was knocked out. When I awoke I was here, and you were on death's door. I healed you, but you needed rest, and I won't leave without you."

Enon frowned. "You should have left."

Siyan raised her chin, pretending his words didn't stab at her. "Maybe, but I didn't."

"You should leave now. You'll be able to travel faster alone."

Siyan shook her head. "I'm not leaving you behind."

"Don't be a fool."

"Enon," she said, looking him in the eyes, "I'm not leav-ing."

Enon set his jaw and his eyes hardened.

Siyan wanted to believe he was just trying to do what he thought best, that him telling her to leave was his way of protecting her. But his severe expression made her doubt herself, and she wondered if that tender moment they had shared after she healed him was borne out of sickness and confusion rather than affection. She wasn't even sure he remembered it; she couldn't bear to ask.

Enon ate some porridge and sipped some tea. The boy must have seen that Siyan had given him her food, for he soon came over with another bowl and another cup of tea and handed them to her. She thanked him, and he nodded and scampered off.

As they ate, Malvin wandered over to them. "I see you are both awake and breakfasting. That is well, for we will soon be leaving."

Siyan scowled at him from behind her spoon. "We'll not be going with you."

"Didn't we already discuss this? I thought it had been settled. Let's not make this difficult. Addigan has business with you that has not yet been concluded. Seeing as she was injured during her pursuit of you, I would be most displeased if her efforts were for naught."

He caught her in an intent gaze. "You have . . . talents. As do I. I imagine if we came to blows, we could do some remarkable harm to each other. But I would prefer to avoid such an event. Look around. You are outnumbered, and while I'm sure you would incapacitate a man or two before we overcame you, know that we *will* overcome you. And, should such an event occur, I would not be able to guarantee your companion's safety, and would have to resort to the unpleasantness of binding the both of you, assuming either one of you lived through the confrontation."

Siyan lowered her spoon, the porridge suddenly tasting ashen. She looked at Enon. His jaw was set and his expression dour. He looked at her, and she knew what he must be thinking: that she should leave him behind and get away from these people.

Setting her own jaw, she looked at Malvin. "Fine. We will come with you. For now."

Malvin smiled. "Splendid. We will be breaking camp as soon as breakfast is concluded. We have a horse your man can use so that he will not have to walk. I think you will find that sharing our company need not be so onerous." And with that, he turned and left.

"You are being foolish," Enon said, his voice low. "You need to leave. Nothing good will come from following these people."

"I know," Siyan said, staring at her porridge so she wouldn't have to meet Enon's gaze. "But you're in no shape to go running through the forest, and I'm not leaving you, as I said. We will travel with them until you are recovered. Then we can . . . reassess the situation." She smiled, forcing a joviality she did not feel. "You'll not get rid of me so easily."

Enon pursed his lips but said nothing. He continued to eat his porridge. Siyan did the same, though her appetite had gone.

Once breakfast was done, the camp was dismantled, the pack ponies loaded with the supplies, and those that had horses pulled themselves up onto the saddles. There was a horse for Addigan, who still hadn't come to speak with Siyan despite Malvin's insistence that the woman had questions for her. The boy that helped around the camp approached Enon, holding the reins to a horse. Enon glowered at him.

The boy licked his lips, glancing from side to side. He then held out the reins to Siyan instead.

"Thank you," she said, taking the reins.

The boy let out a breath and smiled. He nodded and ran off towards the ponies.

She turned towards Enon. "Get on the horse."

Enon turned his glower upon her. Then his frown faded. "We can both get on the horse and use it to get away from here."

The idea was tempting. "And then what? We'll get away, and then they'll come after us. The last time they did you were stabbed and nearly killed. Maybe the best way out of this is to find out what they want."

Enon watched her a while. Then, taking a deep breath, he pulled himself atop the horse. He sat a moment, his eyes closed and breathing ragged. Then he calmed and, looking at her, nodded his head.

They traveled, slow and steady, throughout the day. Siyan walked alongside Enon. She glanced up at him from time to time, to see how he was faring. His face looked ashen and grim, though she wasn't sure if it was because he was in pain or because he was displeased with having to remain with these outsiders.

When the light began to wane, they stopped to set up camp. Enon eased himself off of the horse. Siyan tried to help him, but he waved her away as he hobbled to a rock and sat down. She lingered nearby, not knowing what to do. She wanted to stay with Enon, to look after him, but she suspected he was upset with her and her decision to stay. She stood there, feeling helpless and useless.

Nearby, Malvin helped Addigan from her horse. Once she was down, Addigan shooed him away. Malvin's mouth tightened, and his hands clenched, but then he turned and left her alone.

Who was this woman? Scarred and foul-tempered, she had a Magister bending to her whim. Yet she didn't seem to want anything to do with him.

Siyan walked towards Addigan, now resting against a tree, her eyes closed. Her bandaged shoulder was in need of changing as blood seeped through the cloth. Addigan must not have heard her approach, for she remained still, her breathing even, though a little rapid.

Siyan took the time to get a better look at Addigan's scar. The entire right side of her face looked bruised, though it was unlike any bruise Siyan had ever seen. Snake-like tendrils of purple and red spidered across her skin, branching out and disappearing in her hair and below her collar. Her dress had long sleeves and long skirts, and she wore gloves on her hands and boots on her feet. Judging the way Addigan dressed, Siyan would be unsurprised if the bruise covered more than her face.

Addigan opened her eyes and looked at her.

Siyan stiffened, feeling awkward having been caught staring, but she refused to let herself be intimidated by the woman's glare. "Your face," she said, touching a hand to her own cheek, "what happened?"

Addigan's jaw tightened. In a low voice, she said, "That is none of your concern."

"I suppose not. Though, by the same token, who I am and where I go is none of *your* concern. Yet you hunted me down all the same, got my friend injured and me clubbed over the head. The way I see it, you answering a simple question of mine seems reasonable. In fact, I'd say you owe it to me."

Addigan's glare sharpened. "I owe you nothing." She tried to get up, but winced and leaned back.

Siyan watched her, trying to harden her heart against this unpleasant woman, but she only felt sad. Addigan, with her bandaged shoulder and bruised face, seemed very fragile just then—little more than a wounded animal who tried to bite any hand that might try to help it. Siyan crouched down in front of her.

Addigan, looking suspicious and angry, leaned back into the tree, as if trying to escape Siyan by going through the wood.

Siyan had intended to demand answers from Addigan. She wanted to know why the woman had been following her, and how she knew a Magister. She wanted to know if there were others searching for her, and what it was that Addigan thought so important that it warranted getting shot in the shoulder with an arrow. But as Siyan looked in Addigan's dark, suspicious eyes, she could see that the woman was afraid. Maybe she didn't have any answers to give—maybe neither of them did.

Addigan seemed to grow uncomfortable. She groped at the leaves on the ground and pulled her legs up underneath her. "What do you want?"

It was a good question. What did she want? Siyan had thought she wanted answers—about herself and her family—and that once she had them, she'd be able to pursue a happy life. But it seemed like whenever she found answers they weren't what she expected, and so she'd cast them aside and her search for fulfilment would start anew. Siyan realized then that she had never known what she wanted. She had only been wandering blindly all this time, chasing after shadows or dust that glittered in the sunlight that then vanished as soon as the sun had set.

"I don't know," Siyan said.

Addigan frowned, looking confused.

The two stared at each other for a time. Siyan, against her better judgment, said, "I can heal that bruise of yours."

Addigan's expression hardened. She gripped a fistful of fallen leaves in a tight grip and leaned forward as her lips peeled back in a snarl. "You cannot possibly heal what ails me!"

Addigan's vehemence startled Siyan. She had expected doubt, maybe even suspicion. But this . . . this was fear, and rage, and hurt.

"What happened to you?" Siyan whispered.

"Get away from me." Addigan looked like she might try to stand, but she remained sitting.

Siyan got to her feet but continued to watch the strange and hostile woman.

This seemed to further anger Addigan, and she lunged forward, throwing a handful of leaves at Siyan that fluttered harmlessly to the ground. "Get away from me!"

Her shout had drawn the attention of the others in the camp. Malvin, looking concerned, took a step forward.

Siyan wanted to avoid a confrontation, so she left Addigan and returned to Enon.

"What happened?" he asked when she approached.

Siyan shook her head. She didn't know what just happened. They had been talking, and then Addigan had been screaming at her. Siyan didn't want to admit how shaken she felt. She had offered to help this woman who had brought her nothing but trouble and was met with hostility. Why did she bother? The sooner she and Enon were away from this place, the better.

They sat while everyone else busied themselves with setting up camp. The boy came over with two plates of food: roast rabbit with roasted turnips and onions, and a slice of bread. He handed both plates to Siyan.

"Thank you," she said. Before the boy could leave, she asked, "What is your name?"

The boy's eyes widened and, fiddling with his hands, he stammered, "W-Walt." Then he hurried back to the fire.

Siyan watched him go, wondering if she was now the sort of person that frightened children. Or maybe it was Enon, who, she realized when handing him a plate, had been glowering at the boy.

"You keep frowning like that and your face is apt to freeze that way," she said.

Enon scowled at her. "I don't like it here. I don't trust these people, that boy included."

Siyan nodded, unable to disagree with him, had she even wanted to.

They ate their food in silence. After the meal was done, Enon started to lie down to sleep when Siyan made him let her see his wound. She hadn't ever healed anyone with such a severe injury, and she wasn't sure if her ministrations would keep or if it had only been a temporary solution. So she was relieved when he lifted his shirt and the wound was still nothing more than a fresh scar, and the pain of the injury was all that seemed to remain. She ran a hand over his healed skin, and Enon tensed and lowered his shirt.

They watched each other. Siyan wanted to say something to him, though she didn't know what. Only something that would let him hold her again like he had yesterday. But then Enon turned and lay down, and the night turned quiet and dark.

Siyan awoke during the night, the forest dark and still. The camp was silent, the fires burned down to embers. She peered at the sky, looking for signs of dawn, but there was only the moon beyond the darkened trees.

She turned over, trying to find a comfortable position on the cold, hard ground when a whispering out in the forest caught her attention. She sat up, listening. Wind rustled in the trees, drowning out the rasping voices. Then the wind faded and the voices returned—a bubbling of sound in the otherwise silent night.

Siyan got up and walked through the camp. The canvas tents stood dark; the horses and ponies still tethered in a line. Everything seemed to be in place; nothing was missing. Who, then, could be out in the forest, whispering in the stark of night? She wondered if she should wake Enon, but decided against it. He had been through much and needed to rest.

Siyan followed the voices as they led her out of the camp. She stepped carefully through the brush, trying to remain silent and unseen. The whispering grew louder, the indistinct voices coalescing into words.

"Remember," a woman said.

Siyan peeked around a tree and saw a man and woman standing together. They were young, perhaps a little older than she was. They both had long, dark hair that had been braided with little amber beads woven in the pleats. Both wore tanned leather clothing similar to that of the Ilvar.

"Remember," the woman repeated.

"Remember what?" the man said.

"Everything."

The man stepped towards the woman, but when he reached out, she faded and blew away like pollen on the wind. He buried his face in his hands and he, too, disappeared.

Siyan lingered in the silence. Then, just as she was about to turn away, a little white rabbit emerged from the brush, followed by a little boy. The boy laughed as the rabbit hopped around him. He picked a leaf and held it out for the animal, smiling as the rabbit nibbled on the proffered fare. The boy then plucked a dandelion from the ground and blew on it until the seeds fluttered around him. The feathery tufts hung in the air, floating on the breeze as if forgetting to fall to the earth. The rabbit hopped to the boy's feet, and the boy laughed. The wind stirred, and the boy and rabbit dissolved into dust, scattering in the breeze.

"Do you remember?" a man's voice said from behind.

Siyan turned and found an old man standing there, watching her. His face was like a riverbed of wrinkles. His long, white hair was braided just as the young man's had been, though fragments of bone were woven in the pleats instead of beads. His eyes, black as the surrounding darkness, told her he was an And'estar.

Siyan licked her lips, fighting her own nervousness. "Remember what?"

"Everything."

"I . . ." Siyan began, but realized she didn't know what to say. The man continued to watch her, his expression expectant, and so she said, "No, I don't think so."

"I never wanted to remember," he said, his gaze turning distant as he looked over Siyan's shoulder. "And I forgot for a time." He looked at her again. "I never wanted to remember."

"Do you remember now?"

The man's brow furrowed, but he remained silent.

Siyan watched him, recalling the little boy and the rabbit that she had just seen. "It was you, wasn't it? The rabbit that followed me. You're the And'estar that I woke."

The man said nothing.

Not knowing what else to do, Siyan continued. "I need your help. I need to teach others about you, about us, the And'estar. They've forgotten, and I need to help them see, but they won't listen to me."

"Why?"

"Because I'm not one of them. They don't think I have anything worth saying."

The man shook his head. "Why tell them? They have forgotten. Maybe it is good that they do not remember."

"Why would it be good?"

The man looked away, his gaze distant once more. "Maybe memories aren't meant to be remembered for so long."

Siyan frowned. "Whose memories?" She wondered if they were even talking about the same thing.

The man shook his head again. He turned to leave.

"Wait," Siyan said.

The man ignored her and kept on walking, so Siyan followed.

They walked in silence for a time. The man looked around as he moved, up at the trees and sky and stars, and below at the ferns and fallen needles. He seemed taken with the forest around him, as if he had never seen it before; or perhaps he had just not seen it for a very long time.

"How long have you been sleeping?" Siyan asked.

He looked at her. "How many times have you blinked since you were born?"

Siyan faltered. "I don't know."

He nodded. "Some things are not worth reckoning." He continued walking.

The man seemed much more severe than Siyan had

expected. But then, her experiences with other And'estar were limited; perhaps she shouldn't have expected anything at all.

They came to an outcropping of boulders that towered above them, the stones covered in moss and studded with ferns. A small tree had found purchase among the rocks, with a tiny waterfall that trickled through the long, tendril-like roots. He stopped and gazed up at boulders towering above him.

After a lengthy silence, he quietly asked, "Why do you follow me?"

"I told you. I need your help to convince a clan to listen to me about the And'estar. I need to teach them about what they've forgotten."

"Why?" he asked, his voice still quiet. It was almost drowned out by the tinkling of the water. "Why do you care?"

Siyan opened her mouth to answer, but words failed her. "I don't know," she said after a while. "I want to understand. Maybe by teaching others I can come to understand myself."

He looked at her. "You sound unconvinced."

She was, but she dared not speak her fears aloud. She considered him as he watched the water trickle through the tree roots. "That was you as a boy, wasn't it? Playing with the rabbit. You seemed so happy."

"That was a long time ago." He reached out and let the water from the stones run over his hand. He put his fingers to his lips.

Silence settled between them again. Rather than feeling awkward, Siyan found comfort in it. She crouched to the ground, watching a beetle scuttle among fallen leaves, as she listened to the water. Words seemed unfitting here, a distant distraction that she was no longer willing to cling to.

When the man again spoke, it was almost jarring. "I was, in many ways, an unhappy boy. 'And'estar' is the first word I ever recall hearing, and I was told it was who I was. I was a Spirit Walker, they told me. Important. Timeless. My memories would live on, even after everyone I knew had turned to dust. I was regarded with awe, and all around people would tell me their stories, so that they might continue to live, in some way, through my own memories.

"I resented this. I didn't like being told who I was, never having the option to choose for myself. I didn't like the burden of listening to these people speak of their lives, their names, their children's names; loved ones they had lost; talents and gifts they wished to have memorialized. I resented them and the need they placed upon me. I resented that I was not allowed a life of my own but instead was left to imagine the lives of people I did not care about. I hated them, sometimes, for putting that burden upon me, without ever asking my opinion on the matter. It was expected. It was my purpose. But I thought it unfair to place so heavy a burden on one single boy.

"I ran away, from time to time. Never far, and never for long. I had found a little glade in the forest to which no one ever came, and so that became my hiding place where I would go to escape and be alone. One day a rabbit came out from the bushes and hopped right up to me. I put out my hand and he sniffed it, and he didn't seem at all timid or afraid like rabbits usually are. After that day, every time I went to the glade the rabbit was there, waiting for me. He became my friend, someone that accepted me for who I was and put no expectations on me or my future. The moments I was there, just me and the rabbit, were the first I remembered feeling happy."

He fell silent, leaving the trickling of the water the only sound between them.

Siyan said, "Was fulfilling your purpose such a burden?

Did others feel as you did?" Maybe not everyone embraced their purpose as Emora would have her believe.

The man tilted his head. "No, I was an aberration, an oddity that disagreed with everyone else. Or at least the only one that was vocal about it. I had a difficult time believing that everyone else so readily accepted the obligations determined for them by others. But then, what other responsibilities did they have other than fishing or hunting? So maybe it wasn't such a burden for them as it was for me."

"What did you do?"

He shook his head. "Nothing. I did as I always had done: I stayed and listened. I took moments for myself and escaped to my little glade from time to time. But I always went back. As much as I resented it, I still wasn't ready to turn my back on my people."

"There was also a woman. You reached out to her and she vanished. Who was she?"

The man was silent a long while. "No. I have answered enough of your questions."

"You still haven't answered my first question of whether or not you'll help me teach others about the And'estar."

"Why should I help you? Unlike you, I don't wish for people to remember the way things were."

"The And'estar are able to do magical, remarkable things. If they are forgotten, then all the wonder they bring is forgotten with them. You don't find that sad?"

"I think it is sad that we are not given a choice in the matter. We sleep, perhaps peacefully so. And then someone like you comes along to wake us, without stopping to consider that perhaps we don't wish to be woken. That perhaps we'd like to forget all the memories that have been burdened upon us."

"But maybe not all And'estar feel as you do. Maybe some of them would like to wake up. How can you know until you try? Would you really be willing to condemn them all to sleep forever just because it's what you want?"

He remained silent, returning his hand to the running water. After a while, he said, "I will follow you, and I will watch. But I will not help you. Not until I choose to, if I choose to at all."

It wasn't quite the answer Siyan had hoped for, but it would have to do. "All right," she said, when a thought occurred to her. "What is your name?"

The man moved his hand through the water, as if trying to hold the liquid with his fingertips. "Names are meaningless—words we attach to a man as if to anchor his place in the world. Call me what you will, it makes little difference to me."

Siyan opened her mouth, but hesitated. She didn't know what to call him; the fact that he didn't seem to care only confounded her further. She tried to think of a name, but the only thing that came to mind was a memory of the little white rabbit and a little boy laughing.

"How about 'rabbit'?" she said and then cringed. That was a silly name. She couldn't possibly call a grown man "rabbit," especially a man that might very well be older than some of the trees that towered above them. "Or maybe something like it."

He tilted his head. "'Tavi' is a word men once used to anchor the animal you speak of."

"All right, I will call you Tavi, then."

Tavi gave a single nod of his head before walking deeper into the forest.

Siyan watched him go, waiting until he disappeared from sight before she hurried back to camp.

Chapter 13

Siyan returned to where Enon slept. She put a hand on his shoulder and gently shook him. "Enon, wake up."

Enon stirred and blinked. Then, as if remembering where he was, he bolted upright, wincing from the effort. "What's wrong?"

"The And'estar," Siyan whispered. "He's awake. He's not just the rabbit anymore, he's fully awake. I talked with him."

Enon stared at her. "What did he say?"

"He seemed unhappy. He . . . didn't want to be woken."

Enon continued to watch her, making her feel uneasy.

"I asked him to help us," she continued, hoping to alleviate the weight of Enon's intent gaze upon her. "With the other clan, that is. I asked if he'd help us teach them of the And'estar."

"Will he?"

Siyan scratched her nose. "No. But he said he'd follow and watch us. So that's something. We might be able to convince him."

Enon watched her a moment longer before his gaze flicked past her. She turned around, finding Malvin rushing towards them, red-faced and looking flustered. Two men from the camp followed him.

"You," Malvin said, pointing at Siyan. "With me. Now."

Both Enon and Siyan rose to their feet. Enon stepped forward.

Malvin glanced at him. "Not you, just her."

Enon's hand twitched towards the knife sheathed on his leg as he stared at the Magister.

The two men following Malvin stepped forward, their hands resting on the hilts of their swords.

Fearing they would come to blows, Siyan put a hand on Enon's arm. When he looked at her, she said, "It's all right." She wondered if she was trying to reassure him or herself.

Enon frowned, but he said nothing as Siyan walked past him and followed Malvin. The two men that had accompanied the Magister remained behind with Enon, presumably to keep him from interfering with whatever Malvin had planned. The thought that Enon might need to be kept away made her stomach sink, and she wondered if she had been too rash in her effort to keep the peace.

Malvin stopped in front of a tent. He pulled aside a flap and motioned for her to step inside. Heart pounding, Siyan took one final look at Malvin and the surrounding trees and ducked into the tent.

A brazier of hot coals smoldered within, casting a ruddy light against the canvas walls. At one end of the tent stood a cot, upon which Addigan lay shivering under a pile of blankets. Walt knelt next to her, dabbing her brow with a damp cloth as his gaze darted between Siyan and Malvin.

"What's wrong with her?" Siyan asked.

"The injury to her shoulder has gotten infected," Malvin said. "When I last changed her bandage, the wound had turned red and swollen, and she had developed the beginnings of a fever, but she still seemed fine. I cleaned her shoulder as best I could and I thought she would be all right. But when I checked on her again she . . . she was not doing well."

Siyan watched as Addigan shivered upon the cot. "You want me to heal her."

Malvin was quiet a moment before saying, "Yes."

Siyan remained still. After a while, she said, "I don't think she'd want me to. I offered to heal that bruise of hers, but she got upset and told me to leave."

Malvin shifted his weight. "The bruise is a sensitive subject."

Siyan turned to look at him. "What happened to her?"

"That is not for me to say."

Siyan rubbed her forehead. She was tempted to turn around and leave. She owed these people nothing; they had brought her and Enon nothing but trouble. Yet she remained, watching as Walt gently dabbed Addigan's brow.

Then, letting out a long breath, she walked over to her. Why did she pretend to hesitate? Siyan had known as soon as she saw Addigan that she would heal her. As much as she would like to rid herself of these people, she could never let someone die. Not if she could do something about it.

Walt scuttled away when Siyan approached. Addigan turned to look at her, though there was no recognition in her eyes. She opened her mouth as if to speak. Instead, she leaned over and vomited a milky white liquid onto Siyan's boots.

"She's been doing that," Malvin said.

Siyan clenched her jaw and swallowed the bile that rose in her throat. She knelt down and pulled back the blankets before unwrapping the bandage around Addigan's shoulder. She put her hand to the injury, ignoring the blood and pus that oozed from Addigan's hot, broken skin.

Siyan imagined the wound healed, that the infection, pus, and fever were all gone. She opened her eyes and put a hand to Addigan's brow. Her skin was cool, and her breathing more even. Siyan smiled, her hand lingering on

Addigan's forehead as she eyed the bruise that marred her face. Once again, she wondered what could cause such an injury. She wondered if she could heal it.

Siyan sharpened her focus. She imagined the spidery tendrils that twined across Addigan's skin healed and gone. She didn't know what had caused the bruise, or where the damage originated, so Siyan focused on Addigan's entire body. She focused at a point on Addigan's head and moved her attention, ever so slowly, downward to her chest and arms, abdomen and legs; her hands and fingers and feet and toes. It was like wrapping Addigan in a cocoon of thought and energy. Siyan willed her to heal—every strand of hair, every drop of blood. She would be whole and hale and strong. Siyan willed it until she could no longer hold the thought, and it fled from her like shadows at dawn.

Feeling tired, Siyan removed her hands from Addigan's body and sat down. Her body shook and, putting a hand to her head, she found her own brow beaded with sweat.

"What happened?" Malvin said.

Siyan opened her mouth to speak, but no words came. She shook her head, though even that seemed an unbearable effort.

"The air turned hot at first," Malvin said, "then cold. Now it's raining, even though the sky was filled with stars only moments ago." He was quiet a moment. "You . . . didn't have anything to do with that, did you?"

Siyan didn't know what he was talking about. Why would she know anything about the weather outside?

Malvin walked to Addigan's side, casting a curious glance down at Siyan as he passed. He put a hand to Addigan's brow and examined her shoulder. "Her fever is gone and her wound healed." He brushed a hand across Addigan's cheek, though the woman remained still, her eyes closed. "Her bruise is gone, as well." He looked at Siyan, his expression a mixture of awe and fear.

Siyan wanted to nod, to say that healing the bruise had been her intention. But her head wouldn't move and words proved to be leaden on her dry tongue.

"Are you all right?" Malvin asked.

Siyan wanted to tell him "no," she wasn't all right. Instead she slumped to the ground, unable to move.

Malvin called to some men, and the next thing Siyan knew she was being carried outside. Water dripped onto her face and hands, and she realized that Malvin was right—it was raining. Why did that seem to matter?

She was put on the ground, and then Enon was there. He said something—to the men probably—though she couldn't hear what it was. His words sounded garbled, blending in with the pattering of raindrops that fell around them. The men left and Enon knelt down beside her. His brow was furrowed; he looked concerned. He said her name, she could tell from the way his mouth moved, but the only sound that came was the sound of rain.

He picked up her hand and pressed it. In her mind, Siyan pressed back, but her fingers never moved. Rain continued to drip onto her face, and Enon passed a hand over her brow and wiped it away. She blinked then, and the rain turned hot as it streaked down her cheeks. Enon said something else, but she couldn't tell what it was.

Feeling helpless and afraid, Siyan closed her eyes and took refuge in the darkness that followed.

She walked barefoot upon the soft soil of the forest floor. Vibrant green ferns brushed against the hem of her gleaming white dress. She ran a hand over the fabric; it felt soft and cold and damp. It felt like clouds and moss, like rain and breath. She tried to laugh, but instead the wind blew, sending a spray of raindrops down from the trees.

Siyan continued to walk. Butterflies and mosquitoes flitted in the air around her. Below her feet, the ground squelched with rain. Worms rose from her footprints and beetles scuttled across her path. In a dark corner of her mind, a thought sparked that this was wrong. But then the wind stirred and the thought faded.

She walked on. The trees around her grew tall and then short; the ground dried only to dampen again. In the distance, a light appeared. Siyan thought it was the moon, and that she would like to walk upon its shimmering surface. But when she got there it wasn't the moon at all. It was an ivory tree, twisted and misshapen yet beautiful all the same.

A woman with long, black hair appeared. She looked at Siyan with eyes of glass. "Siyan."

"Mother." She looked different than Siyan remembered, yet still the same. She looked more real, somehow. Like a layer of dirt had been wiped away.

"You shouldn't be here," Iyen said.

"Why not? It's nice here. You're here."

Her mother shook her head and rain pattered all around them. "No. It's not right. Not yet."

"Of course it is." Siyan looked around. "Is Father here, too? Is he well?"

Iyen's eyes turned sad. "He is well."

Siyan smiled. "I'm glad."

Iyen walked up to her and wrapped her hands around Siyan's face. "Wake up, daughter."

"I am awake."

Iyen brushed Siyan's hair back and left a hand against her brow. She then lifted her hand, leaving a single finger upon Siyan's forehead. "Wake up," she said and then pushed her finger into Siyan's skull.

Siyan opened her mouth to scream, but the only sound she made was the screeching cry of a falcon.

"Siyan," a voice said.

Siyan clenched her eyes shut. She didn't want to look and see her mother's hand covered in blood.

"Siyan, wake up."

She recognized Enon's voice and opened her eyes. The sun was up, the day bright. From above, the cry of a falcon echoed around them.

She looked around. They were in a camp, the white canvas tents looking out of place among the greenery of the forest. Then she remembered Addigan. "What happened?"

Enon shook his head. "I don't know. You left with the robed man. You were gone only a short while when they brought you back, saying you were unwell. You did not move, you did not talk." He stared at her. "You barely breathed."

Siyan put a hand to her head. It hurt, and she half-expected to find a gaping hole there from her mother's finger, but the skin was smooth and unbroken. It was just a headache. "I . . . I healed Addigan, the woman you shot. She was ill. I healed her."

Enon frowned. "I thought you were dying," he said, his voice low. "You mean to tell me it was because you healed someone? Is that what happened when you healed me?"

Siyan shook her head. "No. I . . . I don't understand it."

Enon's brow furrowed, his gaze sharp. He looked angry, though she didn't know why he would be. Then he got up and walked away.

Siyan felt like she should feel concerned over his departure, but she was too tired. She lay back down, finding comfort in the smell of the earth and the dampness in the air as sleep came to take her.

Chapter 14

Addigan awoke on a cot, sweating underneath a pile of blankets. She kicked off the covers, but the air in the tent was too stifling to give much relief. Sunlight filtered through the canvas walls and filled the tent with muted light. Malvin sat in a chair in a corner as he pored over a book that lay upon his lap. As she sat up, Addigan noticed her shoulder no longer throbbed with pain. She put a hand to it, finding the bandage gone and the wound healed.

"What's happened?" Addigan said.

Malvin's head snapped up when she spoke, and he closed the book and smiled. "You're awake."

Addigan frowned. "Of course I'm awake. What . . . happened to my shoulder?" She closed her eyes and took a breath, struggling to keep calm as she tried to understand. The last thing she remembered was enduring a throbbing, burning pain that radiated from her wound and down her arm.

"That girl you've been following healed you."

Addigan returned her hand to her shoulder, searching for the wound and for the pain, but found only a dull ache that might have been nothing more than a bruise. "Healed? How is that possible?"

"There's more, Addi." Malvin got up and walked to a narrow table. He picked up a mirror and held it out to her.

She scowled at him. "I don't want that thing. Get out and take it with you."

Malvin sighed and closed his eyes. "Addi, please. Just look."

Addigan tightened her jaw. Malvin knew better than to hand her a mirror. She had gotten rid of all the mirrors she could within the Tower, all to avoid looking at herself for the past three years. He knew this, so why was he so insistent that she look at one now?

"Please, Addi."

Not seeing any other way to get him to leave, Addigan took the mirror, though she held it down at her side.

"Look at yourself."

Addigan didn't want to look at herself. She knew how she looked. The fact that Malvin was trying to coerce her made her want to dash the silver-handled monstrosity across his head.

Malvin took the mirror from her hand and, slowly, raised it in front of her.

Addigan blinked at the reflection she saw. It was a woman in her middle years, her brown hair a wild mess and streaked with grey. Her eyes were brown and narrow, some might say pinched-looking, though Addigan had always thought them restrained. She thought she knew this woman—it was the woman she saw in her mind whenever she thought about herself. But it couldn't have been her, because this woman didn't have the horrible purple scar that marred half of her face.

Addigan cringed and backed away. "What is this?"

"Your wound got infected, remember? You became sick, delirious with fever. That girl healed you, Addi. She healed *all* of you."

Addigan's mind reeled. She remembered enduring the increasing, throbbing pain in her shoulder, and the way Malvin had fussed over cleaning her wound and changing her bandages. She remembered feeling ill, and, following that, a series of disturbing dreams. She didn't remember anything about being healed, and certainly not by that girl. How could any of this be true?

She snatched the mirror from Malvin's hand and threw it across the tent. "Get out."

Malvin deflated, his eyes sad.

Addigan felt a twinge of guilt for causing him pain, but that only made her angrier. "Get out!" she cried, closing her eyes and clenching her fists. Only when she heard Malvin walk out did she open them.

She looked around. The mirror lay on the ground, the glass cracked. Addigan walked up to it and reached out to pick it up. Instead she sank to the ground, burying her face in her hands.

She remained there a long while, trying to find that part in her mind where the Art had once been. She didn't feel any different, but then she feared to look too closely. What would she find if she did? Would she find the Art? Or would she find only a broken and scarred mind?

Addigan got to her feet and staggered to her satchel on the narrow table. She picked it up and shook it, sending her journals clattering to the ground as loose papers and letters fluttered after them. She fell to her knees as she found the dreaded book she so rarely looked at. She rifled through the pages, not wanting to look at the writing too closely, looking only for one line in particular. And then she found it:

It's as though a blanket has been pulled over my mind. Where the Art should be is only a stifled mass of woolen thoughts.

Yes, woolen. That was how she had felt. Whenever she had reached for the Art, her mind had always felt so clouded and heavy. It was like a tightly wound ball of string, tangled beyond repair. Was that how she felt now? Addigan didn't think so, but maybe she had gotten so used to it that she no longer knew what anything else felt like.

What would happen if she reached for the Art? Would she find it there, waiting for her like she had dreamed about so many times before? Or would her mind again turn clouded and numb? Addigan felt sick with the hope that stirred in her gut. She felt even more sick at the thought of having that hope extinguished. She hated sitting there, not knowing what to expect. She hated the fear that had grabbed her by the heart, turning her into a witless woman that sat there trembling and quailing over what she needed to do.

Not giving herself time to think, Addigan stood and turned toward the brazier in her tent. She spoke a rune, *Ignis,* and the blackened coals flared alight before slowly extinguishing again.

Her heart raced as she stared at the coals, wiping her sweaty palms on the skirts of her dress. Licking her lips, Addigan repeated the rune. She spoke it over and over, until the coals finally caught and smoldered on their own.

Addigan ran a shaking hand over her matted hair. She was healed. Honestly, truly healed. She stumbled over to the cot and sat down, staring at the walls as she tried to understand what it all meant.

She could use the Art again. Everything she had been struggling to regain for the past three years had seemingly been restored to her. So why didn't she feel happier? She should be elated, shouldn't she? She would be made a Magister—the first female Magister to ever walk the halls of the Eleventh Tower. It was what she had been working towards nearly her entire life.

So why did she still have that empty, cold feeling gnawing at her heart?

Addigan put a hand over her eyes. It wasn't supposed to be like this. Regaining her ability with the Art was supposed to mean something. It was supposed to make her happy. It was supposed to make her feel whole. But Addigan felt as she always did. She might have laughed at it all, had it been the least bit funny.

Was it because of that girl? Addigan had always thought once she regained her ability with the Art, everything else would fall into place. But then, she hadn't really regained it, had she? Not on her own. The girl had meddled, and now Addigan was sitting there, her heart as heavy as it ever was. Would she even be made a Magister? Or would the girl's meddling compromise that as well?

Addigan closed her eyes, gripping the edge of the cot as she struggled to keep her temper cooled. It couldn't all be ruined. She could use the Art again. That had to count for something, didn't it? As much as Addigan wanted to believe that, her heart wouldn't let her. She had suffered too much disappointment in her life.

So what was she supposed to do now? Question that girl on the construction sites of the Towers? Ask her what this And'estar business was all about? Addigan found it difficult to care. It seemed so trivial now that she could use the Art again, and the thought of speaking to that girl made Addigan's stomach tighten. For the first time since her recovery from the Threshing, Addigan felt lost, lacking the direction and purpose she had been clinging to all these years. It made her sick. It made her angry.

It wasn't supposed to be like this.

Chapter 15

Siyan awoke to the sound of someone walking through the brush. Night had fallen, all else in the camp was still. The noise was careful, considered—not the aimless wandering of someone crashing through forest. She sat up, thinking it was Enon returning, but then she saw his shadowed silhouette lying upon the ground as he slept.

Concerned, Siyan got to her feet. Her legs trembled underneath her weight and, fearful they would give out from under her, she knelt back down.

A light shone on the surrounding trees and then Addigan appeared. She held a stone in her hand that glowed pale blue. Siyan's mouth turned to acid. Only Magisters used stones to light their way.

She was about to shrink into the shadows when Addigan saw her.

"They tell me you healed me," Addigan said. The light from the stone illuminated her face in a gaunt manner, her wild hair giving her the look of a crazed, waifish ghost. The bruise on her face was still gone.

Siyan remained silent, digging her fingers into the soft soil.

Addigan walked up to Siyan and looked down at her. "What did you hope to gain?" she said, her voice taking an angry edge.

Siyan frowned. "Nothing."

Addigan tried to smile but instead she looked pained. "Everyone hopes to gain something."

Enon stirred. When he saw Addigan, he reached for his knife.

"No need for that," Addigan said. "I'll not be staying." To Siyan, she said, "I'll not be beholden to anyone. To you least of all. I owe you nothing. That you healed me means nothing."

Siyan gripped the soil between her fingers. "I don't want anything."

Addigan barked a mirthless laugh. "Don't take me for a fool."

Enon came to stand beside Siyan, his knife in hand.

"You're right," Siyan said. "I do want something. I want to be left alone. I want you and your friends to go back to Roelith or wherever it is you came from and leave us alone."

Addigan's mouth worked as if she chewed on her words. "So leave."

Siyan frowned at her, wondering what the woman was up to.

"Both of you," Addigan said. "Leave. No one will stop you."

Siyan narrowed her eyes. "I thought you had questions you needed answered."

"There is nothing I want from you. I'll have nothing more to do with you." Addigan turned to leave.

"We need a horse," Enon said.

Addigan turned to glare at him.

"She nearly gave her life healing you. You owe her that much."

Addigan twisted her face, looking as if she might spit on him. "I owe her nothing!" she hissed. Then her expression settled into a stony calm. "I don't care about you or her," she said, nodding towards Siyan. "And I don't care about the horses. If one of them should disappear, I don't see how that would affect me in the least." With that, Addigan turned and walked away.

Once she was gone, Siyan pulled her hands from the ground.

Enon knelt down next to Siyan and looked her in the eyes. "Wait here," he said before rising and disappearing among the trees.

Siyan stared at the darkness where Addigan had gone. She tensed as she listened for footsteps, or for the voices of men from the camp coming to take her.

A Magister. Addigan was a Magister, and Siyan had healed her. It was bad enough healing Enon in front of Malvin, and now this. She had a difficult time believing they would truly let her go. Everything she knew about Magi told her they would never leave her alone.

Siyan held her breath when she heard snapping twigs and rustling brush, exhaling when Enon arrived holding the reins of a horse. When he reached her, he stopped and extended a hand. Siyan took it and he pulled her up.

Kneeling in front of her, Enon put out his hands, his fingers laced together. "I will lift you up."

Siyan licked her lips. She had never ridden a horse, let alone been hoisted onto one. She did as she was told, however, and put her left foot in Enon's hands. He lifted her up and she swung her right leg over the horse and settled onto the animal's back. She grinned, feeling very tall and enjoying this new outlook on the world.

Enon rummaged around in the darkness until he found his satchel. He slung it over his shoulders along with his bow and quiver. Taking the reins of the horse, he then led them away from the camp.

They kept a leisurely pace, but Siyan struggled to keep her balance. Her legs felt weak, and trying to stay seated on a horse with no saddle only tired them further. Siyan hugged the horse's neck, fearing she'd otherwise fall to the ground.

Enon stopped as he looked up at her. "Are you well?"

She nodded. "I'm just tired, is all. I'm not used to riding horses."

Enon watched her. Then, after a while, he handed her the reins.

Siyan was about to ask what she should do with them when Enon walked behind the horse and, taking a deep breath, ran a couple steps and vaulted up behind her. He grunted when he landed and held his breath for a while. Then, slowly, he started breathing again.

"Are you all right?" Siyan asked.

He was quiet a moment before replying, "Yes." He reached around her and took the reins.

Siyan tensed, feeling awkward at having Enon so close to her.

Then he said, "You may lean on me if you are tired."

Siyan's face grew hot. "What?"

"We must continue. If you are tired, you may rest upon me. I will not let you fall." Then he flicked the reins against the horse's neck, and the horse started walking.

Siyan sat rigid and upright, gripping the horse's mane to keep from falling. But her weakened legs only grew more tired, and her perch more precarious. Not knowing what else to do, she leaned against Enon.

Siyan remained tense, holding her breath as she waited to see what he'd say or do. But he said and did nothing other than put an arm around her waist and hold her to him. After a while, her tension eased and Siyan relaxed.

It was nice sitting there with him. His body warmed hers, and his breathing in rhythm with the horse's walking soothed her uneasy mind. She rested her head against his shoulder and closed her eyes and drifted off to sleep.

Siyan awoke as Enon slid off the back of the horse. Groggy and disoriented, she nearly fell and gripped the horse's mane and hugged its neck to keep from tumbling to the ground.

Enon held out his hands. "I will help you down."

Feeling shaky, Siyan took one of his hands and swung her leg over the horse's back before sliding off. Her legs buckled when she landed and she very nearly fell, but Enon still had her hand and he helped keep her upright.

They had traveled through the night and the day had broken some time ago. The sky was bright and birds chirped in vigorous chorus.

"We will stop here for now," Enon said as he tied the reins to a nearby tree. "The horse needs to rest, and you need to eat."

"Do we have any food?"

"No." He took his bow in hand and, with a final look at Siyan, headed off into the forest.

Siyan wished she could help him. She looked to the sky and whistled. After a few minutes, Fal appeared and alighted on her outstretched arm. She smiled as she stroked his breast with a finger, realizing then that she had missed his presence. With all that had been happening, she had nearly forgotten about him.

"What have you been up to all this time?" she said.

The falcon glanced at her before his gaze darted elsewhere.

"Enon and I are out of food," she said. "So, if you happen to find any squirrels, or maybe even rabbits, we'd be grateful if you'd share." She lifted her arm, and Fal flew away. Then, taking note of where the horse was tethered, Siyan also ventured into the forest.

Walking was difficult. Healing Addigan seemed to have taken quite a toll on Siyan—her legs were still uncertain about supporting her weight. She looked around the brush as best she could while looking for edible plants or berries. But her legs grew only weaker the more she bent and squatted.

She stopped and rested against the trunk of a tree. She closed her eyes and listened to the breeze stir in the trees and to the birds chirping. Beyond those came a faint trickling of water. Edible plants often grew near streams, and Siyan was thirsty. She got to her feet and made her way towards it. Her pace was even slower than before, and Siyan worried she would lack the strength to return.

She came upon a stream wending its way through the forest. It gurgled over rocks and eddied around roots. She knelt at the bank and put her fingers in the water. It was icy and felt good on her throat when she drank the liquid from her cupped hands. She splashed some on her face, her skin tingling from the cold.

Siyan sat a moment, watching her distorted reflection on the water's surface. She only caught glimpses of herself in the moving stream, and she wondered if maybe that was her true reflection. Maybe she really was only a collection of warbling and broken shadows. Maybe what she saw in the water was real, and the world in which she lived was only a reflection of something else.

Movement caught her eye and Siyan looked up and saw a stag drinking from the water across from her. His antlers were new, branching only once, and covered with velvet. The deer looked up at her, and they remained there for a time, watching each other. Then an arrow pierced his side and the animal bolted. He hadn't gone far when another arrow pierced his hind leg, and the stag stumbled and fell. The deer thrashed along the ground, trying to get up but failing.

Heart racing, Siyan splashed across the stream and ran over to him. She put her trembling hands to an arrow and was about to pull it out when Enon approached. He held his bow in one hand, his knife in the other. He looked at her, and then she understood.

She looked down at the stag. She wanted to remove the arrows, heal his wounds and let him run off into the forest again. But they needed food. Siyan lifted her hands and leaned back, watching with tear-filled eyes as Enon knelt down and slit the deer's throat.

Enon watched her a moment. Then he turned to the animal and cut open its belly.

Siyan stumbled away. She had found some strength when the deer had been wounded, but now that it was all over, she felt weaker than before. She crawled along until she could no longer hear Enon working and sat against a tree.

What was wrong with her? Why did she feel so shaken? They had hunted animals before, and it had never upset her. Not like this. Why did it upset her this time?

Siyan turned at a rustling of brush and saw Tavi walking towards her. He looked younger than she remembered, though he was still in his elder years.

"Where did you go?" she asked.

"I have gone nowhere."

Siyan looked away. She wasn't in the mood for riddles.

He sat on the ground next to her and looked up at the sky. After a while, he said, "Why did you heal that woman? Addigan."

Siyan frowned. "How do you know her name?"

Tavi blinked. "How do you know the wind rustles in the trees?"

Siyan closed her eyes and shook her head. Why couldn't he ever say anything plainly? "She was sick. I couldn't let her die."

"But you are afraid of her."

"She's a Magister. I didn't know that, though."

"Would you have healed her if you had?"

"I don't know." Siyan rubbed her eyes and let out a breath. "Probably. I don't know why."

"Yes, you do. You healed her for the same reason you wanted to heal that deer."

"Because I don't like watching things die," Siyan whispered.

"Yes."

"I don't understand it though. I've watched things die before. I mean, I've never liked it, but I've always understood the need of it. Now . . . I still understand the need of it, it's just . . . it seems so much more . . . unbearable."

"That is sometimes the way for And'elan."

"And'elan?"

"One who is spirit, or one who heals spirit."

"I thought all And'estar could heal."

"We can. But And'elan give more of themselves."

Siyan stared at him. "Is that why I felt so weak after healing Addigan?"

"Yes. To heal the woman, you gave a part of yourself. It is how all And'estar heal. But you gave too much and weakened yourself. And so part of you faded from this world and went into the spirit world. You healed the woman, and the And'estar spirit healed you. You returned, but part of you remains there still. It will always remain. You will forever be changed from it. This is not a terrible thing."

Siyan blinked. "You mean it was real? The dream about my mother—it actually happened?"

Tavi waved a hand. "'Real' is a word men use to anchor themselves in order to pretend they understand. Beyond that, it has no meaning."

Siyan licked her lips. "Is that what it's like? Is what I saw what it'll be like when I . . . die?"

Tavi tilted his head. "'Death' is another word men use to anchor themselves in order to pretend they understand. As for what you saw, I cannot speak to that, for I do not know what it was. It is different for each And'estar. What I see is not what you saw, or what you will see again. What your mother sees is not what you saw. Each And'estar shapes his own world, and sometimes even shapes the world around others. It is the way of things."

The way of things. He sounded like Emora. Yet Siyan wondered how much Emora knew of what Tavi was telling her. Did she also know about And'elan, or what it was like in the spirit realm? Or had this, too, been forgotten, even among Emora's people? Siyan suspected that neither she nor Emora really knew all there was about the And'estar. If Siyan hoped to understand—truly understand—then she needed Tavi. They all did.

"Will you help us understand?" she asked, turning towards him, but the forest was dark. Tavi had gone.

"Understand what?" Enon said as he walked towards her. He looked around, his expression puzzled.

Explaining her conversation with Tavi seemed like an unbearable burden just then. She shook her head.

Enon studied her a moment. "I have made a fire near the water. You should come there, you will be warmer."

Siyan was unsure if her legs would support her. She wanted to be alone, anyway. "I'm fine."

"You are being foolish."

Siyan closed her eyes. She was too tired to argue. "Fine, I'm foolish. Now leave me alone."

Enon remained looming over her, pressing his lips into a fine line. Then, crouching down, he picked her up.

"What are you doing?" Siyan said.

Enon said nothing. He walked back to the camp he had made by the waterside and put her on the ground in front of the fire. He looked angry. Siyan returned his scowl, refusing to be intimidated by him glowering at her. Then she realized he was breathing a little too heavily, his jaw clenched a little too tightly.

"How's your stomach?" Siyan asked, feeling guilty for having forgotten about it.

Enon shook his head. "I came with you to protect you from danger, not to follow a foolish girl who puts herself in harm's way for no other reason than that she can."

Siyan stiffened her back. "I don't need you protecting me," she said, her voice low. "The choice for you to come along was yours, not mine."

Enon set his jaw and his eyes hardened. "You don't know what you need. You are lost. You have said so yourself. You better figure out where it is you are going, and what it is you are after, because it will only get worse for you if you don't." He walked away and continued butchering the deer.

Siyan stared out over the fire, listening to the flames crackle as she waited for the sting of his words to fade.

But it never did.

Chapter 16

Addigan stood in her tent, watching Malvin as he rubbed his forehead.

"What do you mean they're gone?" he said, his voice strained. He struggled to remain calm, but Addigan could still hear the anger in his tone.

She lifted her chin. "I mean just that. I told them to leave. I want nothing more to do with them."

Malvin covered his face with his hands and turned away. "I don't understand it, Addi. You went through all the trouble of tracking them down. You got an arrow in the shoulder. You nearly died! And now, when the answers you've been looking for are within your grasp, you let them go?!" He rounded on her. He was angry now, all pretense of calm seemingly forgotten. "Did you ever stop to consider that none if this is about you? That girl could use the Art, Addi. The Art! In a way that Magisters have only dreamed about. Maybe you don't need her, but *we* do!"

Addigan flinched. It was not lost on her that by "we" he meant Magisters, a group to which she did not belong. "Interesting that you should take note now, when you feel it will benefit you and you alone. If not for me, you'd never even know that girl existed. And yet you dare stand there and accuse *me* of not understanding her importance when you should be *apologizing* to me for dismissing the information I had about her!"

Malvin closed his eyes and shook his head. "Is that what this is? You getting even for having your research dismissed at the Tower?"

"It has nothing to do with 'getting even.' I sought out the girl, hoping to get some answers about certain similarities of the construction sites of the Towers. It turns out I no longer wish to pursue those answers. I feel they're not important anymore and that other, more pressing matters must first be attended to."

Malvin stared at her. "I don't understand you, Addi. You're not making any sense. Who *cares* about the construction sites of the Towers? That girl healed you, Addi! Do you understand that? You were dying, and she healed you with nothing more than putting her hands upon you. Questions about construction sites of the Towers can go rot a thousand bloody, painful deaths for all they matter! What matters is finding out how she did it. I cannot believe that you of all people do not see that!" He grabbed her by the shoulders and said, quietly, "You can use the Art again. Don't you want to know how she did it? Don't you care?"

Addigan stiffened her back. "No."

"What?"

She wrenched herself out of Malvin's grasp. "I don't want to know. I want to forget she ever put her hands upon me!" Addigan took a deep breath, trying to calm her racing heart and rising fury. But Malvin's open-mouthed, dumbfounded stare only fueled her anger.

"It wasn't supposed to happen like this," she said in a low voice that was almost a growl. "I was supposed to recover myself. I was supposed to get my ability back myself! That was the only way I was ever going to get the respect of the others in the Tower, and that *whore* has taken that from me!"

Malvin's expression turned from one of confusion to shock. He took a step towards her and Addigan backed away.

"Don't you see what she's done?!" Addigan was yelling now. In a distant corner of her mind, she saw herself as the crazed woman that Malvin must see now, but she didn't care anymore. "Everything I've been working towards, everything I've struggled with, she has diminished and ruined! The others in the Tower aren't going to see me as a Magister who has regained her ability with the Art. They're going to see a feeble woman who is only able to use the Art through the meddling of some backwards forest witch! I've worked my whole life to be worthy of a Magister robe. And now, for the first time, I feel like not only am I unworthy, but am a disgraceful abomination that isn't even worthy to walk the Tower halls!"

Hot tears streamed down Addigan's cheeks. She couldn't bear to look at Malvin and his saddened eyes and, when he reached out for her, she turned and ran.

Addigan fled out of the tent and into the surrounding forest. Her long skirt caught on a fallen branch, tearing the fabric and sending her to the ground in a tear-soaked heap. She lay there, crying like a new-born babe, all small and mewling.

Pathetic. This wasn't her. She never cried. She hadn't cried when her younger brother had been born and the adoration of her parents had shifted to him. She hadn't cried when he had been given everything, and she nothing. She hadn't cried at the look of relief on her parents' faces when she told them she wanted to leave and become a Magister. She hadn't cried when she saw that look in their eyes that said even if she tried, she still would amount to nothing. She had never even cried after the Threshing, when she had been paralyzed and bed-ridden for months before she began to mend. She had never cried at all, not once. She used to be strong, but now she was a pathetic weakling, bawling in the middle of the forest like a lost little lamb.

She grabbed hold of a nearby bush and spoke a rune that sent the plant up in flames. Part of her felt joy and relief at being able to use the Art again. Another part of her only felt angry that she had not been able to do so on her own. She had been an invalid after the Threshing, but she had recovered entirely by her own hand. Regaining her ability with the Art wouldn't have been any different. Given enough time, she would have done it. And when she had, then she would have finally seen the look of respect in the eyes of her colleagues and of her parents. It was a look she had been waiting to see her entire life.

And now that had been taken from her. All her years of struggling were for nothing. It had all been a waste. Was she supposed to be grateful, as Malvin's perplexed look seemed to suggest? The girl had saved her life, true. But her life would have never been in danger in the first place if that bastard wilds-boy hadn't shot her with an arrow.

She touched a fern leaf and whispered a rune that coated the delicate frond in ice. She might not have any-one's respect, but she did have the Art. Shouldn't that be enough? Could it be enough? She wanted it to be, but that empty feeling she felt in the pit of her stomach was still there, that emptiness that had been there for as long as she could remember. She had thought that becoming a Magister would fill that hole; that once she regained her ability with the Art, everything else would fall into place and Addigan would, for the first time in her life, be happy.

But she wasn't a Magister, and being able to use the Art without being recognized as one was meaningless. She didn't care about the Art; it was only a means to an end. She wanted respect. She wanted deference. She wanted people to see a powerful individual when they looked at her, not a weak woman who they assumed knew nothing beyond embroidery and drawing.

Footsteps rustled through the brush and Addigan scrambled to her feet, wiping her eyes and cheeks before hastily smoothing her skirt. Malvin appeared, and Addigan set her jaw and clasped her hands.

Malvin looked at the burned bush and frozen fern. Then he looked at her and said, "Are you all right?"

Addigan raised her chin as she clasped her hands tighter. "I am fine."

Malvin walked to the ice-covered fern, now dripping water as it thawed, and ran his hand over it. He rubbed his fingers together and turned towards her. "I don't understand how you can be upset over what happened. Isn't this what you wanted? To be able to use the Art again?"

Addigan said nothing. She didn't trust her voice to speak, and she would not cry in front of Malvin.

He took a step towards her. "You'll be a Magister now, Addi. All that talk about how you won't be accepted is nonsense, I'm sure of it."

Addigan closed her eyes and shook her head. "You are the only one who ever thought I would become a Magister, Malvin. What you think and what the others think have never been the same."

"But you completed the Threshing, you *are* a Magister."

Addigan clenched her hands so tightly she feared she might draw blood. Malvin's refusal to see the obvious only hurt her further. "I completed the Threshing and lost my ability as a result. That might as well be the same as failing. To succeed, I needed to regain my ability on my own, not have it restored to me by someone else."

Malvin sighed and rubbed his head. "I don't agree. But then I suppose that doesn't matter. It never has."

Addigan stiffened her back. She would not be made to feel guilty about this.

"So, what do you want to do?" Malvin asked.

Addigan was quiet a long while. "I don't know."

"Let us go back to the Tower. I believe you will be made a Magister upon your return. But even if you are right and you are not, we can decide from there what to do next. Such decisions are always better made in comfort and security rather than out here in these cold and miserable wilds."

Addigan blinked, staring beyond Malvin's shoulder. She didn't want to go back to the Tower. That was the very *last* place she wanted to be right now. But she was tired; she didn't have the energy to argue. So she nodded and let Malvin lead her back to camp like the feeble woman she was.

Malvin herded her back to her tent, calling to someone on the way for tea and food. Addigan didn't know to whom he spoke. She didn't care. It was all she could do to keep moving forward. Her heart felt heavy, equaled by the leaden pit that had settled in her stomach. She felt like she was walking to her doom. That each step she took by Malvin's side was only bringing her closer to her undoing.

It was a foolish notion. The Eleventh Tower had been her home for most of her life, having gone there to apprentice when she was a little girl. It had been more a home to her than her family's house had ever been.

They reached her tent and Malvin escorted her inside and ushered her into a chair. "You sit down and rest. I'll be back shortly." He ducked back outside.

Addigan sat on the edge of her chair, waiting for Malvin to return. Walt came in, holding a steaming mug. He held it out to her.

Addigan ignored him. She didn't want any tea.

Clearing his throat, Walt placed the mug on the table and hurried back outside.

Addigan continued to watch the entrance. What was Malvin doing? She got up and pushed the flap aside. She scanned the camp and the surrounding trees until she found him. He stood away from the other men of the camp, speaking with Jash. Jash looked around as he listened and his eyes met hers. His mouth twitched into a smile, and then he turned back to Malvin. Jash nodded, then he said something and walked away. Malvin also turned, and Addigan lowered the flap before he saw her.

What had Malvin said to Jash? What would happen to her when she returned to the Tower? She had thought her reluctance to go back was borne out of her failure to regain her power by her own hand, but a new thought occurred to her.

She was a failed apprentice, one with capability with the Art. Those who could use the Art who were not yet Magisters were not allowed to leave the Tower—not without supervision. She had undergone the Threshing, but failed. Her only success was that it had not killed her. But she had lost her ability with the Art, and so she was not a Magister. Now that she had regained her ability, would she have to undergo the Threshing again?

The thought of experiencing the Threshing all over again filled her with an indescribable dread. She had nearly died the first time around, she couldn't face it again. Never again. But if she refused, she would never be allowed to leave the Tower.

Suddenly her reluctance to return to Roelith and the Tower shifted to fear. She fidgeted with her hands and her skirt. When Malvin walked back into the tent, Addigan stared at him, as if seeing him for the first time. She had known Malvin since they were children. They had apprenticed together. He was, by all counts, the only friend she had in the world.

Yet, as she looked at him, Addigan couldn't help but wonder if she knew the man at all. Was he trying to help her? Or was he insistent they return to the Tower because he knew she shouldn't be out in the world—a woman capable with the Art who was not a Magister.

"You didn't drink your tea," he said, handing her a plate of food.

Addigan took the plate and blinked at it. She wasn't sure what she should do.

"Are you all right, Addi? You look a little pale."

Addigan looked up from her food. She studied Malvin's face, his tone of voice for any indication of deceit. She knew Malvin. He wouldn't take her back to the Tower knowing she would be locked up, would he? They were friends, that had to count for something, didn't it?

Then she remembered all the times she had been cruel to him, each time her ill-spoken words had caused him pain. After her failure with the Threshing, she had tried to push him away in an effort to protect herself from the pain he unwittingly caused her. She had thought it was loyalty that had caused him to stay, but now she wasn't so sure.

How could they possibly be friends? Addigan wouldn't have remained friends with anyone who treated her as horribly as she had Malvin. She wondered, now, if she truly knew him—maybe his motivation to remain near her wasn't one of friendship.

"You should really try to eat something," Malvin said. "You look like you need it."

Addigan looked down at her plate, though she couldn't have said what he had given her. All she saw was hidden motives and calculating plans. When she lifted the food and took a bite, it tasted of nothing. She managed to eat it, somehow, all the while making polite, if distracted, conversation with Malvin. She had no idea what he was saying, but she nodded her head and said, "I see," at certain intervals when she thought such responses were expected from her. It must have been enough, for Malvin continued talking until the day faded and he left to go sleep in his own tent.

She remained in her chair after he had gone. Only when she was sure that most of the camp slept did she sneak out of her tent. Once outside, she stopped, looking around and listening for any footsteps. But the camp remained quiet and dark, save for the campfires that had burned down to smoldering coals.

Addigan made her way to where Jash slept. She knelt down and shook his shoulder.

Jash rolled over, frowning as he blinked at her. "What—"

Addigan clamped a hand over his mouth. Leaning close, she whispered, "What did Malvin say to you?"

Jash pushed her away and sat up. "Burn me alive, woman, what do you want?"

Addigan scowled at him. "Be quiet or you'll wake everyone."

"Good, let them wake. Maybe they'll have the decency to take you away and let a poor man rest."

Addigan gave him a flat look. "Please. When were you ever a 'poor man'?"

Jash grinned. "Yeah. I suppose never." He rubbed his eyes and looked around. "What hour is it?"

"Late."

"And yet here you are." He grinned again. "Have you finally realized you can't live without me?"

Addigan narrowed her eyes. "Hardly. I need to know what Malvin said to you."

"Malvin? He didn't say anything to me."

"Don't lie. I saw you talking with him. He said something to you earlier today. I was watching from my tent. You even looked at me and . . . smirked."

"Oh *that*. Hardly worth mentioning. I had nearly forgotten all about it."

"What did he say?"

"He told me he was awfully keen on you, and was wondering if you were keen on him too. If so, he was going to shirk taking Sally Miller to the turnip festival and take you instead. He thinks you have a good chance of being crowned the Turnip King and Queen."

"Be serious."

Jash feigned a look of pain and clutched at his chest. "I am serious. It hurts me so that you think otherwise."

Addigan sat on the ground and covered her face with her hands. She couldn't handle Jash and his impossible antics. Not now. It was all she could do to keep her emotions in check and prevent herself from screaming at him.

After a while, Jash said, "Are you all right?"

Still covering her face, Addigan shook her head. When she felt like she could, she said, "Please, just tell me what he said."

Sounding confused, Jash said, "Look, he didn't say much to me. Just wanted me to keep on tracking that girl we'd been following earlier. I thought you knew about it, and that you sent him over to talk to me so that you wouldn't have to."

Of course. Malvin was refusing to let the girl go. She wondered, when the time came, if he would do the same to her.

"Take me with you," she said.

Jash waved his hands and shook his head. "Burn me a thousand times, no."

Addigan grabbed a hold of his sleeve. "You have to."

He wrenched his arm out of her grasp and scowled at her. "I don't *have* to do anything. As it was your man I spoke to, and not you, I consider myself in his employ, not yours."

Addigan clenched her hands and took a deep breath. "Please. I can't be here right now. I need time to think, and I can't do that here . . . with him. He wants to return to the Tower and I'm not ready to do that. Not yet." She closed her eyes. It galled her having to explain herself to Jash. To say such personal things. He was likely to mock her within an inch of her life.

He sighed and said, "Fine. But I'll not suffer you mouthing off. If you come along, you do what *I* say. If not, I'll leave you behind, and I won't care how far away from civilization we are."

Addigan set her jaw. "Fine." Then, just as Jash was about to lie back down, she added, "We need to leave tonight."

Jash laughed, dry and mirthless. "Of course we do. And of course you're still telling me what to do. Stay here then, I don't care."

"After this, I'll hold my tongue. But we need to leave tonight or else Malvin won't let me go. We need to be gone before he realizes it."

Jash narrowed his eyes. "Why do you want to leave without him knowing?"

Addigan raised her chin. "My reasons are my own. Will you help me or not?"

"No. I'm done with you."

"I can pay you extra when I return to Roelith. I'll be quiet like I said, and pay you double what Malvin's paying you for the trouble."

Jash closed his eyes as he rubbed the side of his head. "I know I'm going to regret this," he muttered. Then, looking at her, he added, "Fine. But you *better* make it worth my while."

CHAPTER 17

SIYAN AWOKE TO THE SOUND of the gurgling stream, a crackling fire, and the smell of roasting meat. She sat up, eyeing skewers of deer meat roasting by the flames. Enon was off a ways, digging a hole in the ground with a sturdy stick. He had removed his shirt, and Siyan caught glimpses of the scar on his stomach, still fresh and pink against his darker skin. She watched him for any sign that he was in pain, but if he was he hid it well.

She continued to look around the camp—at the fire and butchered deer, and the horse she had left behind. Yesterday, Siyan had worried about returning to the mare to set up camp, but she had never needed to—Enon had fetched the animal and set up camp around her. Now he was working hard towards some other task, despite the injury that only yesterday had still given him pain.

Siyan regretted what she had said to him last night, when she said she didn't need him. Without him, she would not be waking to a warm fire, or to a breakfast of roasted meat. She probably would have been fine if he had never come along. It would have been harder, but she would have managed. Yet, now that he was here, Siyan didn't want to think about what it would be like trying to do everything alone. Especially weakened as she was.

She should apologize to him, but Siyan was afraid he'd

tear her down if she showed her heart, or that she'd make matters worse and he'd decide to leave. Maybe he wasn't even angry. Maybe she was more upset about it than he was, and he had already forgotten the words had ever been spoken.

Enon put down the stick and walked to the stream to splash water on his head and chest. He returned to the fire and warmed himself by the flames before he put on his torn shirt. He took the meat that had been roasting and handed her a piece.

Siyan took the food. "Thank you," she said, gauging his reaction.

But Enon merely gave a slight nod, his face impassive as usual.

They ate in silence. Enon, after he finished, resumed digging the hole. Siyan hated watching him work while she sat and did nothing. She got up on her trembling legs and walked over to him.

"Do you need help with anything?"

Enon stopped working and looked at her.

Siyan fidgeted with her hands. Even after all this time, she still felt unsettled under his gaze whenever he just *looked* at her like that. She began to regret having asked him when Enon replied, "Yes."

He led her back to the fire and pulled from the stream some of the deer meat he had been storing there. He put her to work slicing the flesh into smaller pieces and laying them out on racks of branches.

When he had finished digging the hole, he laid it with wood and lit a fire. When the fire had died down, he then took the branches with the meat draped over them, and fitted them into the hole. He then covered it with smaller, leafier branches, and left the meat there to smoke. He returned to Siyan and took some meat she had not yet cut, and set it roasting near the fire.

Enon sat with his feet flat on the ground, his elbows resting on his knees and his head hanging down. He looked tired. She wished she could ease his burden.

"I'm sorry for what I said last night," she said before she had a chance to talk herself out of it. "I didn't mean it when I said I didn't need you. I'm glad that you're here . . . with me."

Enon remained still. Siyan hurried to her feet and walked away. She already felt awkward; she didn't want him to say anything or, worse still, say nothing at all. Still, she was glad that she had said it, even if she did feel like a fool. He deserved an apology, and she had given it. Maybe now she could put the whole thing behind her.

She walked over to the horse, untied the reins and took the mare to the water so that she could drink. Enon remained by the fire, and so Siyan remained by the horse, walking her around so that she would find fresh greens to graze upon. It wasn't so terrible a task. Siyan liked tending the animal, and it helped her feel like she wasn't avoiding Enon. No, she wasn't avoiding him at all.

They spent the next few days at the camp, smoking the rest of the deer meat as well as treating the other parts of the carcass for use. Siyan's apology didn't seem to have any effect on Enon. He was the same as he always was, and she accepted that her apology had probably been more comforting to herself than it had been for him.

Enon spent much time showing her how to prepare the various parts of the deer—from smoking the meat, to tanning the hide, and even using the tough sinew and inner lining of the intestines to make strong and durable cords and thread. With a needle Enon kept in his satchel, Siyan was even able to repair the hole in his shirt.

She was weaving together rope made from the fibrous strands of broken down sticks when Enon walked up to her with another bundle. He dropped it on the ground and then held out his hand.

Siyan peered up at him, and his mouth quirked into a small smile.

Her brow furrowed even though she couldn't help but smile back. "What's going on?"

Enon said nothing, though his smile deepened as he held out his hand.

Siyan studied him for a moment. Realizing he wasn't going to tell her, she took his hand and let him pull her up.

With her hand in his, Enon ventured back into the forest. They walked for a time at a leisurely pace. Siyan's strength from her ordeal after healing Addigan was much improved, and she felt much more like herself. The slow pace was nice, regardless. After a while, they came to an outcropping of stones set within a hollow. Enon ducked behind a tree and pulled her down next to him.

What was he up to? His attention was fixed on the stones. She followed his gaze, trying to see what he saw, but she saw only rocks and moss and fallen pine needles. "What is it?"

Enon put a finger to his lips and Siyan clamped her mouth shut. Then he brought his head near hers and, stretching out his arm, pointed at a darkened area within the stones.

Siyan looked and, at first, saw nothing. Then the shadows moved, and out tumbled two baby foxes. They were brown and red with soft, fluffy fur that had not yet known the harshness of the elements. They yipped and pranced around on stiff legs, biting at each other's tails. She grinned and looked at Enon, grinning all the more when she saw he was also smiling.

"Look," he whispered, and nodded towards the hollow.

Out from the stones came another kit, this one white as snow, who looked at the world with little pink eyes. He ran up to his brothers and pounced on one and bit at his neck. Soon the air was pierced with the cries of the kits as they wrestled and played.

They watched the foxes for a time, and then Enon said in a low voice, "Three is often thought to be a number of fortune, and a white animal is always a sign of good things to come. My mother once told me a story of a fox that, three times, managed to get itself into trouble. Each time it was in danger, a kind man helped it and returned it to safety. When the man helped the fox for the third time, the fox then granted him a long and fruitful life. When I saw the foxes here, it made me think of it." He smiled again.

Siyan watched him as he spoke. As wonderful as the foxes were, she found it difficult to pull her gaze from Enon. He seemed so unguarded. He seemed happy. When he looked at her, Siyan averted her gaze as her face flushed. They remained a short while longer before Enon rose and extended his hand to her.

Siyan hesitated. It was nice there with him, she didn't want to leave. Even so, she put her hand in his and, once again, he pulled her up. Once she was standing, Enon remained close to her, looking down at her hand that he still held in his own.

After a lengthy silence, he said, "I have also said things I regret. I was wrong about you."

Siyan swallowed, unsure what to say.

Enon looked at her. "You are not an outsider, I was wrong about that. You are not Ilvar, either—not really— but you are not an outsider." He peered at her, as if trying to see her. "You are . . . different. But maybe that is what my people need right now. Maybe we need someone different to help us out of this rut we are in." He looked down again.

"Enon . . . I . . ."

He shook his head. "And you are not selfish. You are naive, perhaps, and sometimes frustratingly stubborn. But you are not selfish, and I am sorry that I ever thought you were." He looked at her again. "I am also glad that I am here, with you."

Siyan's heart raced. She swallowed again, afraid to speak and say the wrong thing.

Enon reached up and touched her brow and traced the line of her face down to her chin. They looked at each other for what felt like ages before Enon's eyes turned sad. He started to turn away when Siyan clamped down on his hand, refusing to let him leave. She wasn't sure what was happening; she just didn't want him to leave.

With a trembling hand, she reached up and touched his brow, letting her fingers caress his temple and jaw and chin. When she pulled her hand away, he stepped closer to her. He leaned in and touched his lips to her own. It was a brief kiss that was over almost as soon as it began. Even so, Enon remained close, his face next to hers. Siyan thought he might kiss her again, but instead he lingered there, achingly close to her. Then, just as he was about to move away, she leaned in and put her lips to his.

Enon brought up his arms around her and pulled her against him. He kissed her, long and deep and with a fervency that startled Siyan. He kissed her, and kissed her, and kissed her again so that the world around them seemed to fade. She put her arms around him and held him tight, kissing him back as she let all else fade into nothingness.

When Enon stopped, it was almost jarring. Siyan closed her eyes, catching her breath, wanting to keep the world away just a little bit longer. He rested his forehead against hers and they remained there a time, leaning against each other as they embraced.

Then Enon pulled away and watched her a moment before reaching out and tucking a lock of hair behind her ear. She smiled at him, and he gave a small smile back, though his eyes looked distant. Then he took her hand, and they walked back to the camp.

Chapter 18

Addigan sat on the ground, etching runes into a branch that now served as a staff. Jash stood behind her, looking over her shoulder as she worked. Addigan gritted her teeth. It was all she could do to not lash out at him and make him leave.

"What are you doing?" Jash said.

Addigan took a breath and lowered the knife. "Carving runes."

"What for?"

"Why do you care?"

"It's my knife."

Addigan closed her eyes, tightening her grip on the branch. "They help me focus."

"Focus what?"

"The Art."

"The art of what?"

"Just . . . the Art." As much as she tried, Addigan couldn't keep the edge out of her voice. The man really was impossible at times. She had to keep reminding herself that she had promised she wouldn't order him around. Addigan wondered if he was purposefully testing her patience. It certainly seemed that way sometimes.

Jash moved away from her and stood off to the side. He munched on a biscuit. "Didn't know Magi were so artsy."

Addigan shook her head and continued to work. After leaving Malvin's camp, Addigan had spent as much time as she could reacquainting herself with the Art. She was long out of practice, and her ability was not what it used to be. She felt like a novice all over again. It was frustrating, but she was also glad. Even though she wished she had regained her ability on her own, she couldn't help but feel glad that it was back. She almost felt like herself again. She had forgotten what that was like.

She was even more glad that she had left Malvin when she did. The more she tried to use the Art, the more she realized how inept she had become. Her conviction was stronger than ever that if she returned to the Tower she would be required to repeat the Threshing. Addigan had barely escaped with her life the first time, she didn't think she'd be so lucky if there was a second. She didn't want to find out.

Addigan continued to carve runes in her makeshift staff. She mourned the absence of the Tower library, where she'd be able to consult the countless tomes and scrolls of all the runes that the Order of Magisters had discovered thus far. She would be able to create a set of runes that would connect her to the Art in a way that complimented her own abilities. She could make it so that her affinity to fire or ice would be stronger, or use runes that would help amplify her efforts in concentration.

Drawing runes generally made it easier for Magisters to wield the Art. They weren't necessary, strictly speaking. Magi could still wield the Art by speaking runes alone. But there was a reason Magisters embroidered runes on their robes and inscribed them on their staves—they made wielding the Art easier. And, at the upper levels of skill, they *were* necessary. The makings of a great Magi was a mixture of both natural skill and an ability to construct runes in a way that allowed him to command the Art with greater efficiency and power.

Without access to the Tower library, Addigan could only inscribe what runes she recalled from memory. It was woefully inadequate, but better than nothing. Her only hope was to regain as much of her ability with the Art as she could. Maybe then . . .

Addigan paused her carving. Maybe what? She wouldn't have to repeat the Threshing? She would be made a Magister without any uncomfortable questions being asked? No. That would never happen. But she needed to do something, and honing her skill with the Art seemed like the best choice. She would probably need it in the coming days, one way or another.

"Are they still there?" Addigan said. "By the stream?"

Jash nodded. "Still smoking meat from that deer. I don't think they've seen us."

They had caught up to the pair a few days ago. Addigan was surprised she and Jash had found them so quickly. Then again, they hadn't had much of a head start.

Addigan stopped carving and looked up at Jash. "What are you going to do?"

He glanced at her and shrugged. "Keep watching them, I guess. I expect they'll move on once they're done with the deer. We'll keep on following them until they settle somewhere, or do something interesting."

"Interesting? What would they do that's interesting?"

"They healed you, didn't they? I'd say that's interesting."

Addigan stiffened.

"You never know with folks," Jash continued. "Especially ones with particular, ah, talents. Sooner or later, they all do something crazy." He grinned at her. "I think you know what I mean."

Addigan scowled at him. "And why do you care?"

"I don't, but your man does."

"He's not my man."

Jash chuckled. "Does he know that?"

Addigan pressed her lips together and resumed carving her staff. "When will you return to him?" she said, trying to keep her voice light.

Jash was quiet a while. "When there's something worth telling."

Not today then, at least. Unless something happens. "And you're sure he's not been following us?"

"I haven't seen him."

Addigan eyed Jash. Given the lengths Malvin took to keep track of her, she doubted he'd give up so easily.

But Jash just returned her gaze with a steady one of his own. "I'm going to go check on our friends again to make sure nothing has changed."

Addigan watched him go before returning her attention to her staff. She worked as long as the light lasted. When she could no longer see the runes she was carving, Addigan put down her work and looked around. Jash was still gone.

"Jash?" she called, quietly though, so as not to be heard by unwanted ears. How long had he been gone? She had been so absorbed in her work that she had failed to notice the passing time. Had something happened to him?

She reached into her skirt pocket and pulled out a small stone. She spoke a rune and the stone glowed with a cold and pale light. With her crooked, makeshift staff in hand, Addigan headed in the direction Jash had gone.

In a near whisper, she called for him again. "Jash?" Her breath plumed from her lips, caught in the sterile light of her stone before fading into the darkness beyond. When had it gotten so cold?

There was a thumping sound, and Addigan held her breath as she listened. It sounded like a drum, faint and distant. She headed towards it, wondering if it was some kind of trickery by Jash. If he leapt out at her from the bushes, Addigan didn't think she'd be able to restrain herself from striking him—and that wouldn't go over well after she had promised to behave. Even if he did deserve it.

She walked for a time, the night growing darker as the drumming grew louder. The more she walked, the more she wondered if she was being foolish for wandering through the forest as the darkness deepened. What was she hoping to find? Not Jash. He wouldn't be out here—not this far from their camp and from their quarry. Addigan didn't know the man well, but she knew he took his jobs seriously. He liked getting paid, and he wouldn't do anything to jeopardize that.

Addigan told herself to turn around, but still she walked on. Curiosity turned to determination. Who was out there? What was going on?

She ducked under some branches and came to a clearing. Scores of lamps hung in the surrounding trees, looking like massive fireflies floating in the moonlit field. The drumming stopped and a man appeared from the forest. He was tall and lithe, his skin dark like amethyst and pitch. Then the drumming resumed, accompanied by a high-pitched instrument that sounded kind of like a violin, or maybe a flute.

He walked towards her. Addigan spoke a rune that extinguished her stone, but then she realized her foolishness. He had already seen her. Even though she stood in the shadow of the trees, he still continued towards her. Addigan gripped her staff, calling to mind what runes she knew, wondering if she would have to use them.

The man stopped when he reached her. He towered over her, though his body was slighter than hers. He wore no clothes that she could see, yet there was no indecency. His body was smooth and even, like polished stone. Even his face was featureless, lacking any indication of eyes, or a nose, or mouth. Should that have frightened her? Part of her felt that it should, but it didn't. He was odd, nothing more.

He held out a hand to her. She eyed his long, spindling fingers and frowned. "I don't think so." She turned to leave, but stopped when the man knelt upon the ground, bowing his head while still extending his hand.

Addigan's frown faded. Malvin had done that once, when they were young. He had wanted to dance with her, and she had refused. So he had knelt upon the floor with his head bowed and arm outstretched. He had stayed like that, looking like a fool, until Addigan finally relented. She had always liked that about Malvin—he never seemed to care what anyone else thought.

Addigan had never cared for dancing, either before that moment or after. But that dance with Malvin . . . it was then she realized she loved him. Or thought she had. She had been young and foolish. What did she know of love?

The memory of it pained her, and she turned and walked back into the forest. Addigan had only taken a few steps when she stopped and looked back. The man was still out there, kneeling in the grass as the strange music floated in the air around them. Why was she hesitating? She didn't even like dancing, and certainly not with unusual, face-less men in darkened woods. And yet, as she stood there, she tried recalling the last time she had been asked. How long had it been since someone looked at her with some-thing other than pity or disgust or disdain? How long had it been since someone had held out his hand to her? There was Malvin, but his hand was one she no longer wanted. Other than him, there was no one. Nor had there been for a very long time.

Setting her jaw, Addigan propped her staff against a tree and returned to the clearing. Before she had time for regret, she took the dark man's hand in her own. His skin was hard and smooth like stone, but pliable like leather.

He put an arm around her waist and, with an alacrity that surprised Addigan, pulled her further into the field.

The lamps in the trees blurred as they twirled and danced through the grass. Addigan held up her skirts with one hand and held on to the strange shadowed man with the other. Up close, she got a better look at his features—if they could even be called that. He had no face, only a swirling of purple against his black skin. It looked like the grain in wood, or sediment at the bottom of a stream.

He held her waist as they moved through the field. Around and around they spun and danced, causing Addigan to grow dizzy. She closed her eyes and let herself forget the world and her problems. She was not Addigan or a Magister—she was just a woman dancing with a man. Maybe she was a little girl, playing in a field. Maybe her entire life had been nothing more than a vivid dream. The longer she danced, the easier it was to push everything aside until the only thing she knew was the wind on her cheeks and the sound of her own breath.

"Addi?"

Jash's voice startled her, and Addigan stumbled and fell into the grass. Her bun had come undone, and her hair tumbled over her face and shoulders. She pushed it aside as she got to her feet.

Jash stood at the edge of the forest, looking at her like she had lost her mind. "Are you all right?"

Addigan straightened her back and smoothed her hair. "Of course I am."

He took a few steps toward her as he looked around. "Why are you out here?" He grinned. "And why were you dancing?"

"I was with . . ." Addigan looked around but the shadowed man was gone, as were the lamps in the trees. The music had stopped. No wonder he was looking at her funny. "It's none of your concern."

His grin widened as he walked up to her. "May I have the next dance?" he said, extending a hand.

Addigan slapped it away. "Don't be ridiculous." She walked past him, heading back towards camp. She hoped he couldn't see how shaken she was.

Chapter 19

Siyan and Enon remained crouched behind a tree, watching as Addigan and Jash left the field and disappeared into the forest. Siyan didn't understand it. Addigan had let them go; she had told them to leave. And yet here she was with Jash. Were they following her and Enon? If so, why had Addigan let them go in the first place?

Siyan rubbed her eyes. She was tired, and the hour was late.

"Who was that man she was dancing with?" Enon asked.

Siyan looked at him, but he kept his gaze on the empty field. "It must have been Tavi. He must have made all that happen. The lamps, the music, everything." They had heard the music from their own camp. It was what had drawn them there.

Enon blinked. "Tavi?"

"The And'estar I woke. That's what I've been calling him. That's who I was talking to that day when you killed the deer."

He frowned. "To what purpose?" He waved a hand towards the field. "Why create all this? What purpose did it serve?"

Siyan considered a moment and then shook her head. "I don't know." It seemed like that was all she said these days.

Enon's gaze softened as he looked at her. Then he rose and extended a hand. "We should return."

Siyan's heart lurched as she looked at his hand, remembering the day when they had kissed. That had been several days ago, but nothing more had passed between them. Enon continued to teach her how to live in the forest, and he was civil, but that was all. Whatever affection he once held for her seemed to have gone. It confused Siyan and saddened her, for her affection for him had only grown.

Every time Siyan thought of that moment between them, she would smile and her heart would flutter and she would feel just a little bit sick. It was a wonderfully terrible feeling, exquisite and anguishing all at the same time. Then the euphoria would fade and her stomach would wrench as she remembered that Enon seemed to want nothing more to do with her. Had she done something wrong? Or did Enon just see what she had always feared was there—that she was abnormal and unworthy of love?

Unable to look at him, Siyan took his hand and he helped her up. Once she was on her feet, Siyan pulled her hand from his. She didn't like feeling so vulnerable around him. She felt like every time he looked at her, he must see the way her cheeks grew hot, or the way her heart pounded in her chest. She hated feeling that way without him reciprocating. She walked past him and headed back to camp.

Siyan fought down her frustration as they walked. She was supposed to be finding other clans and telling them of the And'estar. She was supposed to be trying to find out what that even meant. Instead she was wandering through the wilds, afraid to act for fear of those who followed her. Yet even if she and Enon weren't being trailed, she wasn't sure what she would do. She needed more knowledge; she needed guidance. If Emora couldn't give that to her, Siyan would need to find it for herself.

It was late by the time they returned to camp, but Siyan didn't want to wait for morning. "Untie the horse, we're leaving."

She knelt down and put her hands to the ground. In her mind, the forest shifted. Paths became hidden behind thickened brush; roots rose from the ground where their tracks had been. The forest became greener, more vibrant; wildflowers blossomed where before there had been none. When Siyan rose, their entire camp looked different. The remains of their fire had been overtaken by a bramble of thorns. What had once been hard-packed dirt was now a carpet of grass and moss and ferns. She wondered why the thought to hide their passage through the forest hadn't occurred to her before now. Perhaps her need hadn't felt great enough.

Enon walked up to her while holding the reins of the horse. He looked around, and then at her. He nodded.

They gathered up the supplies. They wrapped most of the cured meat into the deer hide they had tanned, and tied it on the horse with the rope Siyan had woven. Enon then filled his satchel with as much meat and sinew as it would hold. Everything else needed to be left behind. Siyan put her hand to the ground near the deer and watched as ivy crawled across the earth, twining over the bones and antlers until it was completely hidden.

She straightened and saw that Enon had been watching her. She tightened her jaw at the way her stomach flipped, just as it always did when their eyes met. Then she turned and started walking.

They journeyed through the night. Fearful of being followed, Siyan did not light the path for Enon like she had before. Their pace was slow as Enon found his way through the darkness. As much as Siyan wanted to take his hand and help him, she kept her distance.

As morning broke, Siyan stopped and put her hands to the ground. Once again she used her power to try and cover their tracks. Roots again rose to erase their prints; rocks tumbled from outcroppings and obstructed their path. She had no idea how long such changes would last. Maybe permanently, maybe only hours, if that.

"Is that how Emora keeps your camp hidden, by changing the forest?"

Enon watched her a while before saying, "Not quite like that, no."

Siyan wished she knew what he was thinking, but it didn't matter. They needed to move forward, and there was only one way she could think of to make that happen. "I need to go to the spirit realm."

Enon stiffened his back. "No."

"There is too much about the And'estar that I don't understand. There is much that I don't think even Emora understands. It's not just the other clans that have forgotten the And'estar. We all have—some more than others. If we want to truly remember, then we need the help of an And'estar who actually knows what that word means. Tavi is old. I know he can provide the answers I'm looking for, if I can find him. Going to the spirit realm is the only way I know how to do that."

"How do you know this?"

"I just do." She glanced at him and then away. "I was there once before, when I healed Addigan."

"You mean when you almost died."

Siyan met his gaze. "I know that's where he is. I need to go there. It's the only way."

"It is not the only way, it is only the most dangerous."

"It is my danger to bear."

"You cannot do this."

"Why not? Do you think me unable? Or only unworthy?"

Enon flinched. He looked hurt. It was the first time she had ever seen him like that. Then he looked angry. "If that is what you think then you truly know nothing."

Siyan raised her chin. "I am well aware of how little I know. That's what I'm trying to change. You can either help me or you can leave. Your choice."

Enon clenched his hands and glowered at her before turning and walking away a short distance.

Siyan watched him as he stood there, looking out at the trees as he rubbed his forehead with the back of his hand. She didn't want him to leave. In fact, she was fairly certain she'd need his help. She had no idea how to get back to the spirit realm, and she'd rather not have to try and figure everything out on her own. But if he wouldn't help her, then maybe it would be better if he just left her alone.

After a long while, Enon returned to her. He watched her a moment and then, taking his knife, grabbed one of his braids and cut it off. He held it out to her.

Siyan looked at the long, dark braid and the shells woven in the pleats. "I . . . I don't understand."

"Among my people, it is customary to present an intended with a gift. You are And'estar. Presenting such a gift to an And'estar should be one of worth, and I have thought long on what I can give you that would be fitting. But I have nothing to offer other than myself."

Siyan stared at him. "Intended? Do you mean . . . a wife?"

Enon tilted his head. "Such gifts are sometimes used to propose a joining, or marriage. This gift, however, is insufficient for that. It is only meant to convey my intention towards you. Nothing more."

Siyan licked her lips, though her mouth had gone dry. "And what is your intention?"

He looked her in the eyes. "I care for you, Siyan. I did not want you going to the spirit realm without knowing my heart. I am yours, and so I give you this piece of myself. What you choose to do with it is for you to decide."

Siyan reached out with trembling hands and took the

braid. She ran her fingers over the hard, smooth shells. "Does this mean you'll help me?"

"I will always help you. Even when I do not agree with you."

She smiled, blinking away the tears that welled in her eyes. "I was unsure you cared for me. You were so distant."

"An And'estar deserves more than fleeting affections. But you have held my heart for some time. Perhaps you have always held it."

"Kissing in the forest seems pretty fleeting."

Enon glanced at the ground and laughed. "I perhaps should have stayed away, but I was curious if you felt as I did. It was . . . difficult . . . pulling away from you."

Siyan smiled as Enon's laugh warmed her heart. She hesitated and then reached out and touched his cheek. Enon remained still.

"And now?" she said.

He looked at her. "You know my intention. You decide what happens next."

Siyan's heart thundered in her ears. She felt both nervous and exhilarated—frightened but also strangely calm. "I don't want you to pull away."

Enon stepped closer to her, so close that she could feel his warmth and breathe his scent. It felt right, somehow, standing there with him. He brought a hand up to her face, and she leaned over and put her lips to his.

He pulled her close as they kissed. His hands moved over her body, tugging at her clothes and exposing her skin. Siyan trembled, both from the chill in the air as well as her nerves. She had never been with a man before, but she didn't want him to stop.

And as Enon laid her down among the soft ferns and moss, Siyan wished for time to stop so that she might stay in that moment with him forever. The way his hands caressed her body, the feeling of his breath on her neck. She wanted to remember every look, savor every touch. Even the pain as Enon took her maidenhood. Especially that, for beyond the pain lay a deeper sense of closeness that Siyan had never known. She wrapped her hands around Enon's face and, locking her gaze with his, lost herself in his beautiful, dark eyes.

Siyan knew then that Enon would forever hold her heart.

CHAPTER 20

ADDIGAN SAT ON A ROCK as the sun rose over the empty camp. She had watched as that girl—that forest witch—put her hands to the ground, causing flowers to grow and roots to shift until the entire area became unrecognizable. If Addigan hadn't been watching, she wouldn't have known they had been there at all. But she had. She had been watching the entire time.

Troubled by her encounter with the shadowed man, Addigan had come here, though she was unsure why. She had no intention of talking to the And'estar—she had nothing to say. But her memory of dancing out in the field with that . . . thing . . . haunted her.

It was all so unnatural, the dark man that looked to be made of stone, the strange music, the mesmerizing dance. It was all very wrong, and yet, at the time, Addigan hadn't seemed to care. In fact, she thought back on the dance *fondly*, and that troubled her most of all.

What had come over her? Was it some kind of witchery and, if so, who was the cause? Addigan could only think of one person who could be responsible, and so she came to this camp to sit and watch.

"Addi?"

Addigan turned at Jash's voice.

He waded through a collection of ferns as he walked towards her. "What are you doing here?"

"I couldn't sleep," she said, turning back towards the abandoned camp.

Jash followed her gaze. "This isn't right," he murmured. He took a few steps towards the camp, then he turned back and grinned. "Must've gotten turned around. I thought to check on our friends, but this isn't the spot." He started to walk away.

"This is the right place," Addigan said.

He turned towards her. "No, it was somewhere else. I remember."

Addigan looked at him. "No, it was here. They were here, I saw them. I saw that girl do some kind of . . . magic and change everything."

Jash stared at her, his brow furrowed and mouth hanging open.

"Go on and look," she said. "You'll find deer remains under that growth of ivy."

Scratching his head, Jash took one more look at her before heading towards the hidden camp. He did as she said and poked around in the tangle of ivy. He must have found the deer, for he backed away, his expression now serious. He looked around at the camp a long while, feeling the ground, looking at branches. He was likely looking for their trail, but, judging by his expression, he failed to find it. He returned to Addigan.

"Where did they go?"

Addigan said nothing.

"Addigan!"

She looked at him.

"Where did they go?" he asked again.

Addigan looked away. "Perhaps you should go and tell Malvin that something interesting is happening."

"What?"

She narrowed her eyes at him. "I know he's been following us. You've been going to check on that girl and boy far more frequently than necessary. I didn't want to admit it at first, but I know he's been following us. As always. You better go and tell him that they're gone before you lose track of them for good."

Jash scratched his neck. "What good will that do? If they're gone, they're gone. There's nothing Malvin will be able to do about it."

"He's a Magister, he might be able to use the Art to find them."

Jash watched her a long moment. Then, exhaling, he muttered something under his breath and headed back to camp.

Half the day had passed by the time Jash and Malvin returned to her. She remained by the abandoned camp the entire time, knowing that if she left she likely wouldn't be able to find it again.

Just sitting there and waiting had been one of the hardest things Addigan had ever done. Every part of her told her to run, to get away from Malvin and Jash. She needed to find herself again—on her own terms, not the Tower's—but she knew that Malvin would never let her go. He would just keep tracking her through the forest; she wouldn't be able to hide from him. If she truly wanted to be free of him, she would have to face him, one way or another.

Malvin made no apologies this time for following her, for which Addigan was grateful. She hated pretense.

"I know where they've gone," Addigan said, looking straight ahead. "I can point you in the right direction, but you and Jash will have to be the ones to find the trail. Given that the girl used the Art to cover her tracks, I suspect the Art will be needed to find them."

"And how am I supposed to do that?" Malvin said.

"You're the Magister," Addigan said.

Malvin remained silent. She could feel his gaze upon her, but she refused to look at him. In time, he turned and left.

Malvin's entourage set up camp around where Addigan sat. Pack horses and ponies were unloaded, campfires lit, tents erected. Malvin withdrew to his own corner of the camp, poring over a number of books he had brought with him. They were likely books of runes. It's what Addigan would have brought, had she had access to such tomes. As it was, she had to fight the urge to walk up to him and ask to peruse the books herself. Knowing Malvin, he might even let her. But she didn't want to ask him for anything ever again.

They remained camped there the entire following day. Malvin pored over his books while Jash constantly raided the supplies in search of food. Addigan kept to herself, sitting and watching the forest where the And'estar and her companion had gone. What would Addigan do when they found them? She needed to do something—she couldn't just carry on the way she had been. Something needed to change, only she didn't know what.

The day faded in quiet monotony. When the sun again rose, Malvin walked up to her, his eyes tired and cheeks flushed. "I think I may have found something."

When Addigan said nothing, Malvin spoke a rune foreign to her ears. He stared off towards the abandoned camp. Then he smiled and, sparing only a brief glance at her, he hurried away.

Addigan flinched as his shouts echoed through the quiet morning, ordering the men to break camp. He had found the trail, he said. They needed to leave at once. This was what Addigan had been waiting for. So why did her stomach suddenly feel so leaden? One way or another, she'd find a way to be free. She only wished she knew what that meant.

CHAPTER 21

SIYAN AND ENON SAT ACROSS from each other near the campfire. Neither of them spoke. Siyan stared at the severed braid she held in her hand, trying not to dwell on the task before her, but failing.

She was to go to the spirit realm. She wasn't sure how she was supposed to get there, nor was she sure how she'd return. When she'd been there before, it had all seemed so real, and she had only managed to wake from her mother's hand piercing her skull. What would happen to her if she went there and couldn't find her way back? Would she die? Would her body sprout into a great white tree, with only the traces of a face in the whorls of the bark?

She looked at Enon. He sat cross-legged with his head bowed. It was so strange, the feelings she held for him. They hadn't known each other long, but somehow that didn't seem to matter. Now that he held her heart, it was like he had always held it, she just hadn't known it. It hurt her to think about leaving him. Siyan wanted to forget everything else in the world and stay there with him. It would be so easy to leave everything else behind. If he asked it of her, maybe she would.

She looked down at the braid and ran her fingers over the smooth shells. Growing tired of the heavy, lonely silence, she said, "I've never been to the sea."

Enon looked up at her, his eyes weary. "Neither have I."

"Where did you find the shells?"

"I traded for them from a traveling merchant. A pair of rabbit pelts, I believe. I was very young."

"You kept them all this time?"

"I liked the look of them, and they were a reminder of the world beyond the forests. It was a world I had hoped to see one day."

"Do you still hope to?"

He tilted his head. "I would like to see such a great expanse of water, but I am unsure it is a world I belong in."

They fell back into silence.

After a while, Enon said, "You do not need to do this."

She wanted to agree with him, tell him she'd given up on this fool's errand and regained her senses. Instead, she said, "Yes, I do."

"Why? This is not what Emora asked of you. She would not want you to put yourself in harm's way." He was quiet a moment before adding, "Nor do I."

Siyan shook her head. "Because I am also unsure of the world in which I belong."

Enon's brow furrowed; he looked both confused and hurt, and it broke Siyan's heart. She closed her eyes. "For the past two years, I've felt as if a shadow has been following me. It's almost like it whispers to me, telling me of all the remarkable things I can do. But when I look at it, it fades away. Yet it's still there, still whispering, pulling me towards something I don't understand. It frightens me; it makes me feel like a stranger in my own skin." She took a breath. "I don't want to be afraid anymore. I need to understand who I am and my place in this world. This is the only way I know that will let me do that."

They sat there for a time, then Enon took the braid from her hands and pulled out the cord of shells. He walked behind her, pulled her hair back, and worked it into a plait.

Siyan put her hand to her hair and felt the shells woven within.

Enon came around and sat across from her again. "Perhaps they will help you return, and then we will see the ocean together."

Siyan nodded, biting her lip against the tears that welled in her eyes. Then she forced a smile. "It's all kind of silly, really. I'm not even sure how to get there. I mean, I think I know how, it's just *doing* it is the problem." She looked at Enon. "Has your mother ever gone to the spirit realm?"

He shook his head. "No. But Minan, my grandmother, did." His gaze turned sharp. "She did not return."

Siyan swallowed. "How did she get there?"

"I do not know." Enon fell silent, his jaw working soundlessly. Then, closing his eyes, he said, "My mother did have . . . methods that helped her take more control over her power."

"What kind of methods?"

"Herbs, sometimes. Ones that would let her mind open more freely, as she put it. Sometimes she would go without food or sleep. Sometimes she would do all of these things."

"Did they work?"

Enon watched her, his expression dark. He looked angry, but also a little sad. "Yes."

"What kinds of herbs did she use?"

"I do not know."

Siyan took a moment to consider. She wasn't really sure how going without food or sleep could help, but she didn't know what else to do. She looked at Enon. "Will you help me? I can give up food easily enough, I think. But I don't know if I can keep myself awake."

Enon closed his eyes, his jaw clenched. He nodded.

They continued traveling until they came to a spot that Enon deemed acceptable. It was near a stream so that they would have water, and nestled against a rise of rocks so that they had protection on one side. Siyan hid their camp as best she could while Enon unloaded the horse. Then she sat and rested against a tree, and the waiting began.

It was easy enough going without food the first day. Siyan felt hungry, of course, but she had gone without food for a day or two before, so it was not unusual. During this time, she would occasionally try to use her power as she had with Addigan, but the thought was slippery and slinked across her mind like oil on water.

As the day waned, her fatigue grew. She managed to stay awake for most of the night, but realized she had dozed off when she awoke to Enon gently shaking her shoulder. She gave him a wan smile, but he just got up and walked away.

Dawn broke behind the trees and Siyan watched with bleary eyes as Enon munched on a piece of meat. He crouched down in front of her as he chewed. He held the meat close enough for her to smell, and her mouth watered. Was he taunting her?

She frowned at him. "What are you doing?"

"You are hungry."

Her frown deepened. "Of course I'm hungry. You're not helping."

He took another bite. "You must complete your task. Go to the spirit realm. When you return, you will be able to eat."

Siyan stifled her annoyance along with her hunger. She put Enon out of her mind and tried, once again, to lose herself to her power. But again, she failed. "You're not helping," she repeated, struggling to keep her voice calm.

With another bite, Enon rose and walked away.

Time crawled by, marked only by the babbling of the stream and the birds in the trees. Again and again, Siyan tried to use her power to her utmost ability, but the means of it continued to slip across her mind and out of reach. It was maddening. How could it seem so simple one moment and impossible the next? Her hunger and fatigue grew, and her temper shortened. Enon leaned against a tree as he watched her. His jaw was tight, his eyes tired and sad. He held a piece of meat in his hand that he seemed to have forgotten.

Daylight faded into darkness and then she awoke to Enon tapping her cheek.

"Wake up," he said.

Siyan rubbed her eyes and blinked at him. She said nothing, and Enon got up and walked away.

Again she tried to use her power to find her way to the spirit realm, but again nothing happened. Around her the world swayed. The trees seemed to have unanchored themselves and moved around, making Siyan feel like she was floating.

The day passed in a bleary haze, and it was all Siyan could do to stay awake. She felt like crying, like crawling into a hole and hiding. Anything that would let her sleep. She just wanted to sleep.

Siyan awoke on the ground with cold water splashing on her face. She sat up, sputtering and coughing. "What . . .?"

Enon dropped the empty water skin and crouched down in front of her. He put a hand behind her head and gripped her hair. "You must focus."

Siyan frowned and closed her eyes. "I'm tired. I can't do it. Just let me sleep."

He grasped her chin and pulled her face upright. "Look at me."

Siyan kept her eyes clenched shut. She didn't want to do this anymore. She was tired. It was all a mistake.

"Siyan," Enon said, his voice gentle. "Look at me."

Siyan opened her eyes and looked into his own.

"You need to focus."

"I don't know how."

"Yes, you do. You just need to let yourself."

She shook her head, as much as she could with his grip upon her. "I can't . . ."

"You are strong, Siyan. You can. You have done it before, remember?"

Siyan remembered when she healed Addigan. It seemed like so long ago, like another person. "Yes."

Enon let go of her chin and stroked her hair. It was soothing. He hummed a tune that seemed to wash around her, carrying her among the trees that weaved around her as if floating on water. She wanted to ask him what song it was, but then it seemed so silly. What did it matter? It was beautiful. He was beautiful.

Siyan looked into his dark eyes, losing herself in them like she had before. She let his voice caress her like his hands had caressed her before. She loved him. She didn't know how it was possible. She didn't care. She loved him and, at that moment, she opened her heart to him. She exposed all that she was to him. She was like sunlight and mist, and he the earth and trees. She bathed him in her light and her love, and, for a moment, the light was all she saw.

And then all went dark.

CHAPTER 22

SIYAN'S EYES REFUSED TO OPEN. They felt crusted shut, as if she had been crying tears that had then turned to stone. She tried to rub them, but her hands were gone.

She took a deep breath and cool, damp air slicked down her throat like honey-water. It smelled of earth and rain, of stone and ash. The taste of salt and meat and grass lingered on her tongue. It was good. She was hungry, though she didn't know why. She tried to bite down on the taste, but her teeth dissolved like clouds of mist.

She sighed. Around her the wind blew, crashing into trees like ocean waves. Siyan twitched and wondered from where the ocean came. Her eyelids fluttered, and the stone sealing them shut turned to sand and crumbled away.

The sky was sepia, shimmering with gleams of light that roiled like storm clouds. Around her tall trees stood darkened and shadowed and half-forgotten. Siyan tried to walk but her legs were buried in the earth. She found her hands and used them to push herself up and out of the soil. The dirt clung to her legs. She started to brush it away but then stopped, realizing the dirt *was* her legs. So instead she walked, wondering when the storm of light would rain down upon her like a shower of stars.

Addigan trailed after Malvin and Jash, hiking her skirts up to her knees so as not to make any noise. They had found the And'estar and her companion and were making their way to their camp to talk. Malvin wanted to be reasonable and try to find a way to make everyone happy, but Addigan knew that would never happen. That wilds-boy— Enon, Malvin had said was his name—was much too quick to draw his bow, and this would be no exception. Addigan tightened her grip on her skirts and her staff, annoyed at herself for feeling so nervous.

The camp came into view, and they ducked behind a collection of trees. The And'estar girl lay upon the ground near a wall of stones. Enon sat next to her while holding her hand, his head bowed. Addigan frowned. Had something happened?

Malvin looked at her and then at Jash. Then, saying nothing, he got up and headed towards them.

Enon's head snapped up at their approach. Seeing them, he grabbed his bow and scrambled to his feet.

Malvin put up a hand. "We only want to talk."

Enon's gaze darted between them. He looked tired and sad, worn and haggard. He nocked an arrow, drew, and aimed it at Malvin. "Leave. You are not welcome here."

Malvin continued to edge forward, eyeing the And'estar on the ground. "What has happened to her?"

Enon's lips twisted into a snarl. "Leave. Now."

"Surely we can come to an agreement," Malvin said.

Enon loosed the arrow. Malvin spoke a rune and the projectile veered into the brush.

Enon's eyes widened, briefly, but then he drew another arrow from his quiver and nocked it in his bow.

Siyan walked through the sepia-stained light. Flowers bloomed in her path and withered as she passed by. Thunder boomed overhead, but no storm came. She walked on. She left the shadows of the forest and came to the pale openness of a field. It was dotted with piles of hay, around which circles of children held hands and danced.

Their bodies were soft and dimpled underneath rough-spun clothes, but the heads resting upon their shoulders were those of goats. When Siyan approached, they stopped to look at her with their yellow, rectangular eyes.

"Hello," Siyan said.

The children stared at her a moment and then scattered in a cacophony of bleats and laughter.

Siyan frowned. What was so funny? She lingered in the field, wondering what to do—wondering why she felt the need to do *anything*. She felt heavy, the stones in her earthen legs aching to return to the ground. She wanted to kneel, to feel the earth upon her knees, to lose her hands once again in the soil. But then a thought twitched in her mind that kept her standing. She needed to be somewhere. She didn't know where that was, or why she needed to go. She just did. And so, like a fish swimming upstream, Siyan pulled herself from the field and kept on walking.

The sky roiled in light and ink-stained brilliance. There was no sun, only an omniscient glow that seemed to pour from the tinted clouds, swirling beyond the darkness like shoals of gleaming fish.

Siyan blinked. Had she seen shoals of fish? She must have, for the memory of them seemed to be hers, though she couldn't recall from where she had gotten it. Unable to remember, she dismissed it and kept on walking.

She walked until the sepia sky turned black, and the stars floated above and around her like glimmering motes of dust. In the distance, the moon appeared, but down in the trees rather than in the sky. Siyan hesitated. She felt the pull of the earthen stream heading towards the moon, and the stones in her legs wished to carry her there. But Siyan resisted. As much as she wanted to go, to kneel upon the earth and dream, it wasn't where she was supposed to be.

She frowned. It made no sense. If she wasn't supposed to go there, then where? There wasn't anything else, was there?

Then Siyan remembered that she had a heart, and remembered that, at that moment, it would be beating. Would it be fast with fear? Or excitement? Siyan didn't feel any of these things. There was only a weak thumping in her chest—a half-remembered sensation that seemed out of place. She was about to tell it to stop but didn't. It occurred to her that it was something she should be feeling, though she didn't know why. Just as she didn't know why she turned her back on the moon, and forced her legs of stone and earth to keep on moving. She didn't understand any of it, but she did it anyway.

Malvin spoke a rune and wrenched the bow from Enon's hands and sent it flying into the brush. Baring his teeth, Enon pulled a knife from a sheath strapped to his leg.

Jash pulled out his pistol and leveled it at him.

"You cannot hope to succeed," Malvin said. "You are just one man, and we are three. You are trying to protect your woman, I understand that. But you cannot protect her if you are dead."

Addigan looked between Enon, Jash, and Malvin. The latter two were not paying her any mind. Only Enon looked at her as his gaze darted between the three of them. Despite Malvin's words, Enon didn't seem to have any intention of standing down. That worried her, because Malvin was right: he would not succeed—not alone. Once he was subdued or dead, then it would all be over. They would have gotten what they came for. They would take her back to the Tower.

Nervous, Addigan licked her lips as she tightened her grip on her staff. If she were to have any hope of escaping Malvin, then she needed to do something, and she needed to do it quickly. More than that, she needed to do it *right*. Her ability to wield the Art was still redeveloping. She would need to cast a rune that she knew would succeed. She would only get one chance.

Not wanting to hesitate too long, Addigan turned toward Jash and grabbed his wrist, speaking the only rune that she knew, without question, would succeed.

Siyan walked through the night forest, waving the stars away from her as she would flitting mosquitos. The path she followed branched into four directions, and Siyan stopped, wondering which one to take. On the path behind her lay the moon, the way bright and even. The three remaining paths lay jagged and shadowed, each one as dark as the next. Siyan knew she would choose one of the shadowed paths, but she didn't know which.

"Where are you?" she said, unsure of to whom she spoke.

From the path to her right a white rabbit appeared. It hopped around the thorny bushes, its nose twitching. Then it hopped away and vanished into the shadows. Siyan followed.

All around her the trees shifted, reshaping themselves into houses and hovels, towers and cliffs. One moment they were grand manors of polished stone that gleamed in the starlight, the next moment they were huts of leather hides and wooden poles. Spiraling towers looked down on her with eyes of colored glass, but when Siyan looked back, all she saw were sheer stone cliffs.

Siyan walked on until the stone and trees melted into pools of silver. From them new trees grew, gleaming and skeletal, with branches like fingers that grasped for the sky. She found the tallest one and walked towards it.

The silver pools darkened into a swampy mire. Vines and thorns sprouted around Siyan's feet, twining around her legs, but could not find purchase among the stones they found there.

Siyan stopped and said, "Tavi." She knew he was there, though she didn't know why. The man was nowhere to be seen. Then another name occurred to her, and she said, "Aren."

The air grew still, empty and vapid. A woman approached, her skin dull, her dark hair streaked with ashes.

"Do not come here," she said.

"I am already here."

The woman tilted her head. "Maybe."

There was something about her that looked wrong. She looked hidden, shadowed, like the half-remembered trees Siyan had seen before. "You are not Aren."

"No one is Aren."

Siyan reached out and touched the woman's brow. She moved her thumb across her head, and the woman's skin crumbled away like dead leaves. Siyan put her fingers into the hole that was left behind—an empty darkness that felt cool and moist. She then hooked her fingers behind the woman's eyes and pulled, and the woman crumbled into a pile of leaves and ashes.

The skeletal trees flashed with lightning, and the swamp flared alight with silvery flames.

Tavi—Aren—stepped out from behind the great white tree. He was young, his dark hair pleated and adorned with amber beads.

"Why are you here?" he asked, his voice quiet.

Siyan opened her mouth to answer, but no words came. Why *was* she there?

"I wonder if you even remember," he said as he walked

towards her. "It is like that here. It is a place of memory and dreams. It is easy to get lost. It is easy to forget." His eyes turned sad. "For some, that is."

Siyan backed away at his approach. There was a way in his demeanor she didn't quite like. "Who was that woman? Why was she here?"

"Why are any of us here? Why are *you* here?" His saddened eyes turned hard. "It would be a kindness to you if you forgot. If you slept." He reached out towards her.

Siyan backed away from his grasp. She didn't want to forget, though she was unsure why. What was worth remembering? What was she holding on to? She searched through her mind, trying to remember, but her memory was vast and sprawling. Thoughts both foreign and familiar twined together and branched out in countless directions. It was chaos and cacophony. It was trying to find a raindrop within an ocean. It hadn't always been like this, had it? Her thoughts had once been simple and quiet, hadn't they? She tried to remember when that was, but the thought was drowned in the storm.

Aren continued towards her. "You shouldn't fight it. It is right to forget. It is the natural way of things. We weren't meant to remember for thousands of years. We were meant to sleep. It is our due."

Siyan backed away again, her hands clenched. The more he wanted her to forget, the more she wanted to remember. The silvery flames around them died and in their place rose a forest of trees, thick and towering like giant sentinels. The wind gusted, tearing at Siyan's skin. She reached out towards Aren, looking for the memory he wished to forget, looking for that drop in the ocean. All around her the trees groaned in the wind, bending as is if they, too, reached for him. She locked her gaze with his, her fingers twining as if working an unseen yarn. Then, with a flick of her wrist, she found it. And Siyan remembered.

Addigan grabbed Jash's wrist and spoke a rune of fire.

He cried out, dropping the pistol as he reeled backwards.

Malvin turned towards them, and Enon scrambled along the ground and retrieved his bow.

Jash bent over, putting a hand to his burned skin. "You bleeding whore!" he said, spittle flying from his lips. He started towards her but stopped when an arrow pierced his back. He staggered a few paces, but then another arrow took him in the neck and he fell to the ground.

Malvin looked at Addigan long enough for her to see the hurt and shock in his eyes. Then he gripped his staff and started drawing runes in the dirt and fallen needles.

Enon leveled his bow at him and loosed an arrow, but it veered off course as if blown by a sharp wind. He loosed another, with the same result. He lowered his bow and, gripping his knife, stood in front of the And'estar, who still lay unmoving upon the ground.

Malvin stood between Addigan and Enon. He glanced back and forth between them while standing within his protective circle, likely gauging who was the bigger threat. Then he turned towards Enon as he swung his staff, drawing runes in the air.

Addigan scuttled along the ground and grabbed Jash's pistol. Firing it from a distance would be useless. Malvin's circle would deflect the bullet just as it had the arrows.

Malvin completed the rune and swung his staff towards Enon. The air before him rippled like waves and Enon was sent sprawling to the ground, his knife knocked from his hand.

Before Malvin had a chance to turn around, Addigan walked up to him and put the pistol to the back of his head.

Malvin froze. Softly, he said, "Have you gone completely mad, Addi?"

Addigan set her jaw. Before she had time to think, before she had time for regret, she pulled the trigger. She wouldn't go back.

The hammer struck the steel, but nothing happened. Addigan blinked, and then Malvin's staff crashed into her face and all went dark.

Siyan smiled, turning her face towards the sun that gleamed in a clear blue sky. The wind stirred, cool and refreshing against her warm skin.

A woman laughed, and Siyan opened her eyes to see Aren walk past her towards a woman lying in a grassy field. The woman held in her hands a bundle of flowers, and, when Aren lay down next to her, she let the flowers fall upon him in a cascade of petals. She laughed again.

"She was your wife," Siyan said, and turned to look at Aren, who was also standing behind her. This Aren was old, his hair white and his face mottled with wrinkles. He regarded her with colorless eyes, then his gaze flicked past her as he watched his own memory.

"I wanted to leave," he said.

The sky clouded over and darkened; the trees turned barren and skeletal; and the lush green grass and flowers withered to dirt and ash.

"We can't leave," Lesya said. Siyan caught the memory of her name like she might catch snow from a cloud. Lesya's belly was heavy and swollen with child.

"Yes, we can," the young Aren said.

Lesya started to walk away but stopped when Aren grabbed her arm.

"I am your husband, Lesya. Your place is at my side, wherever that may be."

Lesya glared at him and wrenched her arm from his grasp. "My place is with my people, as is yours. Any husband of mine would know that." Lesya stalked away and the light faded until only night remained.

"I was angry," Aren said, still looking at where Lesya had disappeared. "Angry that my own wife did not understand me, did not support me. She chose the clan over me, and so, in my anger, I chose myself over the clan. I left without her." He shook his head. "A foolish thing to do. Childish. It was like I was a boy all over again, running to my secret grove to play with my rabbit. Only this time I had no friends to greet me, and as my temper cooled, I saw my foolishness for what it was."

The night deepened, eclipsing the surrounding trees in an inky blackness. The wind stilled; all was quiet. Then, in the sky, a red moon rose. It hung low on the horizon, bloated as if heavy with blood. It stained the forest with its rusted light, falling upon the crimson flames of a fire. All else remained shrouded in darkness.

Siyan walked towards the fire. She knew that Aren followed her, even though he made no sound. As she drew closer, she saw that the flames belonged to a pyre. Upon the burning wood lay the form of a body, its charred hands clutching a smaller form to its breast. Nearby, young Aren kneeled, his hands on his legs, his gaze staring out into the darkness beyond. Then the wind blew, and the great flames of the pyre flickered and died, as though it were nothing more than a candle blown out by a gentle breath.

"She died," Siyan said into the darkness, "because of you." She could see the memory of it now, as plain as if it were one of her own. Maybe it was one of her own. Maybe it had been there all along, and only now was she recalling it. "She birthed your child while you were away sulking and died during the labor. They both died. And you were gone, unable to heal her, unable to help her, because you were selfish and thought only of yourself. It cost you everything."

Siyan reached out and waved the darkness away, and they were back in the swampy marsh among the skeletal trees. She turned toward Aren, who was now young again.

"You're hiding here," she said. "You want to forget, but you can't, can you?"

"I did for a time. I slept. Then you came and woke me." He closed his eyes and shook his head. "I will sleep again. You will not wake me again."

The ground beneath Siyan's feet turned to liquid, and the stones in her legs pulled her down into the cold, murky depths.

Chapter 23

Siyan floated in darkness. The branches of memory and thought had gone, leaving her in mute solitude. She liked it. It was soothing, calming. There was nowhere she needed to be; nothing she needed to do. She just was, and that was enough.

She floated. On occasion, a thought passed through her mind, a fleeting thing of shadow and hurt. She could never see it, not directly. Nor did she want to. Nothing would be gained by looking at it. So, each time a thought surfaced, Siyan would breathe in the dark water, feel as the cool liquid filled her body until she could no longer tell her own limbs from the water that surrounded them. She and the water became one, and that was good.

She floated, breathing in the water and exhaling the thoughts until she no longer realized she floated at all. She just was, and that felt right. She remained there, perhaps an eternity, perhaps a few minutes. It was all the same, and none of it meant anything at all.

Then the world tilted, and Siyan was knocked through the water as if someone had pushed her. She opened her eyes, and the darkness around her receded. Her stony legs were embedded in sandy ground, while reefs of coral and tendrils of seaweed surrounded her. Above, shoals of fish careened and flitted, gleaming with a light of their own.

Siyan smiled. She had wondered where she had seen shoals of fish before, and now she remembered. It was the ocean. She was in the ocean. Somehow that seemed important—a thorn that embedded itself in her mind, refusing to let go. She breathed in the water and tried to expel the thought, but still it remained. She needed to tell someone. She didn't know why, she didn't know whom, yet the thought persisted.

Siyan stared out into the water, watching the seaweed sway as if caught in a gentle wind. Her black hair floated around her, melding into the darkness of the water beyond.

She needed to tell someone.

Frustrated, she let out a heavy sigh, and the seaweed bent and swayed and the fish swirled in a furious mass. She pushed away her hair and found tangled within the locks a string of shells. Siyan blinked. She knew there was a memory attached to it, but it was hard to find amidst the memories that surrounded her as deep and fathomless as the ocean itself. She reached out and took the string, the shells hard and smooth underneath her fingers.

She needed to tell someone. She needed to leave.

Siyan looked up, past the shoals of fish and through leagues of murky water until she saw a light. Sunlight, shining through the water above. It was faint, but it was there. She tried to swim towards it, but her stony legs anchored her fast.

She put her hands to her legs and dug out the stones with her fingers. It hurt. Siyan screamed as tears streamed from her eyes. The ocean took her voice and her tears, leaving her mute and cold. Still she continued. The more it hurt, the more she was convinced that it was the right thing to do. She shouldn't be there on the ocean floor as silvery fish coalesced around her.

She needed to leave.

She clawed the stones from her legs, until what was

left of them crumbled into dust and settled on the sandy floor of the ocean. With her arms, Siyan pulled herself up through the water. Her body felt dense and heavy and only got heavier the further she went. Her arms burned until she could no longer feel them, and she feared that they had turned to water and spread out into the sea. But still she pushed on. Upward and upward she clawed. She didn't know how far she had gone, but she dared not look down, fearing her eyes would turn to stone and pull her headlong back into the soft sand below. She kept her gaze upward, breathing out the water that she had only moments ago so deeply breathed in. She wanted it out. She needed to be out.

She needed to tell him. She needed to find him. Enon.

The sunlight grew brighter as she drew closer. The water glimmered green as feeble light filtered through the liquid. Then it turned blue, then golden. Then, just as her hand broke the surface of the water, the sunlight turned white and radiant, blinding her as she opened her mouth to take her first breath of air.

Siyan jolted awake, gasping and coughing. She writhed upon the ground, trying to expel the water she still felt in her lungs, though no water came out. Panic filled her mind. She was drowning. She was going to die. Here, underneath the sun and trees, she would drown on dry land.

"Siyan."

She looked up and saw Enon looking down at her.

"Breathe," he said.

Siyan opened her mouth. She wanted to breathe, but instead she choked and tried to cough up the water that filled her lungs.

Enon put his hands to her chest, his fingers slipping between the buttons on her shirt and finding her skin. "Breathe," he said again. "You can breathe."

Siyan felt as if the warmth from his hands spread though her body, and she calmed. Ignoring the feeling of water in her lungs, she breathed. And as she breathed the air, the feeling of water choking her subsided. She breathed, again and again, until it had gone.

She lay still on the ground, waiting for her racing heart to calm. Enon looked tired and worn. Even so, he gave a small smile and reached out and tucked a stray lock of hair behind her ear. That was when she saw his hands were bound.

Siyan tried pushing herself upright, but her wrists were also bound, and her arms were weak and shaking. Enon grabbed her hands and helped her sit up.

"What happened?" Siyan said as she looked around. There were men all around, tending campfires and horses and pitching tents. It looked like they were back in Malvin's and Addigan's camp. "Did they find us?"

"Yes," Enon said.

"Are you all right?"

Enon's eyes darkened. "I am fine."

"When did they come?"

"After you had gone. I killed one of them. But the other one, the one in red, he also calls spirit. I was not strong enough. Neither was she." He nodded towards the camp.

Siyan followed his gaze. At the other end of the camp sat Addigan, propped up against a tree, her hands bound behind her back and her mouth gagged. Even from where she sat, Siyan could see her bloodied face, all swollen and bruised. "What happened to her?"

"She tried to kill the man in the red robe. She did not succeed."

Siyan looked at Enon. "How long was I gone?"

He continued to stare outwards and did not meet her gaze. "Two days."

Two days. It seemed like both an inordinate amount

of time and no time at all. It had all happened so fast, and yet, now that she was back, she felt as if she had been gone for ages.

Siyan brought her bound hands up to Enon's face and touched his cheek.

He looked at her, the anger melting from his expression. "I feared you would not return."

Siyan nodded, wondering how close she had come to that. "You helped me back."

Confusion shadowed his eyes, but he remained silent. He took her hands in his own, his head lowered as he held them. Then, at the sound of approaching footsteps, he let go, his expression grim once more.

Malvin looked down at them. "So, you're awake."

"What do you want?" Siyan said.

He crouched down in front of her. "From you, I want answers. From him," he nodded towards Enon, "I want justice."

"Justice?"

"He killed one of my men. He would have killed me given the chance. He needs to be brought to account."

"He wouldn't have killed anyone had the situation not called for it. You shouldn't have followed us."

Malvin tilted his head. "I find it interesting that you can comment on the situation, considering you were unconscious the entire time. What happened to you?"

Siyan stiffened her back. "None of your concern."

"Except that it is my concern. I've a duty to the people, and it won't do having two dangerous misfits roaming about. You both have much to account for."

"We've nothing to account for. Your 'duty' is to your own selfish purpose. Don't pretend it is otherwise."

Malvin narrowed his eyes. "You think you know much, but you are just a foolish little girl who couldn't possibly understand. You need to show more deference to your betters." He watched her a moment before reaching out and grabbing her by the chin. "Why *are* your eyes so odd?"

Siyan yanked her head out of his grasp just as Enon got to his feet, grabbed Malvin by the collar of his robe and threw him back.

Malvin stumbled through the brush, his face reddening. He spoke and drew a rune in the air and Enon's head whipped to the side as if struck.

Siyan tried getting to her feet but her legs wouldn't move. Enon breathed heavily, his bound hands clenched into fists. He looked like he might charge after Malvin when three men from the camp came over and stood behind the Magister. One man was bearded, the other short, and the third had long hair pulled back in a tail.

Malvin said, "I think we've given our guests a little too much freedom. See to it that they're properly bound and won't cause any more trouble."

Enon hunkered down and, as the men approached him, brought up his fists into the shorter man's jaw. He then wrapped his hands around the man's neck until the ponytailed man pulled him off. The short man rubbed his neck before bringing his own fists to Enon's stomach and face, again and again.

Heart pounding, Siyan put her hands to the earth but was pulled away and lifted up. Someone held her, pinning her arms against her body. She tried to kick him, but her legs felt leaden and didn't want to move. Instead, she thrust her head back and heard a crack and a muffled cry as her skull met with her captor's nose.

She fell to the ground, and again she burrowed her hands into the dirt. The trees groaned and the ground shivered. Then a hand was again upon her, pulling her away and turning her over. Siyan caught a glimpse of a man with blood running through his beard when he brought up a fist and everything went black.

Chapter 24

Night had fallen when Siyan awoke. Two men held her by the arms, holding her upright as they dragged her through the camp. She tried to get on her feet, but her legs still felt numb and wouldn't respond, so they dragged along the ground behind her.

Her body hurt. Her face throbbed with pain, her arms ached, and the binds around her wrists cut into her skin and made her hands tingle. Siyan tried bringing up her head to look around, but even that seemed to be more than she could bear.

Then Malvin said, "This will do."

The men stopped and let Siyan fall to the ground in a heap. The bearded man that had knocked her unconscious stepped forward, holding a length of rope. He tied one end to Siyan's binds. Then he threw the rope over a tree branch and hoisted her up.

Siyan cried out as pain seared though her arms and shoulders. Her feet still touched the ground when the man stopped and tied off the rope, but Siyan's legs were too feeble to hold her. So she hung there, gritting her teeth against the pain shooting through her wrists and arms.

Malvin arched an eyebrow. "You'd be better served to

stand upon your feet and not drag them like a petulant child." His voice was calm, as if he were giving her advice.

Siyan's heart raced as the wind kicked up and the air chilled. Her breath plumed in a flurry of clouds. Snow drifted down from the sky, and the two men that had carried her shared uneasy glances.

Then, in a wide circle around Siyan, Malvin drew a series of runes in the dirt. Siyan gasped. She felt . . . different. The air warmed and the snow stopped.

"What have you done?" she said.

"I've been thinking much about you," Malvin said. "About the differences between us. I wasn't sure what to make of you, at first. You are clearly not a Magister, nor do you use the Art in the way that Magisters do. A lesser-educated man might think you some kind of forest witch." He glanced at the other men who averted his gaze. "But I am not such a man. Despite our differences, it is still the Art you are wielding, and I know much about the Art."

Siyan reached for her power, but it was gone. She blinked, uncomprehending. It wasn't just the elusive feeling of when her power evaded her—it was not there. Her breath came quickly, panicked and ragged.

"What have you done?" she said, trying to keep the fear out of her voice.

Malvin folded his hands and gave her a level look. "I do apologize for all of this." He waved at the rope and runes. "But you have proven you cannot be trusted, and so that is why we find ourselves here, with you tied up such as you are. I've developed a set of runes that I think will prevent you from causing further trouble." He paused, pressing his lips together before saying, "I am not an unreasonable man. Convince me you are not a danger to myself or my companions, and I am sure we can come to a much more . . . dignified arrangement."

Siyan closed her eyes, struggling to keep her breathing calm. "Where's Enon?"

Malvin sighed. "He had to be restrained, much like yourself, though nothing this drastic. It would be best if you forgot about him. His fate is all but sealed for murdering my man, which he will meet upon our return to Roelith. A young woman such as yourself should think of her own future and not tie herself to such unlucky fellows. Nothing good will come of it." He held her gaze with an intent look. "Think on what I've said." Then he turned and left.

The two men that had carried her there exchanged nervous glances with one another before shuffling off.

Siyan stared at the line of runes twining around her. Again she reached for her power, but it was gone. Her mind felt dark and padded, as if the memory of her power had been wiped away. She tried to kick out her leg to smudge the runes, but her legs only twitched. The runes were likely too far, anyway.

Siyan flexed her hands, working against the numbness and tingling that deepened in her fingers. The bindings around her wrists were too tight, made even worse by having her weight on them. Her entire body burned, all except her legs, which felt numb and cold.

She looked around the camp. The bearded man sat on a folding chair nearby, smoking a pipe as he watched her. The rest of the camp was still. The tents now stood dark—the only light came from glowing embers and the moon.

Siyan closed her eyes. Where was Enon?

Malvin had told her to forget about him, as if that were a simple thing to do. A choice she could make that would wipe him from her thoughts and memories, as if he had never existed at all.

Forget about him. She knew what those words really meant—they were going to kill him. Malvin had called it justice, but Siyan wasn't fooled. They were going to kill him, and she was trussed up like a pig for slaughter.

Siyan again struggled against her binds, but the rope only dug deeper into her skin and she almost wept from the pain. She wanted to call out to Enon, but she dared not, afraid that if she did she would only be met with silence.

The night deepened. The bearded man slept in his chair, his chin resting against his chest. Again Siyan reached for her power, but again there was nothing.

Movement caught her eye and Siyan turned her head to find Tavi—Aren—walking towards her. He stopped upon reaching the circle of runes, watching her with dark eyes.

"You are in a bind," he said.

Siyan stifled her rising anger. Was he trying to be funny? "Help me out of here."

"No."

Siyan's breathing grew heavy and ragged. "What do you mean? Help me out of here!" Siyan hissed the words, fearful of speaking too loudly and waking the camp.

Aren tilted his head, his face calm. "I cannot help you."

"You can't or you won't?"

He waved a hand, seemingly dismissing the question.

"Then why are you here?"

"I am here because I have always been here. I am here because you woke me. Perhaps you should ask yourself why I am here."

"I think you are here because you are finding a perverse pleasure in seeing me bound and helpless. Otherwise you'd be helping me instead of standing there and watching."

"I watch all things. Pleasure—perverse or otherwise—does not matter."

"I think you are lying."

Aren once again tilted his head, as if he were considering her words. He looked down at the runes on the ground.

"These designs, they create difficulties for you?"

Siyan frowned. "What do you know about them?"

Aren bent down to run a hand over the runes, taking care not to touch them. "Curious constructs. They resonate with the power of the spirit world, yet they are not of that world. They are a mimicry, an echo of the power they seek to harness, yet the power they return to us is distorted and bent. Most fascinating."

"How does that help me?"

Aren smiled though his expression lacked warmth. "Not everything is meant to help you." He straightened and turned back towards the forest.

Siyan swallowed, trying to calm her racing heart. "Don't leave me here."

If Aren heard her, he gave no indication of it. He continued walking until he disappeared among the shadowed trees.

"Don't leave me here!" Siyan shouted, panic and fear overtaking her. But it was no use; Aren was gone.

The bearded man started awake. He got to his feet, scowling at her. "You talking to someone?"

Siyan swallowed the bile that rose in her throat. "No."

He peered at her and out towards the darkened forest. Then his eyes turned hard and cruel. "You best keep quiet, or I'll have to shove a gag in your mouth. And I doubt you'd much like that." He sneered at her. "Though I just might." He pulled his coat around him and lay down on the ground.

A calm dread settled over Siyan, as still and cold as a wintery night. She was alone. Powerless. Tied up and discarded at the edge of camp, with only a sleeping man to watch her and a scribbling of runes to keep her power in check. It seemed she was of no concern. They had her well in hand and could sleep easy that night, free of any burdensome worries of her breaking free.

How dare they? What had she done to warrant this? They were the ones who had tracked her down; they were the ones who had situated themselves in her life. And now they had taken her, bound her, separated her from the man she loved, and told her that *she* had much to account for.

How dare they?

She stared at the runes as the bitter taste of acid filled her mouth. She searched for her power, but still it was gone.

Was it really because of the runes? Or was there another reason? Emora had said their power was based on need, because without it, the mind wasn't willing to let go. She needed to let go—she needed to become something more. And she had. She had traveled to the spirit realm, walked upon legs of stone and breathed the ocean's water.

Her power was still there—it had to be. It was a part of her, inseparable from her being. Even death could not take her power from her, but rather transform it. The runes must be masking it—numbing her mind to the power that lay within her, but it was still there.

And runes could be broken.

Magisters had restrained her own mother with runes, and she had broken them, in time. Siyan tried not to dwell on the cost of such an act. Her mother had died and transformed into a disfigured tree. Would the same happen to her?

Yet what choice did she have? They had taken Enon and would kill him once they reached Roelith. And what would they do with her? Take her to the Tower? Prod her mind with their Art to see how her power worked? Would she ever see the sun again? Would she ever feel the wind of a falcon's wings against her cheeks?

She looked to the sky and saw Fal up in the branches, looking down at her. Siyan wished that she had wings of her own. She could fly up and release the burning pain that tore through her arms. If she were in the spirit realm, maybe she would have wings. She had walked upon legs of stone—why not fly with wings of a falcon?

Siyan peered at the runes that surrounded her. Aren was right—they were curious constructs. Scribblings of lines in the dirt, how strange that such things could keep her power from her. And yet they didn't. Her power was still there—it would always be there—she just couldn't feel it. Could she learn to use her power, even while blind to it? Would she ever be able to let go of herself, and give herself to this power that she no longer sensed?

She had to. It was the only way.

Siyan glanced at the bearded man on the ground. He lay still, his breathing even. Tightening her jaw, Siyan gripped the rope with her numb hands. She gritted her teeth and pulled herself up.

She clenched her jaw against the searing pain as the rope dug deeper into her wrists. She wanted to cry out, she wanted to stop, but she kept going. It was the only way. She needed to surrender to her power. Surrender or die. Her arms shook and burned, her legs twitched uselessly in the air as she pulled herself up. After what felt like an age, Siyan managed to bring her chin up to her bound hands.

With only a moment to consider if it was all a mistake, Siyan hooked her chin between the rope and her bound wrists, and then she let go.

The rope from the tree and her wrists pressed against her neck and she was unable to breathe. Panic flooded her mind and Siyan closed her eyes as she tried to control her terror.

She needed to surrender.

Her lungs and neck burned. All sound faded save for the thundering of her racing heart.

Surrender, Siyan.

Her heart calmed. In the distance, a sound floated on the wind. She opened her eyes. Men were shouting, pointing. Then they faded and the world quieted.

And Siyan surrendered.

Chapter 25

Siyan drifted through shadows. They felt soft and cold, brushing against her skin like whispering voices. Was she flying? Or was she anchored in place as the world around her floated by?

She opened her eyes, looking for the sky, but instead found her own body dangling from a tree. Was she dead? Her body was not a tree, so maybe she still lived. But she felt no connection to it. It was like looking at a withered flower. Unimportant. Unremarkable.

Men came running to the body that hung there. As Siyan backed away, she bumped into a wall. She turned and found it wasn't a wall but a circle of runes on the ground. They glowed mutely in the soil—like sunlight through thick, dirty glass.

She bent down and, as she drew near them, shadows clung to her skin. Her hand faded and warped, twisting like the gnarled hands of a crone. She pulled away, rubbing the coldness from her fingers. Siyan needed to break them, though she was unsure how.

Wiping them away looked to be impossible. They were etched into the spirit of the world itself, like a vile tattoo upon porcelain skin. To remove them she'd need to remove that part of the world, and Siyan knew she lacked the strength.

She put her hands to the ground, calling up roots from the trees to tangle and mar the runes. But the roots only sprouted from the soil as stunted, twisted shrubs. She remembered her mother—her tree a twisted and mis-shapen beauty. Siyan knew then how to break the runes. It was how her mother had done it, and Siyan would need to do the same.

She needed to let go, to become something more. She needed to die.

The men cut down Siyan's body and Malvin hustled over, putting his head to her chest. He said that she still breathed, faint though it was. One of the men suggested moving her to a tent. The Magister seemed to consider it, but then said he dared not move her from the runes. She still lived, and so she would remain, though they would watch her more closely.

Let them watch. It would have been better if they had moved her, but Siyan would succeed regardless. She would break the runes. She would be free.

She leaned over the pale form of her body, touching the shells that were wound in her tangled hair. They would both be free.

Siyan knelt to the ground and put a hand to the bruised and battered face that had once been hers. She felt a pang of emotion. Was it sadness? Regret? She would never again feel Enon's hand around her own, or his touch on her cheek. Part of her ached at the thought, but then she pushed it aside. It was the way of things. It was her time. If she did nothing, then Enon would die, and she would not let that happen.

Siyan moved her hand down to her body's chest and felt the feeble thump of her heart. She told it to stop. Then a weight settled over her. It clouded her vision, pulled at her mind. She could feel the world around her, pressing on her, enveloping her. It gave her strength.

She put her hands to the ground, but still the runes remained. They were weaker, though—the light shining from them more tenuous and strained. Siyan sent her sight into the soil, examining each rune from within. They looked to be shifting, pulsing with ebbing shadows, but still solid and whole.

Around and around Siyan went, watching the runes. Waiting. And then she saw it—a fragmented shadow. A broken edge of a rune. It wasn't much—a crack in a window, a draft through a door. But it was enough.

Siyan closed her eyes and pressed her thoughts against the fragmented runes. It was like trying to pass through a keyhole. She couldn't get out, not all of her. She backed away and pulled from herself three tiny drops. It was an odd sensation, being in one place but also another. It was disorienting, and the drops Siyan had severed from her spirit strayed and veered as if lost.

She sharpened her focus and let go of the idea of being a single form. She was the drops. She was the body that lay dying on the ground. She was the wind in the trees and, like the wind, she passed that small part of herself through the crack in the runes.

She was free. Siyan soared up to the sky towards the stars and moon. As she passed the trees and the forest fell away before her, she realized there was more light in the world than just in the sky. The trees themselves glowed— veins of light that quilted the ground clear to the horizon. It was like looking at a map of stars, at rivers of moonlight. It was beautiful, and Siyan again felt a pang of sorrow.

She floated back down among the trees and to the camp. She saw her bruised and bloodied body lying on the ground, shadowed and fading. It looked pitiful and drab, made all the more so by the brilliant form of white light that sat next to it. Was that herself she was seeing? Could she really be so beautiful? It must have been, for it sat in a circle of twisted, tainted spirit. The light was fading, however, bleeding into the drab husk that was her earthly body. Or perhaps it was the darkness bleeding into the light. Siyan couldn't tell.

She touched the ground and gave herself the shape of a fawn. On long, thin legs she moved through the camp. Most of the men slept, but a few wandered among the tents, watching the ground where Siyan's body lay. She wished to remain unseen, so she pulled the shadows close as she walked through the night.

Siyan wandered among the tents, looking for a familiar sight, sniffing for a familiar scent. She smelled dirt and meat, sweat and ashes. She saw men with whom she felt no connection, their light foreign. She walked on, passing a woman on the ground, bound and gagged. Siyan lingered a moment as she looked at her. The woman gazed back, her eyes defiant, struggling against the fear that lingered there. Siyan walked on.

It was difficult to focus. Siyan wanted to leap and run through the forest. She wanted to split herself into a pair of butterflies and flutter away on the night wind. But there was a light she needed to find. A light that she could not let go out.

And then she smelled it: earth and spice, leaves and musk. His scent, the one for which she had been searching. She nudged open a tent and walked inside.

He sat in a corner, his hands and feet bound, his mouth gagged. His chin rested against his chest. He looked to be sleeping, but his light was so faint that Siyan feared it would soon go out. She walked up to him and nudged her nose against his cheek.

He stirred, and when he looked up at her, his light flared bright in shifting shades of blue and amber, gold and green. Siyan realized then just how beautiful he was. Enon. He was hers. His light was her light. And as she looked upon his bloodied face, she felt as if a storm broke within her.

The part of her she left behind now again fought to escape the runes. She no longer wanted to be split; she wanted to be strong and whole. She wanted to unleash her fury upon the camp, make the earth tremble beneath her. But again it felt like she was pressing herself against a wall, unable to get out. She couldn't be whole, not while the runes were still intact.

Siyan felt as if she were being pulled back. Her hooves were too feeble to fight against it. Again she changed. Now she was a little girl, curling up on the ground and hiding her face, just as she used to when she was alone and afraid. After a while, the pulling stopped and Siyan looked up.

Enon stared at her, his eyes wide. She got to her feet and removed the gag from his mouth.

"Siyan," he said. There was a tone in his voice. Was it wonder? Fear? Siyan couldn't tell. She put her pudgy fingers to his binds and tried to untie them.

"You need to leave here," Enon whispered. "Leave me."

"No."

"Siyan, look at me."

She stopped her work and looked into his eyes.

"You need to leave. Now. Please."

Siyan felt small and helpless. She hated being little. She hated being weak. Again she felt the pull as the rest of her being tried to become whole. Fearing she'd be pulled back, fearing she'd lose him, she cried, "No!"

The tent flap pulled back and a man with a lantern stepped inside. He frowned as his mouth dropped open. "Where did you come from?"

He reached down for her, and Siyan darted past him. She ran out of the tent and changed into a falcon and soared up to the sky.

She perched in a tree, looking down on the camp. She wanted to bring a storm, a flood to wash them all away and ease her fury. But her power was still clipped and restrained. Siyan looked down at her body that lay upon the soil. The ground around the runes was beginning to change the more her body faded. In time, the runes would be broken—but by then, it would be too late. They would have taken Enon and dispensed their justice. There was no time to wait. She needed help.

Siyan again took flight and soared above the trees. She hung on the air, coasting on the currents of wind. How she wished Enon could be up there, flying with her. Then she could turn her back on the earthly world forever. But he wasn't, nor would he ever be. Siyan eyed the trees, looking for a particular light among the glowing web that was the forest. When she found it, she dove towards it, finding strength in her new-found purpose.

Chapter 26

Siyan circled over the Ilvar camp, quiet and still in the dark of the night. It seemed like a lifetime ago when she had last been there. So much had happened. She hardly recognized herself when she thought about that girl who had stood before the clan Elder, intimidated and unsure.

The clan had remained in the same location, and Siyan found the Elder's hut among the others. She coasted down and alighted on a pole before hopping to the ground.

Taking a moment to consider, Siyan decided she'd like to stand before the Elder as herself—or at least as close to herself as she could manage. She tried to remember what she looked like, but all she could recall were broken and shifting shadows as she peered at her reflection in a stream. It seemed fitting, to be ever-moving in such an uncertain world. So Siyan shifted into a reflection of that memory and entered the hut.

It was darker inside without the moonlight, but Siyan could still see. Furs padded the ground around the charred wood of an extinguished fire. Beneath the furs lay a form, its dull amber light dim in the darkness. She put a hand to his shoulder and the light brightened.

The Elder stirred, but still did not waken.

Siyan touched his shoulder again and said, "Wake up, Elder."

The Elder groaned. Then, letting out a heavy sigh, he sat up. He looked at Siyan and froze. He stared at her a moment, then frowned and said, "I am dreaming." He started to lay back down when Siyan grabbed his arm.

"You are not dreaming," she said. "I need your help."

The Elder chuckled and shook his head. He waved his hand at her, but froze when he touched her arm. The sleep that had clung to him now seemingly faded. He gazed at her, looking bewildered and a little frightened. "Who are you?"

"We have met before. I came to you, wishing to tell you of what you had forgotten, but you didn't want to listen. Your people stabbed my love and nearly killed him. Then you left us to the mercy of Magisters."

The Elder's look of confusion deepened. "That girl, the one with so much uncertainty and fear in her heart . . . that was you?"

"She was a fragment, just as this form you see now is a fragment. But we are part of the same whole."

The Elder stared at her. She may as well have just told him that she was made of molasses. Then his confusion faded and was replaced by a look of anger. "Impossible." He got up to leave but stopped when Siyan moved in front of him. She stared at him, watching his amber light, finding the thread of his memory.

"I remember you," she said. "Your name is Kosa. You have a son here in the camp, but you and he have not spoken for some time. You've had a disagreement."

Kosa glowered at her. "What would you know of that? Have you spoken with him?"

Siyan stared past him, trying to find more of the memory. "He thinks something needs to change. Your people struggle here in the forest, year after year. He thinks you should be leading them differently. Yet you disagree, you want to keep on as you always have. You think it has served you well, and that nothing good will come from changing it."

"Nothing good ever comes from change. We do well enough. My son is young, with bold and foolish ideas. He will see my way of things in time."

Siyan tilted her head. "Perhaps. Or perhaps he will grow more discontent. Perhaps he will leave, and take along those who agree with him. You will likely never see him again. Or your granddaughter. Your people will be divided. You will be weaker. What will you do, then?"

Kosa said nothing, his eyes dark.

"Change will come to you regardless," Siyan said. "But you can choose how it will come to you."

He gazed at her a moment longer then walked past her and stepped outside. Siyan followed.

The sky turned grey as dawn approached. Kosa looked out at the trees and towards the rising sun. "What do you want from me?" he said, his voice quiet.

"Your help."

"Why?" He turned to look at her. "What could I do to help you? You seem to have all the answers."

Siyan shook her head. "I don't. I'm still learning, just as you are. Just as we all are. I can help you, though, find some of your own answers, just as I've found them for myself."

He peered at her. "How?"

Siyan looked down at her body, nothing more than shifting shadows and broken light. Sadness settled over her then—a distant yet familiar feeling. "I'm dying."

Kosa's severe features softened, yet were still troubled by confusion.

Seeing his questioning look, Siyan continued. "I'm fading from this world, becoming something more. I can see things I've never seen before. Memories, mostly, but there's knowledge there within them. I can help you learn new things, you could provide for your people in new ways.

You could mend the rift that has broken between you and your son and granddaughter. I can help you with all of this, but first you must help me."

Kosa raised his chin and met her gaze with a steady one of his own. After a long while, he said, "What do you need of me?"

Addigan watched as the dark sky turned a deep blue, then grey, then gold and pink. She had been unable to sleep that night. How could she? She was tied up on the ground like nothing more than a sack of potatoes. The binds cut into her wrists, and she could barely breathe around the gag in her mouth and the blood that clogged her nose. It was all Addigan could do to remain calm. Any excitement made her feel as if she was suffocating, and she didn't much care for that.

She glanced at the And'estar's body still lying on the ground. Stupid girl. What had she been thinking, choking herself on her own binds like that? Addigan didn't know whether she still lived or had died. Given that her body had lain motionless throughout the night, she was more than likely dead.

Stupid girl.

What was so terrible to warrant killing oneself? She was captured, yes, but there was still a chance for escape. And even if escape was impossible, there was always a chance for reason. Malvin was usually a reasonable man. Addigan may have ruined her own chances for reasoning with him, but she was sure the girl had not. So why would she kill herself?

Stupid, stupid girl.

Yet, deep down, Addigan couldn't help but feel a spark of admiration for her. They were in the same situation, only Addigan arguably had it worse. Having attempted to kill

Malvin—a well-respected Magister—there was no redemption for her. Addigan's family had all but severed ties with her; she doubted they would come to her aid. The best she could hope for was to return to the Tower and be locked up for the rest of her life. What kind of future was that? It wasn't one in which Addigan wanted to live. And yet the thought of taking her own life filled her with such dread that the idea of actually doing it was unthinkable. She just didn't have that kind of courage.

As the day broke, the camp came to life. Men left their tents to light fires and cook breakfast. Every now and then, one of them would walk up to the girl and nudge her with a foot, but still she didn't move. The fact that the men kept checking on her meant she must be alive. Even Malvin walked up to the girl and stooped down to put a hand on her. He remained a moment and then, casting a cold glance at Addigan, got up and walked away.

Addigan deserved that look, but it still stung. Malvin had always been so loyal to her, even when she hadn't wanted his loyalty. But, now that it was gone, it still gave Addigan a pain in her heart she wished she didn't feel.

The morning wore on and the men ate their breakfasts. Addigan's stomach constricted when she smelled the roasting meat and earthen tea. She expected she wouldn't be given any food, so she was surprised when Walt came scampering up to her, accompanied by one of the men. The man had greasy hair that had been pulled back into a tail, and a scar over one eyebrow. He peered down at her as he unsheathed his sword.

"The boy here's got some food for you. You'll not speak a word or cause any trouble or you'll get my sword in your chest and I'll leave you here to rot. Understand?"

Swallowing, Addigan nodded.

The man nodded to Walt and the boy came up to her and removed the gag from her mouth.

Addigan sucked in a deep breath, tasting the fresh air, relaxing at being able to breathe unhindered. Walt then put a cup to her lips and tilted it. Addigan tasted warm, salty broth thick with onions and rosemary. She gulped it down, reveling in how it warmed and filled her stomach.

When she had finished, Walt pulled the cup away. He untied a small cloth parcel, within which lay a chunk of bread and cheese. He broke these into small pieces, placing each bit in Addigan's mouth and waiting while she chewed.

Addigan looked around the camp as she ate, avoiding the gaze of Walt and his chaperone. It was demeaning, being fed like a child, but she dared not complain.

After Addigan had finished, Walt gave her an apologetic look before putting the gag back in her mouth. It was particularly vile on her tongue after the pleasant taste of cheese and broth. He then turned and left, and the pony-tailed brute followed after him.

Addigan closed her eyes and shivered. The warmth from the broth had faded, leaving her feeling colder than before. Perhaps it would be better if they let her starve. Perhaps they really should just leave her to rot.

She clenched her fists. No, she would not be left behind. She would not die and unburden them of their responsibility to her. She would find warmth again, and then they would be brought to account for ever making her feel so cold.

Morning passed into afternoon, but they never broke camp to continue traveling as Addigan expected. Malvin spent much time near the girl. She remained lying on the ground, unmoving and unresponsive. Malvin seemed distressed about what to do with her, but ultimately he did nothing. He just left her there, lying alone on the hard, cold ground.

It was ridiculous, making the whole camp stop and wait for a single, stupid girl. Strap her to a horse and bring her along; leave her behind and forget about her. But don't just sit and do nothing. That was probably the worst part of it all—the waiting. Just sitting there, bound and cold and uncomfortable. She had no idea what fate awaited her when she returned to Roelith, but she'd rather find out and get it over with.

Time passed, unbearably slow. Afternoon faded into evening, evening into night. Addigan had nothing to do other than watch everyone move around the camp. She bit down on her gag every time she saw Malvin walk out to check on the And'estar. It was maddening, watching him display so much care yet not actually *do* anything. He had been the same way with her after the Threshing—always coming by, always asking if there was anything he could do. There never was, and yet he kept coming, kept asking.

Addigan wanted to spit out her gag and tell him how useless he was being. She wanted him to take action, one way or another. She wanted something to happen—anything other than just sitting there, waiting.

It was almost a blessing, then, when movement out in the forest caught Addigan's eye. Her gaze darted towards the trees, but it was too dark to see anything clearly. Maybe she had only imagined it. Maybe it was just a wild animal. Then twigs snapped and Addigan jerked her head, meeting the black eyes of a girl.

She cried out in surprise, but the gag muffled her voice. Addigan stared at her. There was something about the girl that looked familiar, but then shadows shifted over her features and the familiarity faded. Then, feeling cold, Addigan knew. She glanced back at the And'estar's body, but it was still lying there, unmoving. She cringed back as the girl reached towards her with her strange, shifting skin.

"You are trapped," the girl said. "I can free you."

Addigan glared at her. Was this some sort of joke?

"Help me, and you'll be free of them. I'll not stop you from leaving once I am done here. Do you agree?"

Addigan flexed her hands against her binds. She was probably lying, that girl. Dangle the hope of freedom in front of her and then take it away. But what other choice did she have? She had to take any opportunity, even if it did turn out to be some cruel joke. Not knowing what else to do, Addigan nodded.

Chapter 27

Siyan untied Addigan's binds and waited as the woman straightened her skirts and smoothed her hair. She looked down on Siyan with a dismissive, contemptuous air. Siyan turned and headed towards the camp but stopped when Addigan spoke.

"Your name," she said. "What is it?"

Siyan turned to look at her. Addigan stiffened her back as she met Siyan's gaze, as if steeling herself for an onslaught. Yet Siyan hardly saw her. The question resonated in her mind, seemingly important, but the answer eluded her. Then she found it.

"Siyan," she said and smiled. "My name is Siyan." She relaxed, realizing only then that she had been tense, but speaking her own name seemed to help her focus. Her mind felt a little calmer, her purpose a little clearer.

Addigan looked around the camp. She glanced at Siyan and then, looking away, said, "I need my staff."

Yes, Magisters always seemed to need their staves. "Where is it?"

Addigan shook her head. "I don't know. Malvin must have taken it. He may have burned it, for all I know."

Siyan peered towards the tents before returning her gaze to Addigan. "We will be going into the camp. You will have to look for it. Until then, you'll have to use your Art with your hands."

Addigan narrowed her eyes. "What would you know about that?"

Siyan said nothing. She edged around the camp and made her way back to her body. It looked so small and weak, lying there on the ground. It looked feeble, inconsequential, made even more so by the luminous brilliance that sat next to it.

Siyan felt more familiarity as she looked upon this latter aspect of herself. But that familiarity was waning as the light faded from its shimmering form and bled into the ground. It pulled at her as it sank into the soil. She was tempted to join it, to stop resisting and let herself burrow deep into the earth. She would be stronger, but she would also be changed. That small, feeble body of hers that lay prone on the ground would cease to exist, and Siyan was uncertain that she was ready to let go.

A man with a lantern wandered through the camp, and Addigan drew closer to her.

"Whatever you're going to do," she whispered, "do it quickly."

Siyan glanced into the forest where the Ilvar hid. She found Kosa, kneeling in the brush with his son, Kenan—their dispute with each other momentarily forgotten. Behind them the other Ilvar waited.

Turning to Addigan, she said, "I need you to remove the runes."

Addigan's mouth worked soundlessly as she looked at Siyan and the runes on the ground. Then, glancing at the man with the lamp, she let out a breath and scuffed a portion of the runes with her foot.

Siyan's spirit became whole and she gasped. It felt like plunging into frigid water, and the world around her faded as the trees and sky bled into each other. She closed her eyes. The pull on her spirit was stronger than before. The transition of her earthly body was still taking place, and now that the runes had been broken, there was nothing hindering the intense pull she felt towards the earth.

All sound faded into a whisper of wind. She felt as if she had fallen into a chasm, with the weight of the earth pressing upon her. It gave her strength, but it also threatened to crush her—to extinguish everything she knew until only darkness remained.

She needed to remain; she needed to fight. She sharpened her focus and opened her eyes. Nearby, the man with a lantern came towards them, his mouth moving as he spoke words Siyan couldn't hear. All she heard was the wind in the trees and the creaking of branches. He moved slowly, as if walking underwater, but the way he carried himself told Siyan there was haste in his steps.

She glanced towards the camp and found the tent where Enon was being held. She could see his light even from where she stood, and heat flared through her entire being. It was a feeling of love—and of fury. Siyan crouched to the ground and let the heat consume her.

Addigan put up a hand to shade her eyes as the shifting shadows of Siyan's body were consumed by flames. Fiery wings erupted from her back, dripping drops of molten light that soaked back into the ground. Siyan stood, holding herself tall and proud, and Addigan moved away to avoid the potent heat that radiated from her. The shadows that had once rippled across Siyan's skin were now a rippling glow of orange, white, and gold.

The man with the lantern that had been hurrying towards them now shrank back. His cries had roused the camp, and the silence of the night was shattered as men scrambled after swords and other makeshift weapons.

Malvin approached, his robe a brilliant crimson in the golden light of Siyan's body. He stopped a short distance away—close enough to look Addigan in the eyes, but too far away to touch.

Addigan swallowed. She didn't want to look at him—she didn't want to face him—but she refused to turn away. So she stiffened her back and clenched her jaw and met his gaze with a cold one of her own.

His gaze shifted to Siyan and to the smudged runes on the ground. "What have you done, Addigan?"

"She has done nothing other than expedite the inevitable," Siyan said. "Your runes will never be effective, not in the way you want."

"I think you underestimate me."

"And I know you underestimate me. Your runes are limited. You cannot stop the sun from shining or the moon from rising. You cannot keep the rain from falling or the wind from blowing. You cannot stop *me*, not with your runes. Let Enon go, unharmed, and then leave this forest. Let us both forget ever having met one another."

Malvin's eyes turned sad. Quietly, he said, "I cannot do that."

"Very well," Siyan said and she turned and signaled to the others.

Siyan remained still as Kosa and the other Ilvar came forward with their bows raised and spears at the ready. She didn't want to be there, fighting the Magister's men. She didn't want to have to bring Kosa and his clan to fight her battle for her. It angered her that Malvin had brought her to this, and that anger flowed from her in blazing light.

The ground below her trembled, and the men gathering behind Malvin put out their arms to keep their balance.

The weight of the earth continued to press upon her, and again the world blurred. Shadows crept into the corners of her vision, leeching light from the world. In her mind, images flashed and voices whispered. They spoke to her of memories from both ages ago and recent days. She closed her eyes. She didn't want to see Edmond or feel the joy he felt from the birth of his daughter; she didn't want to know the pain Lennus felt when his wife died from fever. Arno's step had been lightened from winning at dice the night before. And then there was Walt—surrounded by a sickening anxiety and ache in his gut in his desire to return home. Siyan didn't want to see these memories; she didn't want to hear them. She didn't want to feel their pain or share their joy. She wanted them out of this forest, and she wanted her fury to drive them from her.

A scratching sound surfaced as Malvin drew runes in the dirt. Arrows hissed as they flew through the air. One man cried out, and then another. Then, Malvin's steady voice as he spoke a series of runes. Siyan felt the heat being pulled from her, manifesting into a ball of fire that was then flung at her. She absorbed some of the flames back into herself, but the rest flew past her, igniting the trees in a conflagration of sparks.

The Ilvar that stood behind Siyan scrambled out of the way, but some were too late. Their screams echoed in the trees, and Siyan felt a wrenching pain. She pushed aside the memories that filled her mind and pulled together clouds in the night sky. The air stifled and warmed, and from the darkness a fork of lightning flashed, followed by a sharp crack of thunder. For a moment, the air turned vapid, and then grew thick and heavy as the sky released a downpour of rain.

Malvin drew another rune, and the remaining Ilvar spread out and disappeared among the trees. But the ball of fire fizzled in the rain, dissipating into smoke and sparks before he had a chance to throw it. He nodded to his men, and they branched out into the forest after the Ilvar.

The rain dampened the smoldering brush into char and ash, but it did nothing to ease Siyan's fury. The earth continued to press on her, strengthening her and fueling her anger. She wanted to give into it, lose herself in the weight of the earth until nothing of her remained. But she dared not. Not yet.

She staggered towards Addigan. "Find Enon. Over there." She pointed to a tent on the far end of the camp. "Keep him safe."

Addigan narrowed her eyes. "And what will you be doing?"

Siyan shook her head. She needed darkness—shadows in which to hide and ice to slake her anger. She closed her eyes, willing the world to quiet, and the murmured memories of the men around her blended into the pattering of rain. She needed to remain; she needed to hold on just a little while longer. She pulled the weight of the world around her like a comforting blanket, and then she pulled the shadows close.

Addigan watched as Siyan's fiery skin flickered and died, plunging the forest into an inky blackness. She lingered a moment, annoyed with Siyan's dismissal of her. Then she let out a breath. Addigan had said she would help, and so that's what she would do. Despite her faults, Addigan always kept her word.

She hurried towards the tent as quickly as the darkness would allow. She dared not run, lest she fall and break her neck, but she dared not create a lightstone, either. She tried to find comfort in the darkness, telling herself that no one could see her, just as she couldn't see them.

The air turned frigid, causing Addigan to cough as the

cold air stung her throat. The rain turned to hail, and Addigan's skin stung as the beads pelted her face and hands. Then, from the trees, shadows thickened and congealed. They gathered on the edges of Addigan's vision, slinking away whenever she turned to look at them. The air grew colder—if such a thing were possible—and Addigan's teeth chattered as she rubbed her hands together.

Lights winked among the trees. Cold light, like a lightstone, yet the spheres were too big, and they rippled with waves of sterile flame. One came towards Addigan. The hair on her skin stood on end and she flattened herself against one of the tents. It floated past her, pulling wisps of hair that had loosened from her bun towards its path. Behind it crept a shadow, holding the light with long and dark tendril-like arms. Once it had gone, Addigan resumed walking and collided with a man in the darkness.

She let out a startled cry and stumbled back. She put out her hands, ready to draw a rune, but the man never came towards her. He followed the flickering flame, the shadowed form of his body outlined by its pale light.

Addigan let out a breath. She wanted to be done with this business and away from this place. From behind, Malvin spoke a series of runes and she ducked her head as she hurried through the camp, trying to avoid whatever attack he might be sending her way. Instead, a light flared in the sky, bleaching the orbs of blue flame and sending the shadows that held them to scatter among the trees.

Malvin's flare flickered and died, but it had been enough to illuminate a path to the tent and, seeing that nothing stood in her way, Addigan ran towards it. She felt her way around the rough canvas walls until she found the opening and stepped inside. She hesitated, waiting for her eyes to adjust to the deeper darkness within, but they never did.

"Enon?" she whispered, but all was silent. Addigan hesitated. She'd rather not fumble her way through the dark, looking for a man that would likely gut her given the chance. She reached into her skirt pocket and pulled out a stone and ignited it with a spoken rune.

Enon was bound in a corner; she hurried towards him. He glared at her as she approached, but he did not cower.

"I am going to untie you," she said. "I suggest you direct your anger at Malvin rather than at me. Your woman is out there with him. If you want to protect her, you'll have to hurry." She studied him to gauge his reaction, but he gave none. Letting out a breath, Addigan knelt down and untied him.

Once free from his binds, Enon leapt to his feet. He stood there, glowering at her as he flexed his hands into fists. Addigan met his gaze. She held her breath as they watched each other, then he turned and ducked outside. Exhaling, she extinguished the light and fumbled through the darkness as she followed.

Malvin continued to send his flares up into the blackened sky. They flashed across Siyan's vision, blinding her and allowing the memories to come flooding back. The way Dennet had smiled when he built wooden toys with his grandfather; the way Gus had cried when he fell down the well. Joy and hurt, fear and love—all of it pressed on Siyan as heavy as the earth itself.

The rain dissipated and died; the air warmed. She was losing her hold. She looked toward the camp and felt her heart lift when she saw Enon's light moving through the darkness. But then another one of Malvin's flares ignited and blinded her in a searing flash.

She tried to pull at the shadows but they didn't want to come. Voices of memories crowded in her mind, and it was all Siyan could do to keep herself from screaming to try and drive them away.

Then a calm descended. The memories dimmed and quieted to a murmur. Enon drew closer, she could feel it like sunlight on skin. Her vision cleared and, looking up, found he had almost reached her. But then Malvin turned to face him, waving his staff in the air as he drew his runes. Fury erupted again in Siyan, and the night paled as fire and light poured from her. With little more than a thought, she stood before Malvin. His eyes flickered with surprise, and then she put her ember-like hands to his throat.

Siyan felt his spirit beneath her fingers. She pulled it from him, siphoning it through her own spirit before sending it into the ground. He tried to pull away, but she held him fast. Blood seeped from his nose and his skin darkened. His eyes paled and his hair faded to waxy strands before he fell to the ground in a lifeless heap.

Siyan stood over his body. She felt hollow and weakened, and Malvin's residual spirit coursing through her body both tainted and confused her. The earth pulled at her. Its grip enveloped her, and it took all of Siyan's focus to remain standing—to remain at all. Just a little while longer. Please, just a little while longer.

She staggered a step and, feeling like her bones would break from the pull of the earth, she turned towards Enon. Their gazes met, and he stared at her with wide and fearful eyes.

Then, letting out a breath, she let the earth take her.

Addigan stood in mute horror as Siyan's fiery form choked the life from Malvin. Then, as he fell at her feet, Siyan staggered and turned to look at them. Her flames flickered and died, and the world again darkened.

Everything turned quiet. Even the fighting had stopped. Addigan stood there, listening to the blood rush in her ears as she wondered what to do.

"Siyan," Enon said, and he ran through the darkness.

Addigan fished out her stone and lit it before trailing after him. One of Malvin's men came wandering through the trees, his expression frightened and confused. Then, when he saw the dead Magister lying on the ground, he turned and ran.

Enon stood over Malvin's body before leaning down and touching his chest. "Siyan?" he called as he stood and looked around. Then his gaze passed over where her body lay, and he ran over to her.

Addigan edged near Malvin's corpse. His skin was ashen. Blood had seeped from his eyes and nose, glistening in the light of her stone. Addigan stifled a gasp with her hand. Was it horror or grief she was feeling? She wasn't sure.

"Siyan," Enon said as he knelt down by her body. He put a hand to her face and chest, but she remained motionless. "No . . ." Enon said and put his arms underneath her neck and legs. He tried lifting her but met resistance. "No," he said again, panic edging into his voice. Again he tried to lift her, but again she would not budge.

"No!" he cried and, with a hollow, ripping sound, lifted her up. He stood, swaying as he held Siyan as if in a daze. Then, turning towards Addigan, he staggered towards her.

"Help her," he said.

Horrified, Addigan took a step back. Siyan's dark skin had turned white as bone, and thin, root-like tendrils dangled from her back and legs. "What?"

"Call your spirit. Heal her as she healed you."

"I can't . . ."

"Please," Enon said, his voice tight. He looked to be summoning all his strength just to speak. "Do not let her die."

Addigan's mouth hung open. His love for the girl was plain, and she suddenly regretted not being able to do what he asked. "I'm sorry, but we are not the same, she and I. I cannot help her."

Enon's face twisted in grief, and he buckled to the ground.

Addigan took another step back as Enon laid Siyan on the earth. He bent over her, resting his forehead against hers as he smoothed her hair. A sob escaped him, stifled and choked, that sounded loud and foreign in the quiet of the forest.

Addigan fidgeted with her hands, feeling awkward and useless. She felt as if she should turn away, but she remained still. Enon's grief fascinated her. Would Malvin have grieved for her so, if she had passed? She thought it unlikely, and even more unlikely that anyone ever would.

Enon remained there, stroking Siyan's hair as he pressed his head to hers. He whispered something, though Addigan couldn't hear what. Then he hummed a tune. It was broken and off-key from the grief that choked his throat, but still he hummed it. His left hand burrowed into the ground, even as his right one continued to smooth Siyan's hair.

Then, still humming, he moved his right hand to Siyan's chest, directly beneath his own. He was so close to her. Had Siyan been breathing, he would have been stealing her breath. His left hand burrowed deeper in the ground and his humming grew louder. His voice steadied, the tune whole and unbroken. His knuckles turned white as he gripped the soil. Enon's eyes must have been closed, for he would have stopped had he seen what Addigan saw.

Siyan's eyes had opened.

Chapter 28

Siyan called the wind, sweeping up the dried needles that had fallen to the ground. She sharpened her focus, and the needles coalesced together, taking on the form of a great winged bird. She smiled.

"You should save your strength," Enon said, "and not waste it needlessly stirring the air."

Siyan smiled even more. "I like stirring the air. You'll be glad of it when the weather turns hot."

Enon shifted his weight but said nothing.

They remained there for a time—Enon leaning against a tree while Siyan sat upon the ground. They were far enough away from Kosa's camp so that silence fell around them—but they were still close enough for Siyan to make it back without Enon having to carry her.

He had been right about that—her strength was now something she needed to preserve.

Siyan tried not to think back on her encounter with Malvin. It all seemed like a horrific dream. Sometimes she could convince herself that was all it had been if she didn't think too long on the matter. But she often did think long on it. She had killed a man. The memory of it saddened her and sickened her, tightening her stomach into a nauseating knot of ice.

She looked at Enon, and the shifting light around him

flared brighter when their eyes met. It still surprised her, seeing the world as it had looked when she was in her spirit form. She still saw the light that surrounded each living thing. She still recalled memories. Some of them belonged to her, some did not. It was confusing trying to sort out her own life from the lives of others. Secluding herself in the silence of the forest was the only thing that helped her make sense of this new world in which she found herself. Sometimes she wondered if she was still in the spirit realm. Maybe she was only dreaming of being there with Enon as the warm breeze circled around them. Was she really alive? Or was she nothing more than a pale tree, alone somewhere in the darkened woods?

Feeling unsettled, Siyan tried to get to her feet, but her legs were too weak to hold her. She clenched the soil in her hands and gritted her teeth. Despite the weeks that had passed, she still hadn't gathered enough strength to stand on her own. Her body was broken and white as bone, her skin callused like knots of wood where the roots had fallen from her. Even her once black hair now gleamed dark green whenever the light of the sun shone upon her.

Enon knelt down beside her and put a hand to her head. His brown eyes were flecked with blue and amber, gold and green. They matched his light; they suited him. Siyan smiled as her frustration faded.

Sen'itere. The name entered her mind whenever she looked at him. It meant "guardian"—or something like it—but the deeper meaning of it remained hidden to her. That was the way of these stray memories. She'd see fragments, but their origins always lay deeper in the realm of spirit than she could see.

"I'm ready to return," she said.

He put an arm around her waist as she threw an arm around his neck. Pulling her tight, Enon helped her up as they rose to their feet.

Their pace was slow as they made their way back to camp. Siyan put one wobbly leg forward, and then the other. It was more a shuffle than a walk, and without Enon there to support her, she wouldn't have been able to do even that.

Her weakness wasn't like after her previous venture to the spirit realm where all she had to do was wait for her strength to return. Her strength was gone. There was nothing left, and each day was a battle to rebuild what she had lost.

She felt so frail, and yet, at the same time, more powerful than she had ever been. It was like the two worlds—the earthly and spirit—had blurred together. As a result, her connection to her power was closer, stronger. But it was also more tenuous. It would be so much easier to give too much of herself. And if she did . . .

She hugged Enon's neck tighter and rested her head against his own. He must have thought she was tired, for he stopped walking. She closed her eyes and leaned against him, letting the heat of his body warm her own chilled skin.

Sen'itere. Protector. Warden. Sentinel. The words surfaced in her mind, as if out from the depths of a deep dark sea. For a moment, it all seemed to make sense. But then she looked at it too closely and it faded away.

"Have you ever heard of Sen'itere?" she asked.

"No. What does it mean?"

"It's you."

Enon was quiet a moment. "What does that mean?"

She shook her head. "I'm not sure yet."

They returned to camp well into the afternoon. Kosa and Kenan stood speaking by a fire as the remaining of their clansmen tended to the various duties of the camp. Kosa's gaze met hers, and he nodded and walked away.

"Where do you want to go?" Enon said.

Siyan looked around. She was about to tell him she wanted to return to her own hut. The walk had been long, and she was tired. She wanted to lie down and rest, but then her gaze fell on Addigan sitting alone on a hill at the edge of camp.

Siyan nodded towards her. "Over there."

Addigan glanced up at them as they approached and then frowned and looked away.

Enon helped Siyan sit down next to her before retreating to lean against a nearby tree.

Siyan and Addigan sat together in silence. A stream wound through the forest below them, its faint trickling sound was soothing.

Addigan pulled at the grass. After a while, she said, "I can't stay."

Siyan glanced at her. "I know."

Addigan continued to rip at the grass. "It's quite foolish, really. I should have left long ago. I don't know why I've stayed."

Siyan smiled. "Yes, you do."

Addigan looked at her, and her frown softened. She pointed at Siyan's legs. "How's the walking coming along?"

"Better," Siyan said, wiggling her feet. "It's been hard, but you know that. I don't think I could have gotten this far without your help."

Addigan's expression turned sober and she looked away.

"Where will you go?" Siyan said.

Addigan gave a short, mirthless laugh. "I have no idea."

"I'm sure I can find someone to escort you, wherever you decide to go."

Addigan nodded, her gaze distant.

They fell back into silence. After a while, Siyan said, "Do you miss him?"

"Who?"

"Malvin."

Addigan flinched. Then she said, "I don't know."

Siyan remembered the way she had drained the spirit from his body, killing him and letting him fall lifeless at her feet. It all seemed so distant. So unreal. And yet, at her core, she felt like she could still feel the taint of his spirit mingling with her own. She swallowed the sickness that such thoughts always brought.

"I wish I hadn't needed to do it," Siyan said. "I wish I had found another way."

"You did what you needed to. That's all any of us can do."

"But you loved him."

Addigan shook her head. "I don't know. Maybe I did, once."

"You still do."

"And what would you know about it?" Addigan said, her voice sharp.

Siyan met her gaze. "It doesn't mean you're weak, letting someone into your heart."

Addigan glared at her. "You think you see everything with those unnatural eyes of yours? If I loved him, I wouldn't have been so cruel and indifferent towards him. I wouldn't have tried to kill him by my own hand. Does that sound like love to you?"

"It sounds like pain to me. And confusion. But that doesn't mean love wasn't there."

"And what if it was? The man is now dead. What would you have me do, break down and cry and mourn him until my dying days?"

"No."

"Then what?"

Siyan smiled and shrugged. "Just accept that part of yourself. You loved him, Addigan. That's not a terrible thing."

Addigan stared at Siyan as if she had just asked her to strip down and wallow in the mud. Then, making a sound of disgust, Addigan got up and walked away.

Siyan gazed out towards the stream as Enon sat down next to her.

"You spend too much time with that woman," he said. "I still do not trust her."

"She's helping me rebuild my strength, teaching me how to walk again."

"You would have learned that regardless."

"Maybe."

Enon looked at her. "No, not maybe. You know this as well as I do. Why do you keep her company so often?"

Siyan looked away. "She carries so much pain with her, Enon. I want to help her heal. I don't know if I can, though. Her pain is not in her body." She took a breath. "But I need to try—for myself as much as for her."

Enon said nothing. Then he reached out and tucked a stray lock of hair behind her ear.

Siyan closed her eyes at his touch. "Sen'itere," she whispered. "Keeper, caretaker, walker, sleeper." She opened her eyes. "Awake."

"Who is awake?"

She looked at him. "You are."

"I am not And'estar."

"No, you're not. You're something different. Something more."

"More than what?"

"More than what you were."

They watched each other a moment and then Siyan rested her head on his shoulder.

Enon wrapped an arm around her and rested his head against hers. They sat together in silence as the shadows stretched across the ground and the blue sky turned golden.

"What does it mean for us?" Enon asked. "For our people?"

Our people. Siyan smiled. "I don't know yet. But maybe one day I will."

Enon wrapped his other arm around her and pulled her tight.

Siyan closed her eyes, quieting her mind to the stray thoughts and memories that floated around her. Right now, she didn't need to be teaching Kosa and his clan all that she knew of what it meant to be And'estar. She didn't need to worry about Enon's awakening and understanding all that it entailed.

Right now, she was warm sitting next to her love with his arms around her. She had found a home. She was happy. She was content.

And that was enough.

Acknowledgments

Writing is a solitary endeavor, but writing *well* and then publishing really does take a village. Many thanks to Jasmine Angell and Ray Deft for reading through an early version of the manuscript and providing valuable feedback. Thanks to Ray Rhamey for editing the manuscript within an inch of its life, and to Melinda DeBoer for flogging it just that little bit more.

Many thanks to the Stockholm Writers Group for welcoming this fledgling writer within their ranks, and for the helpful guidance I've so far received. Thank you, Celine Jeanjean, for becoming my Blurb Buddy and for being a general voice of support. Thank you to everyone who will undoubtedly help me with the cursed Blurb that, as I write this, *still* isn't done.

Thank you, Ferdinand Ladera, for creating such a beautiful cover image. Again.

Thank you, Anders Nyström, for being both my biggest supporter and biggest critic. None of this would be possible without you.

Thank you to everyone who hangs out with me on my blog or on social media, and for helping me feel like I can actually pull this writing thing off. Lastly, thank *you*, dear reader, for reading this book—even the boring acknowledgments at the end. You make this whole writing gig worthwhile.

ABOUT THE AUTHOR

SARA C. SNIDER IS AN AMERICAN AUTHOR living in Sweden, where she gets to wander dense, cold forests that serve as inspiration for her stories. She loves fairy tales, odd and quirky things, and has a slight obsession for vegetarian dumplings. You can connect with Sara and find out what she's up to at www.saracsnider.com.

Also By Sara C. Snider

Hazel and Holly

Hazel and Holly are two witch sisters trying to find a way to free their mother's soul trapped by their necromancer father. Currently a serialized novel on saracsnider.com, *Hazel and Holly* is a magical family drama with a little bit of whimsy and humor, and a little bit of darkness. Read on for a preview of the first chapter.

Death Before Dawn

Hazel peered at the twilit sky as she wandered along the wooded path. She clutched her lantern, even though the way lightened with the approaching dawn. She quickened her step. It would be a brief visit this time. She knew she'd been too liberal with the valerian tea. She wasn't one to oversleep, but restfulness had eluded her lately. Too much on her mind.

The skirts of her dress rustled against the brush and bushes, a rasping whisper as if the woods themselves hushed her ungainly approach.

"I won't be long," she said. No one was there, but one never knew when out in the woods.

She came to a cast iron gate set within a crumbling stone wall. It wouldn't be long before the gate was rendered useless and one could just hop over the stones. But it wasn't today. She reached into a pocket and pulled out an iron key nearly the size of her hand. She put it in the lock and, using both hands to turn it, unlocked the gate and pushed it open.

The rusty hinges screeched and Hazel clenched her teeth, cursing herself for forgetting, yet again, to bring a pot of grease. She returned the key to her pocket and, leaving the gate open, followed the wall until she came to a little stone cottage nearly overtaken with ivy and brambles of sweet briar. The water-warped door stood propped against the doorframe into which it no longer fit. Hazel slipped passed it and stepped inside.

The room was gloomy within, but Hazel knew the way. She walked to the hearth and, fetching a handful of sticks from a corner of the room, used her lantern to ignite them. She blew on the gentle flames, prodding with a poker until the cold coals flared alight.

Hazel lingered by the fire. It was always so damp in this place; she felt like she could feel the chill in her bones as soon as she stepped over the threshold. But she was late, and it wouldn't do to tarry too long.

She walked to a table at the other end of the room, upon which sat an ewer and basin. Water from a hole in the roof had filled the ewer, and Hazel poured some of the water into the bowl. Then, from another pocket, she pulled out a piece of honey cake wrapped in cloth. She untied it and crumbled the cake into the water.

She looked out the window and at the lightening sky, but the sun still hadn't risen.

"You are late."

Hazel turned and found Willow warming her pale hands by the feeble fire. "I overslept."

Willow smiled, turning her back on the hearth and sauntering over to Hazel. She reached out to touch Hazel's hair, but Hazel moved away. "Still frightened, daughter?"

"I'm not afraid," Hazel said. "I just prefer not to be touched by the dead."

Willow waved a hand and then leaned over the bowl. She took a deep breath, opening her mouth as she lingered over the water. She straightened. "Honey cake." She smiled. "What did you used to call it? Sunny cake?" Willow laughed. "You always thought it made the day brighter."

"That was a long time ago."

"Not that long."

"We don't have much time. The sun will soon be up."

Willow sighed. "Very well." She put on a serious expression, clasped her hands together and, in a stern voice, said, "What is your progress?"

Hazel frowned. "I'm doing this for your benefit, you know. I'm not the one with her soul trapped in a geas. One would think you'd care more about your own wellbeing."

Willow gave a short laugh. "Wellbeing? My dear, I am dead. I am not a being at all, well or otherwise."

"So, you're happy, then? Is that it? You're happy to haunt this decrepit, rotting heap, waiting with each new moon for me to come by with a crumb of cake and to stir the fire? Because that's all you'll ever have, and when I'm gone, you won't have even that. That doesn't concern you?"

Willow tightened her jaw and closed her eyes. "Leave it alone, Hazel."

"I will not leave it alone! He did this to you—your own husband! My father! Was this part of your arrangement? Is this what you bargained for? What was it you used to tell me? He'll come when needed? Well, where is he now?!"

Willow stood there, her body trembling and her eyes clenched shut, but she said nothing.

"Answer me!"

A cold wind gusted through the room, extinguishing the fire and knocking the air from Hazel's lungs.

Willow bared her teeth and grabbed Hazel's chin in an icy grip. "The geas cannot be undone, whatever you might think. It is done, and I will *not* give him the satisfaction of my misery!" She let go of Hazel's chin and put her hand over her eyes.

Hazel rubbed her jaw, working warmth back into her chilled skin. "There is a way, Mother. I will find it."

Willow gave a mirthless laugh. "And what *is* your progress, daughter? What have you found so far?"

Hazel opened her mouth but hesitated. "I *will* find it."

Willow turned away and walked to a window with ivy growing through the glassless panes. "The sun is rising, Hazel. Give Holly my love."

"Mother . . ."

"Do not bring honey cake next time." She slipped out the door just as sunlight streamed through the shattered windows.

Hazel stood there, watching as the dawn chased away the gloom, lessening the damp that hung in the air. Outside, birds began to chirp, but their melody did nothing to soothe the sorrow that had settled in her heart. She picked up the basin and threw the water and cake crumbs out a window before returning it to the table. Then, casting a single look behind her, Hazel slipped out the door.

For more *Hazel and Holly,* head on over to saracsnider. com and read it for free!

www.ingramcontent.com/pod-product-compliance
Lightning Source LLC
Chambersburg PA
CBHW020107310726

48970CB00002B/509